Touching Evil

Touching Evil

Hugh Miller

CORONET BOOKS
Hodder and Stoughton

First published in Great Britain in 1998
by Hodder and Stoughton
A division of Hodder Headline PLC

British Library Cataloguing in Publication Data

A CIP catalogue record for this title
is available from the British Library

ISBN 0 340 71570 7

Typeset by Palimpsest Book Production Limited,
Polmont, Stirlingshire
Printed and bound in Great Britain by
Clays Ltd, St Ives plc

Hodder and Stoughton
A division of Hodder Headline PLC
338 Euston Road
London NW1 3BH

PART ONE

Eddie Franklin, seven years old, zipped up in a scarlet bubble jacket, daydreaming. He stared at a clear December sky, his eyes crinkled against the brightness, held by the movement of a drifting feathery cloud.

Then a bunch of kids ran past. They bumped Eddie, breaking the trance. He turned to where his ball lay and booted it across the grass.

Yards away on a bench beside the swings, Carol Franklin, Eddie's mother, sat rocking her younger one in the pram, small-talking to her friend, another mum. Intermittently Carol looked round, keeping track of Eddie. She watched him slam the ball at a gap in the bushes and turned back to her friend, smiling at what she said, nodding.

When Carol turned to see Eddie again her smile shrank. He was nowhere in sight. She stood up, frowning, craning her neck.

No sign.

She ran to where she had last seen him, then ran in the opposite direction, getting anxious. Her head pivoted. Kids seemed to be everywhere, on the swings and the climbing frame and the roundabout, running and leaping in noisy bunches across the park. None of them was Eddie.

1

She hurried to the tarmac path behind the swings, half convinced he had run past her when she wasn't looking. She stopped on the path and looked both ways, twice.

No Eddie.

A hurt sound escaped her, making white vapour on the air. Breathless now and distressed, she turned back, seeing all those kids with not a red windcheater among them.

'Eddie!'

Her voice wouldn't carry. She was shaking. She went back to the place where she had seen him last. He had been *there*. She walked round the spot, trying to conjure him. He had been on that very patch of worn grass when he kicked the ball at the bushes.

She stopped suddenly and stared, feeling a jolt across her heart. The ball was where he had aimed it, lying in a gap in the bushes, motionless in all that commotion.

'God, Eddie . . .'

To Carol's stinging eyes the ball looked forlorn. It looked like something that no longer had an owner.

1

The emergency siren started up as Detective Inspector Susan Taylor strode across the ground floor at the Organised and Serial Crime Unit headquarters. She bowed her head a fraction as she adjusted her expression. It was important to arrive looking intelligent as well as presentable, even after sleeping badly.

She joined the flow of personnel on the marble stairs, catching the sounds of mayhem up in reception. A man was bellowing over the noise of the siren. Other men were shouting and grunting; there were sounds of scuffling and bodies impacting on the shiny stone walls.

At the top of the steps Taylor slid her ID card through a swipe machine. In the middle of reception three uniformed police officers struggled to restrain a powerfully built man in a greasy raincoat. Taylor watched dispassionately as the man dragged the panting constables eight feet across the floor. He snarled and screamed as they huddled round him in a cordon, trapping his arms.

'I want to speak to Creegan!' he howled. 'I want to speak to Creegan!'

Taylor did an automatic estimation of his age – about forty-five – and noted the terrible haircut. 'Anybody fancy anything from the canteen?' she shouted.

Nobody responded. The struggle intensified.

She turned away. 'Just give us a shout if you need a hand, lads.'

Detective Constable Mark Rivers came up the stairs, blue with cold. He stood for a minute and watched the conflict. 'A tenner on the big guy,' he said.

'I want Creegan!' the man screamed, landing on his back, pulling two of the constables to their knees. *'I want to speak to Creegan!'*

'Why doesn't somebody just get Creegan?' a man yelled.

'Because we don't have a bloody Creegan!' somebody bawled back.

'Yes you have.'

Taylor and the others turned. Creegan, in shirt-sleeves and wide grey braces, came towards them from the office area beyond reception. He was slim, dark-haired, broody-featured. A thick vertical line of scar tissue was visible on his forehead, over the left eye.

'I want to speak to Creegan!' the man on the floor bellowed, forcing the sound past a choke-lock. 'I want Creegan! I want Creegan!' He started to cough violently.

Creegan stepped close and bent down into the man's line of vision. 'Cyril,' he hissed sharply. 'Cyril!'

The man stopped struggling. He stared at the upside-down face above him. The siren died. Everything went quiet.

'You're scaring a lot of people, man,' Creegan said in a clipped North-Eastern accent. 'You want to just calm down.'

The officers relaxed their grip on Cyril. He got up, panting heavily.

'Five deep breaths,' Creegan said. He put his arm round Cyril's shoulder.

Cyril did as he was told, hauling air in through his wide-open mouth.

'Three,' Creegan said, keeping count.

Cyril took two more and grinned, shoving his face close to Creegan's. He chuckled. 'They said you weren't here.'

'Well, they should know better.' Creegan returned the grin. 'They know now.'

'Aye.'

'Let's grab a coffee.'

As they moved away Cyril made a harsh animal growl at one of the officers

'Decaff might be an idea,' Creegan said.

He shepherded Cyril towards the inner offices, past the big OSC sign on the wall. Under the sign were smaller ones, listing the subdivisions – Behavioural Science, Fraud Unit, Drugs Unit, Violent Crimes. Creegan led the way along an echoing corridor and into an office with dark walls and polished wooden furniture. In a corner and along one wall, newly arrived boxes and bags were piled, waiting to be unpacked.

Cyril took a chair by a table, clasping his hands and gazing around him. Hazy daylight filtered through the old window, a muted blue that made the lamplight on desks and tables look golden.

Creegan got coffee. As they drank it Cyril described a recent vision and Creegan listened, making occasional squiggly notes on a pad.

'It . . . it's like, um, all over the place,' Cyril said, 'and then here.' He put a mittened hand in front of his face, staring with wide mantic eyes between the

spread fingers. 'Everywhere. And then straight in front
of me. And it's really dark. And I get frightened. Really,
really black.'

'Dark or black?' Creegan said.

'I get frightened. I get pushed out the way. Because I
don't mean anything. I'm just trying to see.'

'Does someone die?'

'Er . . .' Cyril averted his eyes. He nodded. 'Yeah.'

'Is it a murder?'

Cyril nodded again.

'And you're watching?'

'Not with my own eyes.' Cyril sounded indignant. He
pointed upwards. 'I'm seeing it through the clouds.'

Creegan squiggled a couple of clouds on his pad and
glanced to the side. Taylor had come in. She was standing
by the desk, watching them.

'You look worn out, Cyril,' Creegan said. He narrowed
his eyes. 'You've had a haircut.'

'Oh, aye.' Cyril grinned shyly.

Creegan made an admiring whistle.

Cyril laughed and blushed. 'I did it myself,' he whispered.

'Looks brilliant.'

A female clerk with grey hair and a stern mouth came
into the office and stacked folders on a table by the
door. Creegan stood and took a wad of notes from his
pocket. He peeled off three tens and handed them to
Cyril, then he asked the woman if she would show his
friend out.

'This lady'll take you downstairs,' he told Cyril. 'Don't
touch her breasts, she won't understand.' He turned to
the startled woman. 'You'll be fine,' he promised, then
slapped Cyril's arm. 'Look after yourself.'

When they had gone Taylor sauntered across the room. 'What was that all about?'

'That?' Creegan jerked a thumb in the direction of the door. 'That was Cyril Golding. Nostradamus of the underworld.' He picked up the phone and dialled a zero for the switchboard. 'This is DI Dave Creegan,' he told the operator. 'I'm new in. I'm on extension two one six one if anybody needs to get through. Thanks.'

He put the phone down and saw Taylor studying his cod shorthand.

'So your snout's what?' she said. 'Some kind of psychic?'

'Look.' Creegan took the pad from her. 'I pretend I can do shorthand. Cyril, he pretends he's a psychic. Yes.'

'Wow.' Taylor propped herself on the edge of the desk. 'Good luck to you.' She smiled and tilted her head. 'Do you want to tell me what you're doing in my office?'

The door opened. Commander Enwright came in. He was tall and thin-cheeked, conditioned for authority, with a switch-on, switch-off smile that widened his mouth without lifting the corners. 'You're a day early,' he told Creegan. They shook hands. 'That's a bad habit for a copper.'

'Keen to make an impression,' Creegan murmured.

'Oh, you've done that. Remind me never to put you on a dawn raid.' Enwright looked at Taylor. 'I'm sorry about this. Inspector David Creegan, Inspector Susan Taylor. You're sharing, by the way, till we can sort space out.' He handed Taylor a folder. 'Read this on the way down and, ah, ring me when you get there.'

Taylor stared at him, mystified. 'From?' she said.

7

'St Albans. You're reporting to CS Tony Beecham. He thinks you're already on your way.'

'Right.'

'Both of you,' Enwright added.

Taylor nodded, deadpan, letting nothing show.

2

It was a forty-minute trip. Taylor drove. After fifteen minutes of silence she sighed elaborately and glanced at Creegan. Since they had left London he had been studying the file Enwright had handed her. It was an assemblage of case notes and pictures of missing children. Creegan continued to read, unaware of Taylor's sighing.

'Have you spent a long time alone recently?' she said.

He looked up. 'Why?'

'Well . . .' She made a face. 'If you're not going to talk, I'll have to grab a couple of hitch-hikers.'

He smiled faintly, as if it were an old problem, not one that could be easily fixed. He took out his mobile phone and tapped a button. He waited with the phone at his ear, watching Taylor. When the call connected he turned away to mutter into the mouthpiece.

Taylor discovered she was grinding her teeth. It was nothing serious, not hard enough to hurt or even make a sound, but the tension was there. If Creegan had simply been playing Mr Moody-and-Silent he would have been easy to ignore. But she could tell that the distance he maintained was genuine, it was not a posture. She didn't know why he was doing it, or if he couldn't help it. Being in the dark amounted to exclusion, and Taylor hated being excluded from anything.

She was sure Creegan's behaviour had nothing to do with her. There was no hint of bad chemistry between them, and she knew he saw nothing unpleasant when he looked at her. She had an objective handle on herself and she worked on her image. Her dark hair was fashionably short, but not short enough to be controversial. It framed her face, the supple face of a woman of twenty-eight who could look twenty-three if she chose, with softly defined cheekbones, big, expressive eyes and just enough of a jaw to be assertive. Her body was slender but not thin; it was lithe in a way that harmonised with the mobility of her face. That was what Creegan saw.

When *she* looked at *him*, on the other hand, she saw something too ambiguous to get a fix on. Swift evaluation was her thing, or one of her things, but Creegan yielded zero. Nothing was established by his face or by the way he used it. Which didn't mean he looked odd – quite the opposite. He was unquestionably a looker. Nicely built, too. He had a dazzling smile, he moved well and his Northern voice, what she had heard of it, was sexily modulated. By regular standards the man was a dish.

But.

Taylor glanced at him again. He was still mumbling to his phone. Strange eyes, she thought, and looked at the road again. Greeny-blue, vivid eyes. Until they went vacant. And they could do that in more ways than one.

She grunted softly and wiggled her backside, adjusting her position in the seat. She would get used to him. She would learn to coexist with the nice face that could smile charmingly, or look through her, or appear lifeless. She'd get accustomed to that scar, an enigma, his only blemish.

As for the silence like a force field round him, she would get used to that, too. If there was to be no alternative, she would adapt to the whole damned package.

Creegan finished his call. She waited for him to initiate something, now she had made her point. But he went silent again, shuffling the case notes, gazing at pictures of smiling lost children.

When they got to Greenwich Park in St Albans the place was alive with uniformed police. An incident van had been set up. Forensic photographers and SOCOs worked behind the bushes at the back of the children's play area.

'Obviously,' Creegan said as they approached the gate, 'I'm rusty on the rules. You'll nudge me if I make any cock-ups.'

Taylor showed her OSC identification to the constable on the gate. Creegan did the same, fumbling the brand-new card out of its polythene.

'We were told to check with CS Beecham,' Taylor said.

The constable went off to find him.

They stood inside the gate and waited. Bright crime-scene tape fluttered like bunting around the play area. Sergeants and constables marched purposefully back and forth, performing their civilising rituals.

'I'm an inspector,' Taylor said, not looking at Creegan. 'You're an inspector. Enwright never wastes resources. Why's he made us partners? Is he trying to tell me something?'

Creegan hesitated, then he said, 'Should he be telling you something?'

'No, he bloody well shouldn't. My track record's impeccable.'

Creegan grinned. 'If you do say so yourself.'

'Oh, I do.'

'Good. Well, if you don't bring it up again, neither will I.' They looked at each other. 'Equal status, equal billing. The Two Ronnies.'

Chief Superintendent Beecham appeared and led them over to the crime scene. He looked old for a policeman, even a senior one. Lined cheeks, a bristly grey moustache and bushy eyebrows reinforced the impression of age. He was in full uniform, the hat pulled down and the greatcoat collar turned up. Vapour plumed from his nostrils as he marched across the frosty grass.

'Commander Enwright brief you?' he asked. His delivery was brusque, almost military.

'Child abduction?' Creegan said, making it sound like a response.

Beecham stopped. He turned and nodded. 'Kept track on the news on the other two. Same form. It's always busy. Nobody saw anything, nobody heard anything. And it's a dedicated safe haven.' He pointed to an array of CCTV cameras covering the main areas of the park.

'Not your first port of call if you're desperate, then,' Creegan said.

Taylor found herself on Creegan's wavelength. She said, 'Unless you knew what you'd come for.' To Beecham she said, 'You've obviously got your reasons for not bringing the OSC in sooner?'

He ignored that. 'Same age, all male,' he grunted. 'This one's Eddie Franklin, aged seven.' He pointed to the bench by the swings. 'His mother was only there when he went.'

Creegan wandered over to the bushes. A man in a car coat and Donegal hat came striding across from the gates.

He was Detective Chief Inspector Frank Dolland – gaunt, pockmarked, grim-faced from habit. He stopped in front of CS Beecham.

'What the hell is going on?' he demanded.

Beecham glared at him. 'Number three is going on, Frank.'

'I'm talking about this lot. Assuming I've heard right. Are you handing this over to the OSC?'

Beecham scowled at him, no love lost. 'You were asked to make contact with—'

'This is my case! It is my groundwork!'

'It's number three, Frank!'

'And it's *my* responsibility!'

'And you were instructed last week to make contact with the OSC!' Beecham shouted. 'You told me you had!'

Dolland's volume went down. 'I faxed outlines.'

Taylor said, 'The brief we got at headquarters said for information only.'

Creegan meanwhile was on the other side of the bushes, standing at the top of a slope, watching white-suited SOCOs work in the grass with their torches and tweezers and plastic specimen bags. He looked past them at the balding stretch of ground between the slope and the fence. Something incongruous caught his eye. A daffodil.

'Hang about, lads.' Creegan turned to one of the SOCOs and took a trowel he was holding in a plastic bag. 'Sorry. Can I?'

He was down the slope before the SOCO could say anything. Taylor, Beecham and Dolland came through the gap. They watched him. He crouched by the daffodil and dug at the stiff ground, throwing up chunks of earth, digging straight down beside the flower's stem. He hit something flexible and put down the trowel. Carefully he pushed aside the longer blades of grass. With his pen he reached into the shallow hole and brought up what he had found. He turned to face the others, holding up his discovery. It was a child's size-nine trainer.

'Germany. February '94,' he said. 'There was an Interpol file flying round. Two kids abducted. He buried their shoes at the scene of the crime.' He revolved the trainer, examining it. 'What triggered us was the daffodil.'

He bent and drew the flower out of the ground, holding it by the folded plastic bag.

'The daffodil?' Dolland looked baffled.

Taylor was on the wavelength again. 'It's December.'

'It's plastic,' Creegan said.

Taylor became brisk. 'Can we go back to the last two sites?'

Dolland stared bleakly at Beecham, no longer sure if he was still on the case.

Taylor drove to a local shopping precinct. Dolland sat in the back of her car and gave her directions. When they arrived in the town centre the three of them got out and took a short cut along the side of a church. It was cold. They walked quickly.

Dolland hadn't lost any of his stiff-necked resentment. As they approached the precinct he said, 'You're all recruited from Cambridge, aren't you?'

'Oxford,' Taylor said.

'Durham,' Creegan muttered.

Dolland scowled and dug his hands into his coat pockets. 'You're worse than the bleedin' masons. Since when did it take a degree to catch Ian Brady?'

14

'They didn't catch Ian Brady,' Creegan said. 'He got turned in.'

'We wouldn't be here unless we could help,' Taylor pointed out.

'Listen, sweetheart . . .' Dolland stopped and jabbed a finger at her. 'I've been swimming down this lane eighteen years. So don't play the double act with me, all right?'

Taylor bristled. 'I met Creegan this morning. I know as much about him as you do.'

'Oh, I know about Creegan,' Dolland said, starting to walk again. He glanced over his shoulder. 'I've checked you out. So don't come in here looking like the patron saint of How It's Done.'

Creegan quickened his step. He caught Dolland by the elbow, spun him round and stepped close. 'You refusing to co-operate?'

For three seconds it was volatile. The wrong response and Creegan, from the look of him, would have thrown a punch. But then his expression softened. When he spoke he sounded reasonable, gently mocking.

'That's very grown up of you, Frank.'

'Look . . .' Dolland's eyes wavered. He looked vulnerable. 'You come in here now and you clean this up, and that's my career.'

'It depends how many times your name comes up on the final report, Frank,' Taylor said. 'Now, I'll be filing the report. Try charming me.'

Dolland swallowed that. He strode on into the shopping precinct. It was a development like dozens of others, roofed and paved, with benches for footsore shoppers. Taylor and Creegan followed a short distance behind Dolland.

15

'They've spent four hundred man-hours on this,' Taylor said.

Creegan sighed. 'They've wasted half the man-hours because they've missed half the bloody clues.'

'Well, they know that. They're embarrassed.'

Dolland stopped under a cluster of lights between facing shopfronts.

'Jerry Casper was last seen here.'

Creegan stopped. He turned his head slowly, scanning the precinct. After ten seconds he stopped moving and stared. Taylor and Dolland took his sightline. In a municipal flower planter six yards away, a lone daffodil stood among the winter flowers and shrubs.

Later that day Taylor and Creegan spoke to Carol, Eddie Franklin's mother. She sat opposite them in the interview room at the local police station. Her friend, the woman who had been with her in the park when Eddie disappeared, sat beside her. The interview was recorded on station equipment, but Creegan's portable recorder was also on the desk. In addition to that, as questions were asked and answered, Creegan took notes on a spiral-bound pad.

At the outset Carol Franklin made a visible effort to keep control of herself. But as time passed and she was obliged to recount the moment when she first realised Eddie was gone, she began to cry. Her friend tried to soothe her and she wept harder. Her shoulders heaved uncontrollably. As the interview drew to a close, her mascara was running down her cheeks.

'Carol, did you see anyone?' Taylor said.

Carol shook her head.

'Were you aware of any single men who might have come near or walked past?'

Again Carol shook her head. 'No.'

'Look,' the friend said, 'Eddie's a smart kid. He knows about nutters. He wouldn't have just gone off with somebody.'

Creegan picked up the framed picture of Eddie that Carol had brought with her to the station. He looked at the cheerful young face. 'We'll copy this and get it straight back to you, Carol.'

As Creegan put the picture down Taylor glanced casually at the notebook he was using. She looked again. His notes were in shorthand. Real shorthand.

3

The next afternoon, walking through the headquarters building with Creegan, Taylor deliberately took the scenic route, giving him a measure of the geography.

'Not your average nick,' she said. 'It used to be an annexe for GCHQ.'

The structure of the place and the design details gave away its art deco origins. Taylor said nothing about that, in case she sounded pretentious. Instead she talked about the renovations that had been carried out before OSC moved in. The original stonework had been retained as far as possible and carefully restored; where repairs were necessary they had been made with matching material, some of it rescued from defunct buildings created by the same architect-builder partnership.

The building asserted its own atmosphere. As Taylor and Creegan passed other offices there was a sense of activity, steady work going on beyond the doors with an occasional thrumming hint of machines, all of it somehow at one with the marble and the grandeur. The presence of extensive front-line technology, in a building straight out of a twenties novel, was an arrangement that fired Taylor's imagination. It made her think, sometimes, of old late-night movies about futures that were already past.

'Pretty impressive, isn't it?' she said, her heel-clicks echoing off the corridor walls.

Creegan shrugged. 'It just makes me want to nick soap.'

They took a turning that led to one of the computer rooms. Taylor opened the glass-panelled door and led Creegan in. The blinds were shut. The room looked cavernous and shadowy, with only a couple of desk lamps for illumination. At a long table a man in his thirties, a detective sergeant, sat before a bank of computer screens. He was using the keyboard of a master terminal to put footage from the Greenwich Park CCTV cameras on all the screens in front of him.

He looked up and nodded. His stubbly beard and placid features gave him the look of a trendy scholar, but the busy eyes were pure policeman. 'These are all repeat-performance tapes,' he said. 'Anyone appearing in the park on more than one day, and more than once in the same day.'

Taylor and Creegan took the two chairs beside him. He tapped the keyboard smartly and brought up footage that showed the park from a camera on the perimeter fence.

'Now,' he said, his eyes on the screen, 'I'm presuming the perp picked his spot, so he must have been on a recce previously.'

Taylor interrupted to make a hasty introduction. 'John – sorry, *Jonathan* Kreitman, Anorak of Fire,' she said.

Creegan reached past Taylor and shook Kreitman's hand.

'He says he knows his keyboard like a woman,' Taylor said. 'But I don't think he's ever had a woman, which is why he hammers it.'

It was untrue, therefore it wasn't offensive, and Kreitman grinned.

Creegan asked him how long the tapes went back.

'They're kept for a week, and then recorded over. This is the most recent hundred hours. The rest are being sent up. So, go on, what are we looking at?'

They watched the big main screen. Kreitman used a selective zoom control to reframe the shots, picking out details.

'Well, that's Mrs Franklin and her friend,' Taylor said.

In the close-ups Carol Franklin looked as Taylor couldn't have imagined her – animated, bright-eyed, enthusiastic. She and her friend were laughing.

The camera moved on.

'And that's Eddie.'

The little boy in his red windcheater picked up his black-and-white football and turned to camera.

'You got a clear shot of that?' Taylor said. 'We've only got a school photo.'

Kreitman tightened the shot until Eddie's face and shoulders filled the screen. He tapped a key and the printer whirred. Two seconds later a big colour print landed in the tray.

Kreitman flitted to another image, then split the screen, showing two shots from separate days.

'That woman there . . .'

Taylor put a finger to the screen. A straggly-haired woman with a broad hairband, edgily puffing on a cigarette, was talking to another woman while two small hyperactive boys jumped around her.

'Yeah . . .' Taylor nodded as Kreitman zoomed in. 'She's on both tapes.'

'She's in the park every day,' Kreitman said. 'I'm sick of the sight of her. She's a nanny for those two.' He pointed to the cigarette. 'That's a spliff, by the way. I reckon her and the kids deserve each other. But there is something else.'

He began tapping keys at speed. High, long-shot images of the play area came up on all of the screens.

'Now concentrate,' he said, 'or you'll miss.'

Taylor had no idea what he meant. She watched the camera pan along the roadside behind the park. Beside her, Creegan stared at the main screen. People were walking in both directions, cars came and went. Kreitman continued to tap keys, varying the image size, upping the replay speed. As he worked he mimicked the *Countdown* quiz show theme.

'Back,' Creegan snapped.

Kreitman reversed the tape.

Creegan said, 'Yellow Volvo?'

Kreitman nodded. 'Correct.'

Taylor was frowning. 'Where?'

'Watch.'

Kreitman zoomed to one car among the many, sitting across the way from the park. An old yellow Volvo saloon. It appeared on both tapes. Kreitman homed in on the registration plate and hit the button marked PRINT.

The OSC conference room was dominated by the central table, a flawless expanse of polished mahogany with six chairs at either side and room for three at each end. On the middle of the table six green-shaded lamps in two rows gave adequate light for note-taking.

That afternoon eight people were seated at the table, four on one side, three on the other, with Commander

Enwright at the end. Susan Taylor stood by the projection screen on the wall directly opposite Enwright's chair. She was summarising the abduction case for her colleagues.

'Jerry Casper,' she said, triggering the slide projector and bringing up a picture of a boy. 'Three p.m. last Tuesday.'

Weak blue daylight trickled through the closed Venetian blinds and glinted on three plastic bags on the table, each containing a child's shoe. The slide blacked out and was replaced by another.

'Stephen Lord, five p.m. Saturday.'

The slide changer rattled again.

'Eddie Franklin, nine yesterday morning.'

Eddie's smile vanished and was replaced by a picture of a daffodil.

Taylor picked up the plastic bags and put them down again, one by one. 'All of them were marked by the presence of the artificial flowers,' she said. 'The only others forensics identified were in the woodland areas. They were weeks or months old, mostly eliminable.'

The door opened and Creegan strode in. He was in shirtsleeves. 'Sorry,' he said, smiling absently at Taylor. 'Sorry.' He went straight to the overhead projector and put a sheaf of papers down beside it. 'I think I've found something.'

Taylor blanked her reaction at being interrupted. She sat down.

Enwright sighed. 'Apologies to anyone I haven't tuned in today.' He smiled awkwardly and cleared his throat. 'This is DI Dave Creegan, new to us but very lived-in. We worked at Devas Street together. He helped me plan the OSC two years back, before he went on a sabbatical. Um, well, I'll . . . I'll let him speak for himself.'

'Yeah.' Creegan glanced briefly at the others, then fired up the overhead projector. He tapped the pile of papers. 'These are all suspects and witnesses from the South Herts team's files. Including a voluntary witness statement by this man.'

He put the witness statement on the projector platen and it appeared on the big screen.

'Ronald Hinks. He was in the shopping precinct when Jerry Casper got lifted. He gave average corroborated information. Cup of tea for his trouble, then he was sent home.'

Creegan removed the witness statement and put down a photograph of the Volvo he had spotted on the CCTV video.

'This car's registered to Ronald Hinks. It's seen here at Greenwich Park the day Eddie Franklin disappeared. Also the day before.'

Enwright jerked forward in his chair. 'Who's duty lawyer?' he snapped

Steve Carroll at the far end of the table put up his hand. 'Here.'

'Right, Steve, get us an arrest-and-search for this guy's house. Kreitman, Rivers, you're with Creegan and Taylor. I'll liaise with South Herts to make sure they're not losing their shopping. We need them on our side.'

Personnel began to move.

'I haven't finished,' Creegan said flatly.

Enwright looked at him. Rivers, a young DC with a shock of ginger hair, looked at Kreitman. Taylor kept her eyes on Creegan. She noticed that he could convey annoyance without looking or sounding annoyed.

'All right,' Enwright said.

Creegan went back to the projector and displayed three

24

pictures in quick succession: a small fat boy, a daffodil, and a small thin boy.

'Stuttgart, Germany, February '94. Two identical abductions. The flowers marking the shoes, marking the scenes of the crime, where the bodies eventually turned up.'

'Bodies?' Taylor said.

'The victims were both found at their original vanishing scenes in plastic bags. Both suffocated.'

Creegan put a standard passport snapshot on the screen, attached to an OSC file sheet. The subject was a balding middle-aged man with cold grey eyes and a prissy mouth. The word pedantic popped into Taylor's head.

'Professor Ronald Hinks,' Creegan said. 'Fifty-six. Geneticist working for Kessler UK. Kessler UK is owned by a Swiss pharmaceutical company. One of Kessler's branches is in Stuttgart. Hinks worked in Stuttgart from '93 to '94.'

'So why stall arresting him?' Enwright said.

'He's not going to talk,' Creegan replied. 'He's made himself visible.'

Taylor said, 'You think he wants to be caught?'

'I think he wants to be chased. There're three roads to the park. He picks the only one on camera.'

'*Just* on camera,' Kreitman pointed out. 'There's no reason he should know it from that distance.'

'He's been planning this for years,' Creegan said. 'He's not going to make any mistakes.'

A serious-faced woman with glasses held up her hand. Enwright nodded at her. 'Marion.'

'It's a double-edged sword,' she said, pushing the specs along her nose. 'On the one hand—' She broke off and smiled at Creegan. 'By the way, welcome to OSC . . .'

He smiled back.

'On the one hand,' Marion continued, 'the flowers and the shoes are obviously compulsive signatures. If he's throwing down the gauntlet, he's expecting a battle. If he's expecting a battle, he's more prepared than we are. It's highly unlikely they're still alive, but whether—'

'I'm sorry,' Enwright interrupted, and turned to Creegan. 'Marion's our psychologist.'

'Get away,' Creegan said, expressionless.

'But whether they are or not,' Marion concluded, 'I'd have serious reservations about leaving him on the street.'

Enwright looked at Creegan again. 'What are you suggesting?'

Creegan stared at the face of Professor Hinks up on the screen. 'Let's disappoint him,' he said.

4

Professor Hinks lived in a detached house on a quiet suburban street thirty miles from central London. That evening, as he turned his Volvo in through the gate and up the short drive towards the front door, a man and a woman appeared ten feet in front of the car. They averted their eyes from the headlight beams. The man held up a standard police ID. The professor switched off the engine and got out of the car.

'Ronald Hinks?'

Creegan stepped forward as a dog in the back of the car barked.

'Henry, be quiet.' The professor turned to Creegan, regarding him coolly. 'Correct.'

'You called a dog Henry.' Creegan seemed amused.

Hinks let the animal out of the car. It was a big soft-eyed brown animal, nowhere near as daunting as its bark. It went to the front door and waited.

'Is this concerning my statement?'

'Yeah.' Creegan and Taylor nodded in unison. 'I know it's a bit boring but we need to go over a couple of contradictions.'

'Really?' Hinks looked sourly surprised. 'Well, please, come in.'

'No stone unturned,' Creegan quipped, playing the affable tec as Hinks unlocked the door. 'You know – Elliot Ness?'

The moment Hinks went inside Creegan back-heeled one of the Volvo's indicator clusters and smashed it. He gathered up the fragments quickly and stuffed them in his pocket. Taylor stared at him, mortified. Creegan hurried into the house, pulling Taylor after him.

'I thought I gave an accurate description,' Hinks said. He took off his hat and overcoat and hung them up. He threw the dog a chewy treat from a tin on the hall table.

'I know it's tedious,' Taylor said. Her eyes were everywhere as she and Creegan followed Hinks into the kitchen. 'But we need to go over that description again.'

Hinks began spooning coffee into a percolator.

Creegan sighed and looked at Taylor. 'Just tell him,' he said. 'He's not gonna bite your head off.' He looked at Hinks. 'We mislaid your statement. And the boss is asking for details . . .'

'It's my fault,' Taylor said, blurting it, simulating relief that she had come clean.

Creegan made an apologetic face. 'She can't find it.'

'I see.' Hinks smiled faintly. He was obviously prepared to be magnanimous. Mistakes happened. 'Well . . .' He frowned, thinking, and waited as Creegan got his notebook ready. 'Light brown hair, early twenties, average height. One of the great unwashed. He looked quite on edge and the only time we connected eyes, he looked quite hostile.'

Creegan finished scribbling. 'That's brilliant, Professor.' He pocketed the notebook. 'Thanks for your time.'

'You're welcome.'

Hinks followed them back along the hall. The dog

barked again and went quiet as soon as Hinks told him to. On the step Taylor turned.

'Where can we contact you in working hours?'

Hinks frowned at her. 'You know I'm a professor but you don't know where I work?'

There was the merest pause, then Creegan said, 'You'd have been cross-checked on the IR register. It's, um, it's a formality.'

Hinks nodded. 'I see. Well, Parmenster Moor. The Kessler building at the university.' He followed Creegan as he turned away. 'The Sistine Chapel's brilliant,' he said.

Creegan blinked at him. 'Sorry?'

'I have an allergy to words like *brilliant* and *fabulous*. Students use them.'

Creegan looked chastened. He glanced awkwardly at Taylor, then at his own feet, then at the Volvo. 'Your light cluster, by the way. It's *not* brilliant.' His voice hardened a trace. 'It's busted, in fact. You could get stopped for that.'

For an instant Hinks's face was blank. He stared at the broken cluster, then launched smoothly into an improvisation. 'Yes, of course, I overshot a bollard at work. I've been meaning to book it in for a fortnight.'

Creegan nodded, looking straight into his eyes. 'Thanks again.'

Hinks watched Taylor's car pull down the drive and out on to the road. He listened to it accelerate away, then he turned and stared at his broken lights. He looked perplexed.

In the car Taylor said, 'What was that all about?'

'I wanted to see his face when he lied.' Creegan dug out his radio. He thumbed the transmit button and put the unit to his mouth. 'It's him,' he said. 'He's got a dog so don't get too close to the house. When he moves, you follow him.'

A voice said OK.

Creegan put the radio down and looked at Taylor. She was smothering a yawn. He suggested he take over the driving. She accepted, and on a quiet stretch of road she stopped the car. They got out and changed places.

Ten minutes later, humming along the motorway, Creegan looked at Taylor again. She was fast asleep.

She woke up as the car braked.

'How are you doing?' Creegan murmured.

'God, sorry.' She pushed herself up in the seat and looked at her watch. She had been asleep for nearly half an hour. 'Where are we?'

'This is where I get out.'

Taylor peered through the window. They were on a street of semi-detached houses. The one they were parked outside had a tidy frontage with clean brickwork and hardy shrubs growing.

The car door clicked and she realised Creegan had got out. A moment later he leaned down by the passenger window and rapped it.

'See you in the morning,' he said.

Taylor nodded and slid across into the driver's seat. She sat for a moment and watched Creegan go up to the front door. He knocked and it was opened by an attractive fair-haired woman in a polo-neck sweater. He kissed her cheek and went in. Before the woman closed the door Taylor saw Creegan go to the stairs. She looked up and saw a lit window with children's curtains and a Mickey Mouse on the sill. Creegan's shadow crossed the curtains.

Taylor put the car in gear and pulled away. One more snippet, she thought. One more patch of light on the picture.

At 7.45 the following morning Ronald Hinks drove his Volvo out through the gateway of his home and turned right towards the junction with the main road. As he turned right again DC Rivers watched him from the roof of a block of flats sixty yards away. Rivers crouched down by the surrounding wall, keeping the wind off his head and off the radio.

'He's just left Langham Lane,' he said, holding the instrument close to his face. 'All clear.'

Back at Hinks's house vehicles seemed to appear from nowhere. There were marked and unmarked police cars, vans and Land-Rovers. Dogs were unloaded from a van and set to comb the big garden at the back of the house. A handler took a small T-shirt from a plastic bag and offered it to a wiry Alsatian as a scent.

Taylor's car drew up behind a squad car. Creegan and Taylor got out and hurried to the front door. Five men were standing in a row against the wall. One of them was DCI Frank Dolland.

Creegan stared at them. 'What are you waiting for?'

'The locksmith's stuck in traffic,' Dolland said.

Creegan walked up to the door. He stood for a moment, shifting from foot to foot, then reached in his pocket and took out a Tesco loyalty card. He pushed the edge against the side of the door, twisted it sharply and sprung the lock.

Twenty-two personnel and two dogs entered the house and began a meticulous search. They worked in units of two and three, concentrating on narrow, strictly defined

31

search areas. Creegan, Taylor and Dolland put on latex gloves and searched cupboards, drawers, bookcases and bags. They checked newspapers, magazines, CD boxes and the backs of picture frames for the presence of irregular matter. Taylor went through every pocket of every jacket and every pair of trousers in the wardrobe. Hinks's fastidious tidiness made it easy to put things back as they were found.

The fingerprint team lifted marks from furniture, from the TV set, the video machine and window-ledges, while the forensic squad took carpet samples, bath-room samples, bed samples and samples from soiled clothing in the linen basket. The blanket where the dog slept was vacuumed from edge to edge; loose crumbs and pieces of biscuit were replaced once the blanket was returned to the dog's basket. Everyone worked without talking, each staying focused on the task in hand.

Twelve minutes into the search the police radio on the hall table crackled. Rivers's voice came on. Everyone froze, listening.

'He's turned around!' Rivers shouted. 'Hinks is coming back to the house! Repeat – Hinks is coming back to the house! Get out now!'

'Shit.' Dolland stared across the kitchen at Creegan. Taylor stood bent over an open briefcase. Technicians were motionless at various angles all over the house.

The frozen moment passed. Reassembly began at speed.

'Get out of the house!' the radio warned again.

Teams scrambled to put things right. They worked to a furious rhythm, maintaining orderly procedures but executing them twenty times faster than usual. Cupboards and drawers were closed, surfaces were wiped, rows of books and piles of journals were straightened.

Forensic and fingerprint personnel packed up their kit and covered their tracks.

As the teams left, Taylor and Creegan exited the house backwards, checking, scanning for anything missed, their eyes sweeping left, right, up and down. At the door Creegan snatched the radio off the hall table and went out, slamming the door. He stood for a second, watching the cars and Land-Rovers take off, seeing the dogs being shoved into the van.

Taylor pulled his sleeve. He ran after her and dived into the car. Taylor started the engine, threw it in gear, swung the car round and gunned it along the detour route before Creegan had time to get the radio back in his pocket.

A minute later the area was deserted and quiet.

Half a minute after that Ronald Hinks arrived. He left the dog in the car, let himself into the house and hurried to the kitchen. He looked at the key hook above the worktop, tutted and strode out to the hall. On a low table by the sitting-room door he spotted a bunch of keys and picked them up.

As he turned back towards the door he stopped. He looked round slowly, as if he had heard or sensed something that puzzled him. He looked into the sitting room, across at the stairs, down at the table where he had found the keys. For another moment he stood there, frowning.

Then he became brisk again. He dropped the keys in the pocket of his mac and strode along the hall. He went out and slammed the front door behind him, pushing it once to make sure it was locked.

5

When Taylor got back to OSC headquarters people were arriving for work. Commander Enwright came through reception behind her.

'Morning,' he said. 'What's happening?'

'The house is clean,' she told him.

Enwright noted that without comment. 'Do you think Creegan's adjusting?'

'Oh, he's adjusting,' Taylor said. 'Ask me how I'm doing when I've caught up.'

'I wouldn't sell you a turkey, you know.'

'That's holding me together, sir.'

Enwright looked mildly troubled. 'I owe you a drink.'

She agreed with a nod. 'One I can swim in.'

Enwright smiled and walked away to his office. Taylor stayed where she was, looking around carefully. When no one was near by, and nobody appeared to be watching, she slipped into the gents' toilet.

The first two cubicles were empty. She opened the door of the third and found DC Rivers. He was sitting on the toilet seat, lid down, nursing a fat manila envelope. He looked up and leered as Taylor came in and closed the cubicle door.

'You smell gorgeous for a cleaner,' he said. 'Want to show us what you can do with your Marigolds?'

'Oh, no . . .' Taylor snatched the envelope from him and edged him off the seat. 'Don't scare yourself, Rivers. Just go and wash your hands, you perv.'

As Rivers went out, laughing, Taylor shouted, 'How can anyone doubt that men lack direction when all their toilets smell like this?'

She made sure the cubicle door was locked, then she stood on the toilet seat and sat down carefully on the cistern. She opened the envelope and pulled out an OSC personnel file. It had Creegan's name and photograph on the front. She opened it and began to read.

On the way back from Hinks's, Taylor had let Creegan out of the car at the end of a narrow street near St Mary's hospital in Paddington. He waited until she drove off then he crossed the road and walked down the street opposite. Halfway along was a small greasy-spoon restaurant with steamed-up windows. When he walked in, a middle-aged waitress was trying to take away the dregs of a glass of milk from Cyril Golding. Cyril sat at the otherwise empty table with his elbows braced on the top, hanging on to the glass with both hands.

'Oh, come on, love,' the waitress moaned. 'A cow don't hang on to its milk that long.'

Creegan came to the table. He nodded at Cyril. 'How you doing?' He turned and smiled warmly at the waitress. 'Large coffee,' he said, 'three glasses of milk and two full breakfasts, please.'

The waitress went away. Creegan sat down opposite Cyril. They waited in silence until the order came.

Creegan had the coffee. The three glasses of milk and two breakfasts were for Cyril. He gulped down half of one glass and started on the first big plate of eggs, sausage, bacon, baked beans and fried bread.

Creegan sipped his coffee and watched. Cyril speared a sausage, cut it in half, dipped the cut end in egg yolk and stuck the whole thing in his mouth. Then he finished the first glass of milk.

Creegan continued to watch and wait.

Cyril got the other half of the sausage on his fork and looked up. 'I don't like where you work.'

'You getting upset because they gave you a hard time?'

Cyril added beans and a sliver of bacon to the fork and closed his mouth over it. He pulled out the empty fork, chewed furiously, paused, gulped down more milk, then chewed some more.

'I'm investigating the disappearance of three kids,' Creegan said. Discreetly he laid the pictures out in front of him: Jerry Casper, Stephen Lord, Eddie Franklin. He turned them to face Cyril. 'What can you give me?'

Cyril began eating faster, staring at the pictures between attacks with the knife and fork. The waitress and two women behind the counter watched, astonished, as he cleared the first plate, pushed it aside and started on the second.

Creegan waited.

Cyril chewed, staring at the photographs. 'They're gonna die,' he said.

'But they're not dead?' Creegan leaned further across the table. 'Cyril, those murders you saw when you came into my office, was it these?'

'I saw it.'

'Yeah?'

'Through the clouds.'

'Yes, but was it these?'

'I don't know,' Cyril said. 'Can I have a pudding?'

Early that afternoon Professor Hinks showed a crocodile of first-year secondary-school children round his territory at the university. Kessler UK had a policy of inviting bright, impressionable children on to the premises to be shown a version of life in a commercial pharmaceutical laboratory. Hinks took the job of hosting them in his stride. He could behave as if the show Kessler laid on was an accurate reflection of everyday life in the world of scientists.

'This is where all the tiresome repetitive work has to be done, thankfully not by me these days.'

He had brought them to an area where cages were laid out in tight rows on tables. The cages contained laboratory rats. The children were immediately charmed. Hinks stood in their midst, hands in pockets, entirely at ease.

'Hands up anyone who's had a vaccine?'

The children looked blank.

'Well, I think if you asked your parents, you'd find that you had. The animals here serve a purpose. That purpose is to provide a means of testing human formulae before they're released on to the market. The rats are the barrier between you, me and untried science.'

The teacher accompanying the children cleared his throat and spoke up from the back of the group. 'But the animals are all very well treated, aren't they, Professor Hinks?'

'Well, we make them very comfortable, yes.' Hinks paused. 'But many of them have to be killed,' he added briskly.

The children who had been smiling into the rats' cages stopped smiling. Hinks walked off, beckoning them to follow.

An experiment had been set up. It was a display of impressive chemical flim-flam with no relevance to the work of serious genetics. It was carried out by soundless technicians who stood aside when it was over and were careful to do nothing that would upstage the professor.

Hinks turned to the children. 'What we're mainly focusing on here is the most basic human structure. Can anyone tell me what that is?'

'The heart, sir?' a small boy said.

'Crucial, yes,' Hinks nodded, 'but this is something even more fundamental to life than that.'

'DNA, sir?' another one offered.

'Correct. You know what those initials stand for?'

A five-second silence.

'Come on,' the teacher snapped. 'We talked about this last Thursday.'

A thin lad in gold-framed glasses piped up, 'Deoxyribonucleic acid, sir.' He smirked and added, *Jurassic Park,* sir.'

Hinks beamed at him. 'Very good.' ——————

As they moved along the lab to the next enticement, Hinks fell into step beside the kid who had first said DNA. 'He's the one to stick with,' Hinks muttered, jerking his head at the clever one who remembered long names. 'He knows all the answers.'

'He does the school magazine,' the boy said.

'Ah . . .' There was a quiet, easy conspiracy in Hinks's tone. 'Is it any good?'

The boy shook his head. 'He's a prick, sir.'

Hinks laughed, strengthening the fast-established bond. The boy for his part grew taller for being quietly in touch with an important man.

That same afternoon, on orders from Commander Enwright, Taylor and Creegan flew to Stuttgart. They were met at the airport by Otto Dreiher, a pensive, melancholy-looking German DCI who spoke excellent English. He welcomed them formally then drove them directly to the Volksfeld cemetery on the outskirts of Stuttgart.

It was intensely cold and a misty gloom was gathering. Taylor and Creegan watched as gravediggers raised a coffin from an open grave halfway along a row of crosses and stone angels. One of the men brushed crumbly earth away from the eroded plate on the coffin lid, revealing the inscription:

Marc Volper
6.1.87
17.2.94

Taylor looked around at the others standing near the graveside. They looked uniformly gaunt and officious. Exhumation orders were only occasionally granted, and they were never undertaken lightly. This was a starkly serious operation, conducted according to the strictest rules of procedure. All police and forensic personnel in attendance wore their English or German ID badges, plus special-issue *ad hoc* badges in yellow.

Taylor glanced at Creegan. He was expressionless, but she didn't think she imagined the discomfort in his eyes.

As the coffin was carried from the graveside by two uniformed policemen, Creegan followed and watched it being loaded into the back of a big white mortuary van. From where Taylor stood she could see another coffin already in the van, caked with earth and clay like Marc Volper's.

When the bodies had been removed to the city mortuary for extensive tissue and fluid analysis, Creegan and Taylor were taken to a warm room at the central police station. They were given coffee and sandwiches, and Otto Dreiher brought them the case histories of the two murdered boys.

'Marc Volper and Kristian Mann,' he said, laying the papers before them. 'They were abducted four days apart. Some of us saw that as significant, some didn't. It was never resolved.'

Creegan stared at the pictures of the two little boys. He looked up. 'Please, will you tell the families we're grateful for their help? We'll do all we can.'

'The only hope they have now,' Dreiher said, 'is that you will show them their children's killer.'

Creegan asked if there was any way of tracking down Hinks's accommodation in Stuttgart.

'We've arranged that,' Dreiher said.

That afternoon, when Hinks returned home from the university, DS Kreitman, DC Rivers and a young CID detective from Dolland's squad were already in lookout position. The roof of the block of flats where they crouched had already been used to keep watch on Hinks's house. The three

41

men had tripod-mounted cameras loaded with high-speed monochrome film and fitted with 300-millimetre lenses. Each camera was trained and focused on a different area of the house.

Inevitably, as dusk approached, the freezing, fed-up CID man began to voice his resentment of OSC and all it stood for. He implied, among other things, that OSC operated an unfairly generous holiday scheme.

Kreitman began to answer, then through his camera he saw Hinks come out of the house with a plastic bag and push it into the dustbin. Kreitman fired three shots, then looked at the CID man, whose name was Bevan.

'OSC get the same holiday as regular coppers.'

Bevan sneered. 'They tell you to say that, do they? So what's this eight weeks' training leave all about?'

'Eight weeks' training,' Kreitman said.

Rivers nodded, confirming it.

'Crap.' Bevan popped a chunk of cold pizza into his mouth. 'My training for this bit lasted about fifteen minutes.'

'Well,' said Kreitman, 'it shows.'

Bevan stiffened. 'What's that supposed to mean?' He glared at Kreitman, waiting for an answer.

It was Rivers who answered. 'You eat with your mouth open,' he said, 'and your feet stink.'

'Piss off,' Bevan said lamely.

Down in his sitting room Hinks had just switched on the TV set. He went to the curtains to close them. Kreitman's lens was watching. He fired one shot.

A moment before the curtains closed, Hinks looked

up at the block of flats. It was only for a fraction of a second, but the expression on his face spoke clearly to a trained eye. He knew he was being watched.

6

Next morning Creegan and Taylor were driven out to Rischling Strasse on the northern outskirts of Stuttgart. It was a street of bungalows, at the centre of an estate made up entirely of bungalows, all practically identical.

'One-eight-five,' Taylor said, pointing one out. 'Used to be leased to Kessler International.'

The car stopped beside a cluster of other marked and unmarked police transport. Creegan and Taylor got out and looked at number 185. It was a profoundly ordinary-looking house, lacking any mark of individuality, but Taylor's expectations of it were daunting.

The occupant was Frau Locher. She took Creegan, Taylor, Otto Dreiher and a group of other police officers on a trip around the interior of the bungalow. She was an old woman, frail and stooped, with the suggestion of a dowager's hump. She wore a bulky, fleecy blue dressing gown and carried a cat in the crook of her arm. Other cats appeared to have unrestricted access to all of the rooms, which were comfortably furnished.

In German Frau Locher said, 'I took the lease over in 1995. Big corporation. Bastards, all of them.'

Dreiher made a quick gesture to Creegan and Taylor, tapping his head, indicating that the old woman wasn't entirely sane. He asked her if it was correct that her previous tenant had been the Englishman, Herr Hinks.

'That's right.' She made a fluttering gesture with her arm. 'He used to clean like a woman.'

As the erratic tour continued Creegan and Taylor went back outside. They checked the garden at the rear, which was small and clearly visible from surrounding properties. They returned to the front of the house, where several police officers stood, a couple of them stamping their feet to keep warm.

There was an abrupt metallic clank and the electric up-and-over garage door began to rise.

'Aah!'

Two officers standing close to the door recoiled violently from the smell that wafted out. A cat bolted past them. Frau Locher was now visible inside, standing by the switch that operated the door. The whole interior of the garage – floor, walls and ceiling – was covered in white ceramic tiles. The floor was covered, in addition, by the excrement of cats.

Creegan and Taylor put their hands over their noses and stepped inside, trying not to put their feet in anything. Policemen began to take photographs. Creegan looked round very slowly, noting the sunken light fittings, the tightly grouted tiling, the old brackets and holders on the walls where equipment had once been bolted.

'It's not always dirty here,' Frau Locher said in German. 'It's cleaned every Friday. *Every* Friday. You could eat your dinner off it.'

Without warning she unhooked a steam-jet washer from the wall and turned it on, sending cat turds flying in every direction. Officers shouted and scattered. Frau

Locher stared at them, bewildered, letting the nozzle of the washer come up, spraying steam at the level of their heads. Otto Dreiher and another man grabbed the washer from her trembling hands and turned it off. An officer led Frau Locher back through the adjoining door to the house.

Creegan looked at Dreiher. 'Do you mind if we shut the garage door?'

Dreiher nodded for them to go ahead. He clearly didn't relish the thought of being in there again with the door closed. He stepped outside with the others.

Creegan hit the switch. The door slowly came down, isolating Taylor and him.

She turned, her nostrils flaring with distaste. 'Creegan, I'm allergic to cats. You've got me standing in cat shit. Why am I letting you do this to me?' She did not add that she was also getting allergic to him pulling stunts like this.

He stood in the dim glow of the diffuse white lights, looking round the garage.

'You wouldn't go to all this trouble,' he said finally. 'You would not make a place like this if all you were going to do was kill them.'

Taylor watched him look around again. He stared at the shiny rear wall.

'I think they're still alive,' he said.

Later, when Creegan and Taylor had done all they had come to do and were back at the airport, they sat in the restaurant with a glass of wine and a snack to fill the time before the flight to Heathrow boarded.

Seated at the long curving bar with Taylor beside him, Creegan got out the copy files on Marc Volper and

Kristian Mann. He flipped through the scene-of-crime pictures.

'He led us here,' he said. 'With that much evidence, he led us to his house.'

'To a clean house, exactly like his other house,' Taylor said. 'If Frau Locher's steam-cleaned that garage once a week for the last four years, we're not going to find any admissible samples there.'

'I know.'

'Enwright's on probation with the Home Office. You won't get him to move on *instinct*. I don't care how far back you two go – Devas Street, Special Branch. He'll need solid evidence.'

Creegan closed the file. 'Happy birthday, by the way.'

Taylor was surprised. 'How do you know it's my birthday?'

'Same way you know I worked in Special Branch. I got your file out.' He clinked his glass on hers. 'Cheers.'

'Well . . .' Taylor shrugged. There was no point in denying what she had done. 'If you talked more, I wouldn't have had to.'

Creegan leaned his elbow on the bar. For once, he began to look relaxed. 'Go on, then.'

'I know you worked on Vice till you took a bullet through the head in a drugs raid,' Taylor said. 'Twelve months' sick leave, then there's a hole in your file. Psychiatric leave?'

Creegan sipped his wine, said nothing.

'Postgrad in criminology,' Taylor went on. 'Got an M.Phil., so if you wanted to pull rank you could wave your certificates.'

'Which would be very cheap and very vulgar. But I wouldn't put it past me.'

Taylor smiled, charting the humour as a defence mechanism. An effective one.

'Enwright drove up to see me in August,' he said. 'He asked me to come and work for your lot.'

'Obviously a fan. He's hoping I will be.'

'You're not?'

'Do you care?' Taylor said.

'Do you?'

'You're not my type, if that's the question.'

'It wasn't,' he said.

'Fine.'

Creegan swirled his drink. He looked at it for a second, then at Taylor. 'What *is* your type? For the record?'

She cleared her throat. 'Younger than you with bigger muscles and no qualifications whatsoever.'

'Fine.'

'So it took you from August to get here?' Taylor said, pushing the talk back on track.

'I was looking for something I could do without having to answer to everybody else.' Creegan looked about him in his disconcerting way. 'My ideal job is selling ice cream.'

Taylor frowned.

'You drive the van yourself,' Creegan explained, 'you mix the ingredients yourself, and the only complication is a greedy fat kid wanting more 99s than you've got Flakes for. Either way, it's one to one. I focus best on one to one.'

Taylor, at that moment, was focusing on the scar on his forehead. 'You joined a team,' she reminded him. 'We *are* a team, Creegan.'

He acknowledged the fact with a dip of his head. There was no sign that he had come to terms with it.

The Tannoy issued an announcement in German, then in English: 'Flight LH514 for London Heathrow is now ready for boarding at Gate Twelve.'

They drained the wineglasses, grabbed their hand baggage and headed for the gate. They were at the bottom of the stairs when Otto Dreiher and two uniformed German policemen came haring after them.

'Inspectors!'

They stopped and waited. Dreiher came panting up to them, waving a photocopied sheet. He took a moment to catch his breath.

'On the original autopsy,' he said, 'Marc Volper's liver revealed traces of a chemical. It was degraded, but it had some characteristics of an anaesthetic.'

Taylor said, 'What about Kristian Mann?'

'Well, Kristian was never tested. Marc had had a tooth extracted the evening before he was abducted. Which explained the anaesthetic. They assumed it was halothane, a gas dentists use. Today they screened Marc's tissue again – the technique has improved a lot since 1994. They discovered the substance was ketamine, a fast-acting *injectable* anaesthetic. Traces of the same were found in Kristian's body.'

'If they were injected,' Creegan said, 'it explains why they never shouted for their mums.'

'Mrs Franklin said there was no way Eddie would go off with a stranger,' said Taylor.

Creegan looked at Dreiher. 'They were abducted four days apart?'

'Correct.'

50

'How long after the second abduction were they murdered?'

'Six days.'

'Our last abduction was four days ago,' Taylor said.

Creegan was nodding. He looked at Dreiher. 'They *are* still alive.'

He turned without another word and ran up the stairs.

Taylor thanked Dreiher, then ran to catch up with Creegan.

'Good luck,' Dreiher called.

He watched until they were out of sight, then walked back with the uniformed officers to the carpark.

7

At 7.45 a.m. on the fifth day of the investigation, Ronald Hinks drove his Volvo out through the gateway of his home, as he did five mornings a week, with the dog in the back and the radio playing. As the car passed the main road junction and disappeared from sight over a hill, police vehicles from three separate side roads moved out to form a convoy. They travelled at speed along the avenue leading to Hinks's house, where they fanned out on both sides of the road and parked.

Police officers and technicians poured out of cars, vans and Land-Rovers. Two forensic teams stacked their equipment ready at the front door. Dogs tugged at their chains, whimpering and barking.

DCI Dolland spoke into his radio as he walked towards the house. 'He's on his way into work. We're tracking him along the A424.'

Creegan was on the other end of the connection. He sat beside Taylor as she drove them towards the campus of Verulamium University.

'Don't be subtle,' Creegan said into the radio. 'Take the door off.'

Dolland said he was waiting for a warrant.

'Don't worry,' Creegan told him. 'I've got it.' He

snatched up a McDonald's bag from the floor and crinkled it near the radio mouthpiece. 'I'm looking at it now.' He rattled the bag some more, then said, 'Take it down to the brickwork, Frank.'

He switched off the radio. Taylor watched him throw the paper bag into the back seat. She shook her head, knowing there was no chance of Creegan seeing her. As far as she could tell, he wasn't aware of her at all. He was hunched forward, glowering through the windscreen, his eyes flicking left and right, showing all the agitation of a man in serious need of a showdown.

Half an hour later, Hinks drove through the main gates at Verulamium University and on to the forecourt of the Kessler building. He eased the old Volvo into the parking spot marked with his name and braked. As he undid his seat belt Creegan appeared at the passenger window.

'Recognise any of these, Professor?'

He slapped a photocopy montage of three pictures on the front windscreen. It stuck to the damp glass. Right in front of Hinks were the smiling faces of Jerry Casper, Stephen Lord and Eddie Franklin.

'Or these?'

Creegan's hand came down with a thump as he stuck another photocopy on the windscreen. This time it was Marc Volper and Kristian Mann. Hinks looked startled.

'What's wrong?' Creegan snapped. 'We working too fast for you? Get out of the car.'

Taylor, Kreitman and Rivers came forward as Hinks pushed down the door lock. They saw him reach inside his jacket.

Creegan pulled his gun from his shoulder holster and pointed it at Hinks. 'Get out of the car!'

Hinks slowly withdrew his hand from his pocket, letting Creegan and the others see he was holding a telephone. He raised the antenna, tapped two buttons and put the phone to his ear. Outside he saw Creegan lowering the gun.

'This is Professor Hinks. I need to speak to the Legal Department urgently.' He listened and sighed. 'I don't know. I'm being arrested. It's all very bizarre.'

Fifteen minutes later, inside the Kessler building, Creegan, Taylor, Kreitman and Rivers accompanied a buxom middle-aged woman along a corridor past a gantry announcing BIOGENETICS. The woman's badge identified her as Dr Wanda Galley, Dean of Medicine. Near the end of the corridor she pointed to a staircase. Taylor went up the steps smartly. The dean put on a spurt to stay alongside her. Creegan, Kreitman and Rivers stayed right behind the dean.

'His room's on this floor,' the dean told Taylor as they got to the top. 'If you don't give me an answer fast, you can whistle for the keys.'

Taylor quickened her pace, heading straight for the door with Professor Hinks's name on it. As she got close she moved faster and turned side-on to the door. She hit it hard with her shoulder and the door burst open.

'Hey!' the dean shouted.

'What?' Creegan yelled in her face.

He walked into the office behind Taylor. Kreitman went in behind Creegan; Rivers stopped to confront the purple-faced dean.

'OK,' he said, 'I need an inventory of all chemical substances brought into the building over the past twelve months. Specifically, psychoactive or sedative substances. I need any clothing, gloves, footwear, head-gear, whatever, that Professor Hinks might have—'

'Are you completely bloody deaf?' the dean demanded.

Rivers peered at her, pushing his face very close. 'Dean Martin, singer,' he said. 'Dean Saunders, centre-forward. Dean of Medicine?' He frowned. 'Remind me.'

Before she could say any more Rivers stepped aside to let a stream of white-suited SOCOs and forensic photographers into Hinks's office. She glared and her mouth worked furiously, but no further sound came out. She turned and stamped away.

While a systematic search and collection of specimens was carried out in Hinks's office, his Volvo was taken to a police garage where mechanics and forensic technicians stripped the body to its component parts. The paintwork, flooring, mats and upholstery were then meticulously inspected and sampled.

As the search at the office proceeded, Rivers sidled over to Creegan, who was picking through syringes and bottles on top of a cabinet. Kreitman was close by, watching. When Rivers was sure that Kreitman was the only witness, he spoke to Creegan.

'I don't know whether you've forgotten the score or just picked up some bad habits while you were out of action, but I think you should relax a bit.'

Creegan chuckled drily. 'Is that right?'

'Well, he isn't exactly throwing evidence at us, is he? Any mistakes on our part, we lose points in court.'

Creegan picked up a measuring cylinder. He looked at it against the wintry daylight from the window. 'And what mistakes have I made?'

'You forced a suspect out of his car at gunpoint. That could trip us up in court.'

'And that's a DC talking to an inspector,' Creegan said. 'Where did your bad habits come from, Rivers?'

Kreitman stepped forward and made his own contribution to the argument, *sotto voce*. 'Any mistakes should be his. We *will* get him.'

For a moment Creegan said nothing. He appeared to be thinking over what they had said. Finally he nodded. 'Point taken.'

'And it's not cool to pull rank any more,' Rivers added. 'And it means you've got to buy the drinks.'

In spite of the effort made by Kreitman and Rivers to behave covertly, Taylor had clocked the whole exchange from across the room. Nobody noticed her do it.

At the detention centre of the South Herts Police District, the physical processing of Ronald Hinks began.

Wearing the shiny, frill-necked detainee's shirt, he was first made to sit in a straight-backed chair and let a trained technician pass a sterile comb through his hair. At appropriate points the technician used angle-nosed forceps to pull out individual hairs from Hinks's scalp, taking care to draw the full DNA-rich bulb of each hair from the follicle. Several scalp hairs were collected in this fashion and transferred to a sterile specimen bag.

Next an orange stick was used to scrape minute particles of debris from under his fingernails. These samples, like the hairs, were bagged.

Next he was fingerprinted on a standard card which would be sent to the SO3 branch at Scotland Yard for processing, match-searching and filing.

Finally he was photographed – full face, right profile, left profile.

Then he was shut in a cell. Throughout the processing

Hinks had remained impassive and expressionless. When the cell door closed he sat in the semi-darkness, stoically hanging on to his straight face. He could hear the sounds of police business, people coming and going, other prisoners shouting and swearing and coughing in adjoining cells.

This was a place and a circumstance beyond Hinks's realm of experience. He was without reassurance and he could control nothing. As the minutes passed he began to look dispossessed and vulnerable.

Creegan and Taylor went directly from the university to the incident room at the South Herts nick. Kreitman went out to Hinks's place to assist in the interviewing of possible witnesses, while Rivers stayed at the university to get an inventory of materials handled and controlled by Hinks.

Creegan was at a desk in the incident room, studying a list of articles removed from the Kessler building, when Marion, the psychologist, arrived with her evaluation of the suspect.

She undid her overcoat, loosened her scarf and wiped the condensation from her glasses. She then opened the bulky folder she had brought and removed the photographs of the five boys. Her notes were underneath, pages of them, some typed, others written in longhand, all copiously highlighted in yellow. She put them on the desk in front of Creegan. He read snatches while she talked to him.

'Obviously, all the victims have similarities,' she said. 'Age, hair colour, eye colour. So we're not looking at generic paedophilia – the image is very specific. And there was no evidence of sexual violation with either of the German kids. So, he's not a paedophile. Or if he is he shows remarkable restraint. We could be looking at some kind of manifestation of grief, something platonic. A friend, brother, father.'

'No. Hinks is an only child.' Creegan took no trouble to hide his impatience. 'Never been married and both his parents are alive and kicking in Tunbridge Wells. If that isn't a contradiction in terms. Um . . .' He looked up from the notes, frowning. 'I need a bit more than this, Marion. Do you want to try again?'

Marion looked wounded, but she continued. 'It could have been the early death of a relative. A school-friend—'

'Could have been the early death of his hamster!' Creegan snapped. He took a careful breath and stood up, dropping the notes on the desk. 'What I need are triggers to get him talking.'

Marion stared at him. 'If you've an allergy to psychologists, I suggest you get that looked at.' She turned to Taylor, who was standing by the window. 'Is there anywhere I could get some food?'

'There's a canteen on the second floor.'

Marion nodded. She threw Creegan another hard look and went out.

'She's as good as the rest of us,' Taylor said quietly. 'You knock her, you knock us. Which reflects on you.' She walked out of the room, following Marion up to the canteen.

Creegan sat down again. For a minute he stared at his hands, clenched on the desktop. Then he sat back, snatched up the bulging folder of Marion's notes and opened it on his lap.

He was still reading ten minutes later when Dolland,

Kreitman and Rivers walked into the room. It was the first time Creegan had seen Dolland without his hat. He was bald. He looked like a different man. He also looked triumphant in a vaunting, gloating way.

'Absolutely nothing,' he said, nearly shouting. 'The only prints in that house belonged to him. The dogs have been walked till their knackers dropped off.'

'We've interviewed a hundred and fifty residents and regulars to a mile radius,' Kreitman said, 'including the estate up the road. They've seen nothing, they've heard nothing.'

Creegan crossed the room, handing Dolland a sheet of paper as he passed. 'Your warrant for the file.'

'Hey . . .' Dolland was peering at the paper. 'This wasn't signed till ten o'clock.'

'Your watch is slow,' Creegan said. He looked questioningly at Rivers.

'The only drugs that pass for anaesthetics aren't controlled by Hinks,' Rivers said. 'If he'd removed that kind of stuff from the labs, there's a triple-signature procedure.'

'Yeah, but he's in charge of the programme,' Creegan said. 'He could have dodged the books.'

Kreitman shook his head. 'He'd still only get access to enough gear to knock a rat out. There's nowhere near enough to sedate a human. Even a small one.'

Dolland was leaning on a desk near by, puffing on a cigarette, openly sneering. 'Well,' he said, 'for a crack team, you've slipped in your own shit fast enough. You've commissioned more man-hours in two days then we've spent in two weeks.'

'But we've delivered,' Creegan said.

Dolland blew smoke at him. 'You haven't had a

single sniff of the bloody victims! And you won't have a suspect much longer. Have you seen who he's got for a brief?'

'Peter Lister,' Taylor said, coming into the room. 'Kessler have just flown him in from Belgium. His chauffeur is in the canteen.'

'So even with evidence,' Dolland said, 'he'd piss you out of court. And you've got nothing.'

Taylor was frowning at Dolland. 'I'm struggling to understand why that should make you smile, Frank.'

'I could smile with that much Scotch inside me before breakfast,' Rivers said.

Dolland stepped away from the desk, squaring up to Rivers. 'Do you want to say that again, you little shit?'

Rivers stared at him. 'I could smile with that much—'

'Rivers!' Taylor snapped. 'Move!'

Rivers threw Dolland a look of contempt before he turned and walked out of the room.

8

Creegan sat at the table in the interview room with Taylor on his right. Opposite Creegan was Ronald Hinks, still wearing the detainee's shirt. On Hinks's left was the bulky figure of Peter Lister, sharp-eyed behind self-important brows, wearing a superbly cut pin-striped suit.

Creegan looked at Hinks and waited for the tape recorder to beep. 'Ronald,' he said, 'you're obviously not going to qualify for legal aid on your salary. But, ah, Mr Lister is a very expensive brief. Have you got that kind of money?'

'You don't have to answer that,' Lister said in a weary, sonorous voice.

Creegan turned to Taylor. 'Do universities pay that kind of money these days? Have I missed a revolution?'

'I represent Kessler UK,' Lister said.

'Oh, I see.' Creegan nodded, looking from client to lawyer and back again. He leaned closer to the microphone. 'On record that Mr Hinks doesn't actually work for the university, he works for Kessler UK at the university. And on record that the bill for Mr Hinks's defence is being footed by said Kessler UK.'

Lister sighed. 'You have no case to make. My client strenuously denies all charges laid against him and you have no evidence whatsoever.'

Creegan blinked a couple of times. 'How long have you worked for Kessler, Peter?'

'Oh, really, this is—'

'As far back as '94?'

Lister hesitated. 'Yes.'

'Stuttgart?' Creegan said. 'Did you work in Stuttgart?'

'Indeed I did.'

'So you were there about the same time he was? About the same time two boys were abducted in identical circumstances.' Creegan pushed the case paperwork across the desk. The pictures of Marc Volper and Kristian Mann were clipped to the top page. 'Both found dead six days later. Were you his brief then, Mr Lister?'

Hinks tilted his head a fraction, managing to look offended and scornful at the same time. 'That's a very crass accusation,' he said.

'It's not an accusation,' Creegan snapped, 'it is three questions. Three pieces of information. Were you interviewed at all in connection with those crimes, Ronald?'

'Briefly. As a witness.'

'As a witness.' Creegan looked at Lister. 'And were you his brief during this piece of history, Mr Lister?'

Lister looked shaken. 'I was not.'

'Oh no, that's right, it was another brief paid for by Kessler International.'

'I don't know what connection you're trying to make,' Hinks said, 'but a voluntary statement made during an extensive police inquiry does not implicate me in any way in any crime whatsoever.'

'I know. But it's twice you've done that, Ronald.'

Hinks glared at him. 'So?'

Creegan looked at his watch. 'Interview terminated at sixteen fifty-three.' He hit the switch and turned off the recorder. He looked at Lister, who was fidgeting uncomfortably, glancing sideways at Hinks. 'Did you want to use the toilet?'

'No,' Lister said curtly. He sat up in his chair. 'Now, please answer my question. Have you, or have you not, any reason to hold my client any longer?'

Creegan looked at Hinks, holding his gaze. He let a couple of seconds pass. He shook his head. 'No.'

Hinks and his lawyer left.

Creegan and Taylor went back to the incident room. There was nothing positive or notably directional in the way they walked there. They wandered into the deserted room and looked around at the littered desks and windowsills, the empty polystyrene cups, the swirling screen-savers on the VDUs. The interview had not propelled them to a course of action. It had left them adrift.

Creegan stood staring at Marion's notes, scattered across the desk. 'Where are those kids?' he murmured.

Taylor was watching him from across the room. 'Creegan, what if we've got all our resources pinned on the wrong guy? What if we can't find any evidence because there's none to find? You know, it's worrying me. Why isn't it worrying you?'

Creegan turned. 'We can't find any evidence, so you presume it's not him.' He studied the floor for a second. Taylor had seen that look on him before, like a teacher trying to find a way to put across what he knew. 'Why isn't it striking you that Hinks is bright enough to keep us from finding evidence?'

'Because without more evidence, a conviction's a fantasy.'

'Based on the fact that all you expect is a conviction?' Creegan spread his hands. His voice had begun to shake. 'Hinks is a freak. He's an intelligent freak who credits himself with being in control of the facts. If all you're waiting for is evidence, then we've got three dead kids around the corner, Taylor. He did it!'

Taylor was determined to hold her ground. 'I think you'd better speak to Enwright before we go any further.'

'If we don't find them, and he lets them die, he won't be blaming himself.' Creegan tapped his chest. 'I will.'

Taylor found his intensity disturbing. 'You need to stand back,' she said. 'We can't take responsibility for all of them.'

'But that's the only reason why I'm here.' He stared at her as if she had said something outrageous. 'The responsibility's the only reason why I came back, Taylor. What are you here for?'

She said nothing. She had no answer he would find acceptable at that moment, in that state of mind.

Hinks had been directed to the police garage where he could collect his car. A uniformed policewoman at the desk pointed it out to him. He walked smartly across the service bay, his overcoat flapping as he picked his way between the other cars.

He opened the driver's door of the Volvo and got in. Immediately the front passenger door opened and Creegan got in beside him. He looked squarely at Hinks. 'The more I come after you, the more we embarrass

Kessler. And the faster they start talking about your early retirement. It's their name they're looking after, Ron, not yours.'

Hinks was visibly startled, but he struggled to sound calm. 'I'm filing a report for wrongful arrest. You're welcome to add threatening behaviour to that.'

Creegan smiled tightly. 'I'll send you the forms.'

Hinks put the key in the ignition. Creegan caught him by the lapel and drew him sharply across the seat. Their noses almost touched.

'They will dump you, Ronald. Because I'm not going anywhere. I'm in your face till we put you away.'

Creegan let go of Hinks's lapel and got out of the car.

Hinks looked at him through the open window. 'Then we'll grow old within sight of each other, won't we?' he said. 'Because quite frankly, I don't think you're up to your job.'

Having delivered a calm, cold statement that amounted to an inadmissible confession, Hinks fired the engine and drove away.

Cyril Golding was in a hospital Casualty bay, being restrained by two male nurses as a young doctor tried to administer an injection. Cyril, breathless, choking, was dragging the nurses all over the room, knocking over tables, kicking aside chairs and upending a treatment trolley. His mouth was wide open, dribbling as he tried to shout at them and simultaneously pull air into his chest.

'It's an injection!' the doctor shouted, trying to position the syringe. 'It'll help you!'

The nurses wrestled Cyril on to a bed and leaned across him to hold him down. He bucked furiously, trying to throw them off.

'Look,' the doctor panted to the nurses, 'if you don't hold him tighter than that I'm going to break this needle. Just get me some flesh . . .'

A nurse leaned on Cyril's left arm, trapping it against the hard rubber mattress. The doctor brought down the syringe and jabbed it into the straining muscle. Another nurse piled on, reinforcing the restraint. The doctor quickly slipped an oxygen mask over Cyril's nose and mouth. Quite suddenly he wasn't resisting any more. The fight had gone out of him, but he still struggled to breathe.

As they wheeled him to a corner and began hooking up the support and monitoring equipment, Creegan was already on his way, speeding, using the siren and blue lamp. He turned in at the hospital sign and braked with a jolt at the Casualty entrance.

Cyril seemed to hear the running feet in the corridor. He turned his head to the glass panel in the door and saw Creegan there, panting, staring at him.

The image swam. Cyril was choking. His chest felt full of hardening jelly. He tried to say Creegan's name but breathing was getting too hard to manage and talking was miles beyond him.

It had to do with the boys, but he couldn't make himself know why. One was talking – Cyril could feel the voice more than hear it, could feel him telling another one not to go to sleep, and the other one saying how cold he was.

Stand up! Don't go to sleep!

And another one couldn't breathe, and Cyril felt that one strongest, he lived that one. He was making Cyril feel this way, making him *be* like this.

'What happened?' Creegan asked the doctor.

'Are you a relative?'

Creegan hesitated, then nodded. He could see Cyril beyond the glass, staring at him, his eyes wide, his tongue lolling behind the steamy plastic mask.

'He came in with a severe asthma attack,' the doctor said.

'What are you talking about? Cyril's not asthmatic.'

'Well, we've given him some of the strongest medication we can, but he's deteriorating fairly quickly.'

'Cyril!' Creegan shouted through the glass, his voice high with distress.

'Look, it's a condition we call dry drowning. He's pulling fluid into his lungs and we're struggling to control it. I'm going to take him up to Intensive Care.'

As Cyril was being taken along the corridor, festooned with tubes and bottles and cylinders, miles away in Greenwich Park, in St Albans, Ronald Hinks played a game with his dog.

He was in the children's play area, among the swings and climbing frames and CCTV cameras, waving his arms to make the dog jump for a stick, grunting with the exertion, his breath vaporising on the air. In the distance, two men in an unmarked car monitored Hinks as he exercised his liberty and made the dog bark.

Later, back at home, Hinks gave the dog a bowl of milk, then he went to the kitchen to wash up the tea things.

As he mopped a plate he paused, hearing a fly. He looked up and saw it near the light fitting above his head. With a sharp flick of the tea towel he brought the fly down on to the worktop, stunned.

Quickly he put an upturned glass over it. He continued to mop and rinse the dishes, watching the fly under the glass, seeing it recover and get itself up on its feet. After a minute it was functioning again, but now it had nowhere to go, nowhere but that narrow space inside the glass. It would stay under there until it died.

Hinks continued to mop the dishes and carefully rinse them, pausing from time to time to watch the luckless fly.

9

In the garage at Frau Locher's bungalow in Stuttgart, a technician wearing breathing apparatus had lit three smoke bombs in the middle of the tiled floor. White smoke billowed and quickly filled the garage. Outside in the cold pre-dawn gloom, a team of German police officers, headed by Inspector Otto Dreiher, stood watching the garage door, their eyes fixed on the seal around the edge. In the hallway of the bungalow, two other officers watched the interior garage door.

After a couple of minutes Dreiher got out his mobile phone and tapped two buttons. He waited.

'Hello? You were right. There's nothing coming out.'

Creegan was on the other end, sitting at his desk in OSC headquarters. 'You're sure?' he said.

'I'm sure.'

'What about the other door inside the house?'

Dreiher called to one of the officers in the hallway. '*Luftdicht?*'

'*Ja,*' the man replied. '*Luftdicht.*'

'No,' Dreiher told Creegan, 'it's completely airtight.'

In the pale light from the desk lamp Creegan looked sick. He swallowed softly. 'Can you find out when the garage was modified?'

Dreiher said they were checking that. Creegan put the phone down. He looked at the window. It was getting light. He stood, put on his jacket and raincoat and left.

At the hospital he showed his ID to the senior nurse outside Intensive Care. 'How's Cyril? Cyril Golding?'

'He's very poorly,' the nurse said. She led Creegan along the passage to Cyril's room. 'He gave us a couple of frights in the night. He can hardly breathe. You'll get nothing out of him.'

As she opened the door a high-pitched tone was coming from the cardiac monitor. The bed was empty and the window was wide open.

Creegan looked at the startled nurse. 'He was *that* poorly?'

At the very moment the nurse crossed the room and stared out at the fire escape, Cyril was half a mile away, running along a busy street, laughing and waving his arms and breathing with no difficulty. He gulped at the air as he charged along, filling his lungs, dodging the traffic as he leapt and skirted his way across the road.

Half an hour later, Creegan and Taylor arrived at OSC headquarters at the same time. They passed their cards through the swipe machine in reception and went together to Kreitman's office. He was expecting them.

'I've been checking on Hinks for a criminal record,' he said, going to the computer. 'Nothing. Then I contacted the regional force at Tunbridge Wells. Again nothing criminal, but his name came up attached to this case. As a witness.'

'Again?' Creegan said.

'Yeah, but he was only eleven when it happened.'

He tapped a key and an image of a newspaper page

came up on the screen. There were pictures of two boys alongside the heading 'ICE TRAGEDY – BOY, 10, LOST HIS LIFE IN LAKE'. Kreitman ran off two print-outs and handed them to Creegan and Taylor.

'"I could see him under the ice but I couldn't break it,"' Taylor read aloud. '"He was looking at me and I couldn't get to him. He just went back under and I never saw him again. Ronald Hinks, December 1954."'

'Is there any more of this?'

Kreitman shook his head. 'The newspaper closed down in 1955.'

'Find the parents of the dead lad,' Taylor told Kreitman. 'Track down the reporter and try and get hold of a copy of the coroner's report.'

Kreitman sighed heavily.

Taylor frowned. 'What?'

'I've been up all night. I could do with some sleep.'

'Fine,' Taylor nodded. 'Get Rivers to drive. Kip in the car.'

Later that morning Creegan and Taylor went to the greasy spoon where Creegan had met Cyril three days earlier. Taylor sat at a table near the door. Creegan sat nearer the middle of the room with his back to her. They separately ordered coffee and sat with their mugs for twenty minutes, waiting. Creegan was trying to catch the waitress's eye to order another cup when Cyril marched in.

Creegan got up. 'Are you all right?'

'Fine,' Cyril said. He went straight to the counter, stuck his face in front of the waitress and said, 'Milk.'

'There's a word,' she said.

'Toast.'

Creegan came forward, smiling. 'And I'll have a coffee,' he said. 'Please.'

They sat down. The waitress brought the coffee and milk to the table. She informed Cyril stiffly that the toast would be about five minutes. Over by the window, Taylor sat nursing the dregs of her coffee, watching the contortions of Cyril's face as he described the ordeal that had put him in hospital.

He threw back his head suddenly and made a loud, raw gasping noise. Creegan got out his shorthand pad and pencil. He looked embarrassed, but he didn't interrupt.

'I couldn't breathe,' Cyril said. 'There's nowhere to go.'

'Is it dark or light?' Creegan asked.

Cyril brought his head forward again and thought about it. 'It's dark.'

'Can you see me there?'

Cyril looked pained, trying to work out his thoughts. 'I'm seeing it through the clouds.' He lowered his voice a fraction. 'I don't like the people you're working with.'

'That's because you don't know them. Do you want to?'

'No.'

Creegan chuckled.

Cyril reached for his glass of milk. He stared at Creegan. 'He's watching them,' he said quietly. 'Your friends. He can see them.' He picked up the glass and started drinking.

'That's impossible, Cyril. We've searched his house, we're watching every bloody move he makes.'

'He can see them!' Cyril shouted, spraying milk, startling everybody. Then he whispered, 'He's watching them.'

The toast arrived and Cyril had nothing further to communicate. Creegan paid the waitress, pocketed his pad and pencil and left. Taylor went out a minute later.

When she got into the car he was on the telephone to Stuttgart.

'Inspector Dreiher, are you in the garage?'

Dreiher said he was.

Creegan could hear Frau Locher in the background, complaining in German at the continuing presence of the police in her home. 'Could anyone see into the garage from outside?' Creegan asked.

'Well . . .' Dreiher sounded as if he didn't understand the question. 'There's no view in from the outside.'

'The door to the house,' Creegan said, 'there's no window in it?'

'No, there's no window.'

Creegan persisted. 'Has there ever been a window in there?'

There was a long pause. Creegan heard a sound like something being torn open. Dreiher came back on the line, sounding a little breathless. 'Yes,' he said. 'There is a window.'

Later that morning there was a case meeting around the big table in the conference room. One by one the investigators took the hot seat directly opposite Commander Enwright and presented the latest intelligence they had put together on the abduction case.

Creegan was first.

'If the garage of the Stuttgart house was rendered airtight,' he said, 'he must have gone to a massive effort to achieve that. A small window was put in the garage door *after* Hinks moved in there in March '93. Over here he paid a local plumber, Kevin Hyatt, to fix a leaking tap, so he's not a DIY man. We need to check with builders' merchants, plumbers, tilers in his area. Somebody must have records of substantial works or deliveries or inquiries.'

Then it was Rivers's turn.

'Surveillance is showing that the only journeys he makes are to work, oh nine hundred, and from work, seventeen thirty. The only stops he's made are Sainsbury's where he buys his food by the day and a local newsagent's where he buys his paper. Now, he never buys a paper in the morning. Always at night. We've got the city engineers going through archive plans to find any boltholes close to Hinks's house.'

Rivers pressed the projector handset and a map came up on the screen. He used a laser pointer to indicate an area marked with a letter A.

'An old water board desalination unit,' he said. 'It was decommissioned and bricked up in 1970. As far as we can tell, it hasn't been disturbed since.'

He moved the pointer to a spot marked B.

'An underground war bunker which, apart from a couple of dead cats, never saw any tragedies.'

Kreitman was next.

'We've interviewed the mother of an old friend of Hinks.' A picture of the drowned boy appeared on the projection screen. 'Peter Weller. They went to school together, best of mates. Weller fell through the ice of a boating lake, December 1954. Hinks was there when it happened. Mrs Weller was far from happy talking about Hinks. She still blames him for her son's death.'

When Marion the psychologist took her turn, she said that if Ronald Hinks had to watch his friend die at the age of eleven, it was feasible that he or anyone could displace that experience into a need to be with children. 'Wanting back the kind of friendship he lost,' she said.

'And then he kills them,' Creegan said flatly.

Marion nodded. 'Possibly.'

The room was silent for a moment. Then Enwright said, 'Am I the only one with reservations about this suspect?'

'No,' Taylor said.

Creegan looked at her. 'What kind of reservations?'

'I worry that we're putting everything we've got into one suspect.'

Creegan looked at the window for a moment, then back at Taylor. 'Twenty-five ex-offenders with form for child-related crimes were interviewed by South Herts police, cross-examined by us and discounted. We're sticking with Hinks because he's the only one moving us on.'

'How?' said Taylor. 'All we've proved is that Hinks doesn't go anywhere. He doesn't do anything. All we know from surveillance is that he isn't making contact with the victims. Now I don't understand how we can treat him as the only suspect without a single scrap of evidence, Creegan.'

'Yeah,' Enwright said, 'I share that feeling. Anybody else?'

'Whoa!' Creegan looked round the table. 'We only got on to Hinks because his Volvo was parked near the scene of the crime. We only got on to the victims in Stuttgart once we started checking Hinks.' He paused, looking at Marion. 'Nobody invented that connection.'

There was silence again, uneasy this time. 'Look, we're under the microscope here,' Enwright said, 'and I'm sensing that people are losing their footing slightly. I think we need to go back over the original list of suspects and absolutely convince ourselves that we're not misfiring.'

'Sir . . .' Creegan was clearly having trouble hanging on to his temper; 'I think that's just wasting time we haven't got.'

Enwright leaned forward. 'Half an hour ago, I was made aware that the parents of Eddie Franklin have gone to the press about our performance. I've been called to a meeting at the Home Office this afternoon.'

Kreitman looked surprised. 'I thought there was a news blackout on this?'

'It's not news,' Enwright said. 'It's no news, which as you well know, the press seem to prefer.'

'Oh, shit,' Rivers muttered. 'I'm with DI Creegan on this. It's a waste of time.'

'Yeah, well . . .' Enwright stood up, signalling the end of the meeting. 'The faster we waste it, the faster we can get on.'

10

That afternoon twenty-five ex-offenders were brought to the South Herts incident room and questioned, for the second time, by OSC officers. Meanwhile a TV news report highlighted the case.

'The parents of the three abducted children, Jerry Casper, Stephen Lord and Eddie Franklin, have criticised the way the police are handling the case,' a stiff-faced newsreader said. 'The OSC, Organised and Serial Crimes Unit, who were called in to supervise the case, are accused of being too secretive by one mother.'

There was a close-up of Carol Franklin, crying. 'I've been told nothing,' she sobbed. 'My son's been kidnapped. And he's out there with someone who shouldn't have him. I don't know what they're doing about it.'

The newsreader said that Commander Stephen Enwright had made the following statement. The picture cut to a shot of Enwright working at his desk with the OSC logo on the wall behind him. He looked up and spoke directly to camera.

'We're pursuing several significant leads, none of which we're able to disclose at this point in time. I would, however, like to assure those parents that everything possible is being done to track the whereabouts of their children.'

Enwright finished with an appeal for witnesses.

'Any clues, any information, no matter how unimportant people think it may be, could be crucial in the resolution of this case. Events. People, faces, vehicles. Anything that may have happened to those boys prior to their disappearance. Please, contact us.'

Earlier that afternoon, immediately following the case meeting at headquarters, Creegan drove forty miles to Tunbridge Wells in Kent. He parked the car halfway along a neat terrace of Victorian houses, got out and walked up the path of number 63. At the door he checked the address on a slip of OSC paper, then knocked.

The door was opened by a woman in her early seventies. Her silver hair had been carefully styled, and she wore a little discreet make-up. A pink scarf was fastened at her throat with a small gold brooch, and her cardigan, a powdery blue, was cashmere. She had the appearance and bearing of a woman who adhered to standards.

She smiled carefully at Creegan.

'Mrs Weller?'

'Yes.'

He held up his warrant card. 'DI Creegan.'

She made to shut the door. Creegan shoved his foot in the gap. 'I know one of my officers has tried making contact.'

'He has, and it's not for discussion.'

'Look,' Creegan said, 'I think Ronald Hinks is responsible for the abduction of three children.' He paused, watching the decisiveness slip away from her face. 'What do you think, Mrs Weller?'

She stepped back slowly. Creegan pushed gently on the door, opening it, stepping into the hall. He closed the door again and waited. Mrs Weller led him into the sitting room.

They sat down and she looked at him, showing not a trace of resistance now. She was ready to be prompted. Creegan asked her if she had seen anything on TV about the three little boys who were missing. Mrs Weller said yes, she had seen the broadcast. Creegan told her that those were the three boys that he believed Ronald Hinks had abducted. Then he asked her to tell him what had happened the day her son died more than forty years before. She gave him the story more or less as it appeared in the newspaper report. When she had finished she dabbed at her eyes with a handkerchief.

Creegan sighed. 'You don't think it was an accident, do you?'

'No. It *was* an accident.' Mrs Weller spoke carefully, her eyes distant as she recalled. 'It was the latest freeze-over we'd ever had. It was meant to be nearly spring. The lake glazed over but it wasn't really thick enough to carry a bird.'

'So how can you blame Hinks?'

'He didn't call for help.'

'And that doesn't count as shock?'

Mrs Weller twisted the handkerchief between her hands. Distress could still take a hold on her after all these years. 'He told the police he screamed for help,' she said. 'He just watched. He told them he came knocking at our door, which backed on to the lake, and couldn't get a reply. I was in the kitchen with the door open when he said he was hammering on it.' She paused and looked at Creegan. 'Even his own mother didn't believe him when

he started crying. His father begged me to let him come
to the funeral, but there was no way on God's earth I
wanted him there.'

By four o'clock Taylor had interviewed three of the
ex-offenders. There were still four on her list. She
decided to do one more before she took a sanity break.
As she walked past a row of tables where low-probability
suspects were being interviewed by junior officers, her
eye was caught suddenly. Ten feet away, Ronald Hinks
was sitting at a table talking to a young female officer.

Taylor strode forward and snatched up the statement
form in front of the officer.

'Hello again,' Hinks said brightly. 'I racked my brains
following the television broadcast and, well, it worked.
I've remembered something else.'

Taylor looked at him coldly, taking in the cheerfulness,
the creepy affability. She found herself suddenly drawn
to Creegan's level of certainty about this man.

'Do you want to follow me?'

Hinks smiled. He got up, politely said goodbye to
the young officer, then followed Taylor to an interview
room. On the way she nodded to Kreitman, who followed
them in.

Taylor told Hinks to take a seat. She sat down opposite.
Kreitman stood at the side, observing. Taylor asked
Hinks to tell her everything he had been telling the junior
officer. He started by saying he was in the park.

'Which park?'

'Greenwich Park.'

'When?'

'Wednesday, December fourth.'

'When?'

82

'Nine o'clock.' Hinks hesitated over none of the questions. He seemed anxious to get on with his story. 'Which is, as you've already got on file, when I told you I was there. And this man, this scruffy man—'

'The same man you saw the day Jerry Casper was kidnapped?'

'That's right.'

Taylor stared at him. 'You just happened to be there when two kids were abducted in separate circumstances.'

'I'm saying I thought the same man was also in both locations.' Hinks glanced momentarily at Kreitman. 'What I'm further suggesting is that because he was carrying two large shopping bags brimming with food, he must live close by there. Mustn't he?'

'So,' Taylor said, 'we put fifty officers on a ground search of the area and we might eventually come up with something vaguely resembling the description you gave us?'

'I'm sorry.' Hinks looked wounded. 'I thought I was being helpful.'

'I'll bet you did,' Taylor said.

Ten minutes later, as Creegan entered the South Herts police station, Rivers spotted him through a set of double doors.

'Sir!' he shouted, waving. 'We've got something!'

Rivers led the way to the incident room. Kreitman and two strangers were standing watching a TV screen.

Kreitman turned when he saw Creegan. 'This is Richard Price and Gavin Broby,' he said, indicating the two young men. 'They're engineers with a TV crew. They were testing a satellite link near Hinks's house when they picked this up.'

Creegan stepped close to the TV. There were zigzags of static, dim daytime television snippets and snatches of transmission test patterns. Then a sharp, full-colour picture filled the screen. It showed three boys in a pure white room, sitting on the floor playing a game of snap with cards. The image stayed for only a few seconds, then it was gone.

The sight of it seemed to have taken Creegan's breath away. 'Is it them?' he said.

Kreitman had brought back the image and now he froze it on the screen. He pointed to one of the boys. 'That is definitely Jerry Casper. And that's what Stephen Lord was wearing when he went missing.'

'That's the bit I recognised from the news,' Broby said.

Kreitman turned to Creegan. 'DI Taylor's got our man in Interview One,' he said. 'He's volunteering new information on the man he *thinks* was responsible.'

Creegan dashed out of the room and ran along the corridor. He found Taylor sitting alone in Interview One. She looked shaken.

'Where's Hinks?'

'I took him out the back and beat him up,' Taylor said.

'You what?'

'I sent him home.'

Creegan pulled out his radio. 'DI Creegan to Surveillance Unit One.'

A surveillance officer responded.

'Get Hinks now,' Creegan said.

He walked out into the corridor with Taylor behind him.

'I've just relayed,' the man on the radio said. 'He's with Two.'

Taylor asked what had happened.

'In his face now!' Creegan barked at the radio. 'Get him!' He turned to Taylor. 'We've found the kids.'

'Alive?'

'For now.'

He got to the stairs and went down them two at a time.

'Where?' Taylor shouted, struggling to keep up.

'We don't know.'

They got in Taylor's car. Kreitman and Rivers took off in another car ahead of them. The TV engineers' van with its dish on top was already on its way back to the vicinity where the signal had been picked up.

En route to St Albans Creegan monitored the radio exchanges while Taylor drove.

The intercept of Hinks's car had appeared to be imminent when Unit Three passed an urgent message to Unit Two: 'We're stuck on the wrong side of the level crossing at Spring Road. You'll have to take him.'

'We're on the way back to base,' Unit Two pointed out. 'I thought you were taking him.'

Creegan opened his radio channel. 'Unit Three,' he snapped, 'name yourself.'

'Sergeant Slater, two one four two.'

'I'm gonna pull your bollocks off when I see you.'

Before Creegan spoke into the radio again he took a deep breath and let it out slowly. Taylor snatched a look at him. This time he didn't look so much impatient as anxious.

'Rivers,' he said, 'where are you?'

'Back road towards Hinks's house,' the radio squawked.

'Unit Two,' Creegan said, 'get on to Jubilee Road. Make sure Hinks can't double back.'

Ronald Hinks was turning in at the gateway of his house when he suddenly became aware that something was descending on him. Police cars were coming from two directions. A black car with a blue lamp on top was racing down the back road. On the spare land behind the house, police Land-Rovers and support vehicles had gone off-road to try heading him off.

Then he saw something that truly startled him. It was a white television engineers' van with a dish on top.

Hinks hit the accelerator and tore along the drive to the front door. He ran up the steps and had his key in the lock as Rivers's car raced along the drive and stopped with a tearing noise on the gravel.

Hinks got the door open and ran inside. He was at the top of the stairs when he heard footsteps thumping in through the front door.

He ran along the upstairs passage and into the front bedroom. He went to the window. A length of coaxial cable led in from the satellite dish fixed to the wall outside, to the right of the sill. Hinks jerked the slack at the top of the cable and the dish swivelled several inches to the left.

He moved away from the window as the footsteps came thudding along the passage. The door swung open and Kreitman and Rivers strode in.

Hinks recoiled. 'What have I done?' He shrank back nervously, looking from one to the other. 'I . . . I don't know what I'm supposed to have done.'

Kreitman took one arm, Rivers the other.

'You're a lying bastard,' Kreitman said as they took him out and dragged him down the stairs.

In the engineers' van, parked ten yards down the road from Hinks's gate, Gavin Broby was at his console, scanning the surrounding air, trying to trap a signal. Creegan and Taylor came in and stood behind him.

Creegan said, 'This is where you were yesterday, yeah?'

Broby nodded. 'This is roughly where we were. But I mean, there's no way of telling where we picked the signal up.'

'And you didn't see it at the time?' Taylor said.

'No. Only when we were spooling through tapes back at the office. I remember a flicker of interference but that's all it was.'

The van began to move forward very slowly as Broby continued to scan. Creegan looked out of the back window and saw Hinks being marched between two uniformed constables to a waiting police car. Behind them, his dog was being put into a dog van.

Broby sat back abruptly and shouted to the driver, 'Stop!' He twisted a filter switch at the side of the monitor. 'Hold on. Yeah, well, I've got something.'

Creegan and Taylor peered. A wavy mist shimmered across the screen. Broby used the keyboard to move the dish on the top of the van. Strong colours surged on the screen.

'There it is,' Broby said.

The picture was bright and sharp. The three boys were clearly visible. They lay motionless on the white tiled floor, the playing cards scattered around them.

'They're not moving,' Taylor said. She turned to Creegan. 'They're not moving.'

For the space of three thumping heartbeats Creegan

stared at the screen, then he swung round, jerked open the van door and leapt out on to the road.

'Creegan!' Taylor shouted, jumping out after him.

He was running hard along the road to where Hinks sat in the back of the police car.

'Stop him!' Taylor yelled as Kreitman and Rivers came out from the house. 'Stop him!'

'Dave!' Kreitman shouted. Creegan pushed him aside and shot past. 'You can't! Dave!'

Rivers started running until he was a couple of feet behind Creegan, then he dived and tackled him to the ground. Creegan struggled free but Kreitman was there, helping Rivers to hold him down. Creegan was staring at the police car. His eyes were fixed on Hinks in the back.

'Where are they, you evil bastard?' he roared.

Taylor walked past the three on the ground and went straight up to the police car. She put her face to the open back window. 'Please, Ronald,' she said quietly. 'Please.'

Hinks turned his head aside.

As the police car sped away with its siren going, Creegan walked out into the middle of the road, dusting leaves and dirt off his coat. He looked at where the dish on top of the engineers' van was pointing. In the distance there were a few tower blocks. One of them was framed loosely with a couple of clouds.

Creegan stared.

Clouds.

Still gazing at the tower block, he reached for his radio.

11

Within the hour seventy police officers in fluorescent yellow jackets were at the high-rise development, pounding the stairways and landings, knocking on doors and talking to as many people as possible. Creegan, Taylor, Kreitman and Rivers co-ordinated the operation and, while they worked, engineers in the detector van half a mile away tried to pinpoint the probable source of the television signal.

Every policeman on the sweep had photographs of the missing boys. Creegan's instructions were that, wherever possible, officers were to get inside the flats and look around. It was an ambitious job, complicated by its scale. From where Creegan had stood, the development looked like a single block, but up close there were four separate towers, all of them in line with the antenna on the engineers' van, all of them within the compass of the nimbus clouds.

The OSC contingent had already searched three empty flats, all lacking front doors and too severely run-down to serve even as squats. It was getting dark; everyone on the search had a torch, and a few startled rats were caught in the criss-crossing beams.

'OK,' Rivers called, 'we've got some numbers from

the council.' He had been talking on his mobile phone and had scribbled on the back of his hand. He read out the numbers of four vacant flats.

'Ask if there's any occupied flats with absent tenants,' Taylor said.

'I have.' Rivers looked at his hand again. 'Seven oh two's the only one.'

They started climbing. On the seventh floor they used a battering ram to open the frail door of number 702. The air in the place was foul. The movement of bodies through the dank atmosphere threw up swirls of dust into the torch beams.

'Stephen,' Creegan called out. 'Jerry.'

They moved from room to room, Creegan, Taylor, Kreitman and Rivers, calling the boys' names, bashing open doors, encountering one empty, smelly, dispiriting room after another.

Finally they emerged on the landing and stood taking deep breaths, Rivers blowing his nose furiously. A group of uniformed men came from the other end of the landing, shaking their heads, spreading empty hands.

'Right,' Creegan said, 'we drag in another hundred officers. We go house to house again.' He stepped back and shouted so every officer would hear. 'I want every flat searched!'

'No.' Taylor shook her head. 'It's going to take days to get that many warrants.'

'You don't *get* warrants,' Creegan said. He was agitated, waving his hands. 'You knock on the door. As soon as they open it you're in.'

'No,' Taylor said calmly. 'We don't. We ask. Tell them as little as possible.' She looked at Creegan. 'Right?'

He nodded glumly, taking control of himself. 'Yes.'

Taylor waved her arm at the uniformed officers and told them to get moving. As they trudged away she turned back to Creegan. 'I'll talk to Hinks,' she said. 'He can't have much left to hang on to now.'

The last time Hinks had sat in Interview One, he had been animated and voluble, apparently glad to pass on information to DI Taylor. Now he sat in his detainee's frilled shirt, completely silent, sullen, avoiding Taylor's eyes as he patterned a coffee spill on the table with the tip of his finger. Lying in front of him was a copy of the old *Wells Herald* press cutting with the ice tragedy headline, the picture of his eleven-year-old self looking up at him.

Taylor sat opposite, her eyes fixed on Hinks, maximising the intensity of the atmosphere. Kreitman was by the window behind him. There was another officer on the door. Hinks had answered none of the questions.

Taylor let the latest silence run to three minutes, then she spoke. 'We know you know where they are.'

Hinks continued to doodle, looking detached and bored.

'Are they alive?' Kreitman asked.

Hinks gave no sign that he had heard.

Taylor said, 'If you give them up, and you help us get to them, it works in your favour on your sentence.' She paused, giving him time to think that over. 'Now you know perfectly well you'll get unconditional life. But where you serve it can be a matter for discretion.'

There was a knock at the door. Rivers put his head round the side. 'His lawyer's here.'

Taylor sighed. She pulled herself to her feet and looked at Hinks. 'I hope you rot,' she said.

As Kreitman went past the table he spat on the back of Hinks's head.

Creegan was waiting for them in the incident room. He was agitated, rolling a stretched rubber over and over between his hands.

'Can I do the interview?' he asked Taylor.

She frowned. 'You don't touch him.'

'I won't touch him,' Creegan promised.

'If you're going to scare him, you make sure your arse is on that chair.' Taylor was not happy about this, but Creegan's agitation was not something she could easily sidestep. 'Promise me, Creegan.'

They went back to Interview One together. Creegan sat down opposite Hinks. Taylor faced the lawyer, Peter Lister, who was all business, stacking folders on the table, uncapping a fountain pen, opening a leather-bound notebook to a fresh page.

Creegan laid out the news clipping about Hinks's drowned friend. On top of that he placed the five photographs, facing Hinks. They showed the three missing boys and the two who were murdered. Creegan then unwrapped a fresh cassette tape and put it in the recording machine beside the table. He waited for the recorder to beep, then he looked at his watch.

'The time is five oh one,' he said. 'This is DI Dave Creegan accompanied by DI Susan Taylor. We're interviewing Professor Ronald Hinks and he's accompanied by his brief, Peter Lister.'

Now Creegan looked at Hinks, saying nothing, compelling Hinks to look at him. Hinks could do that for only a second. He looked away again.

'Ronald.'

The eyes came round slowly, reluctantly holding on Creegan.

'Did you abduct Jerry Casper, Stephen Lord and Eddie Franklin on the twenty-sixth and thirtieth of November, and the fourth of December?'

'No.'

'You've no knowledge of their whereabouts?'

Hinks shook his head. 'No.'

'And you'd nothing to do with the murders of Marc Volper and Kristian Mann in February 1994?'

'I did not.'

Creegan nodded curtly. 'Thanks. You can go.' He looked at his watch. 'Interview terminated at five oh two.' He switched off the recorder, got up and marched out of the room.

Hinks looked shocked. 'What's going on?'

Taylor got out of her chair and ran after Creegan.

'What the bloody hell's going on?' Lister demanded. 'Is this some kind of joke?'

Taylor ran down the stairs after Creegan but he was moving too fast for her. She shouted at him as he strode along the corridor to the fire doors at the end, and she yelled at him again from the steps outside as he fired the engine of his car and drove out of the carpark. She stood there for a while, watching his exhaust dissipate on the cold air.

Minutes later, in the station's custody area, Ronald Hinks, back in his civilian clothes, stood beside his lawyer and signed for the return of his property. He was patently aware that behind him Kreitman, Rivers and several other officers were standing by the wall and in the doorway to the cells, staring, making their loathing plain. Hinks ignored them. Peter Lister tried to do the same.

At the sound of panting Hinks turned and smiled. His dog had been brought from the kennels. He hurried across and knelt by the animal, fussing it, cooing affectionately as it licked and nuzzled him.

That was almost too much for Kreitman. He turned and marched away.

Hinks went home in a taxi. He paid off the driver at the gate and walked smartly up the drive. The dog tugged on the leash, restless at the prospect of being fed.

The timer had already switched on several lights inside the house. As Hinks opened the door and looked along the hall, he was motionless for a moment, seeing the disorder left by the police.

He went in, closed the door and let the dog off the leash. It padded through to the kitchen, stood by the pantry door and whimpered. Hinks took off his hat and raincoat and hung them in the hall.

He turned and looked into the sitting room. Lampshades were askew, papers were scattered across a table and on the floor.

Hinks caught his breath. On the table in the middle of the sitting room was a vase filled with daffodils. As he stared at it a man walked into view and stood by the table. It was Creegan.

Hinks turned on his heel and snatched up the telephone from the hall table. He pressed it to his ear, began to dial, then he stopped. He looked at the receiver, put it to his ear again, then sighed and put it back in the cradle. He turned to Creegan, who was standing in the sitting-room doorway, his hands in his coat pockets.

'If you could have proved anything you wouldn't be here,' Hinks said.

'If you'd been clever, I'd never have been here at all.'

Hinks swallowed visibly. 'You can't threaten me, Creegan.'

'No? What makes you so special?'

'You've done enough damage.'

Creegan laughed as he came out into the hall. 'I'm just laughing at something one of our psychologists said.'

'You're trespassing,' Hinks said. He made a show of confronting Creegan, facing him square on. 'If you don't get out of my house now, I'm within my rights to set the dog on you.'

Creegan looked towards the kitchen door. 'Henry!' he called, and pulled a packet of Maltesers from his pocket. He held them aloft and rattled them. The dog barked and came running. 'Good boy!'

Creegan walked to the vestibule door, rattling the sweets, rustling the packet.

'Good boy! Good boy!'

The dog followed. Creegan let it get ahead of him, and once it was in the vestibule he shut the door on it. He pocketed the Maltesers and turned back to Hinks. On the other side of the door the dog whined.

'Yeah, we keep shrinks on the payroll to speculate on the abstract mind, Professor. Imagine having a job like that.'

'I want to make a phone call.'

'Fine,' Creegan said.

He followed Hinks into the sitting room and stood behind him while he tried another phone. It was dead, like the one in the hall. 'You're getting ready for work thinking I've three abstract minds to get sorted today, and if I do it by five, I can get to Sainsbury's. It's a scream, isn't it? It's like your job. Biogenetic engineering. Ah, it's all *Thunderbirds* to me, you know.'

Hinks turned and strode out of the sitting room. Creegan followed him upstairs.

'Go on. Talk me through it.'

Hinks was panting when he got to the top. He hurried along to his bedroom and picked up the extension on the bedside table.

'You've fed the dog, you're having a shave, it's a precision lifestyle. But what are you thinking? I need to get in early, I've got an ear to grow on the back of that rat? Or don't forget to reduce human life to a single molecule at least once today?'

Hinks slammed the phone down.

'What shape's the rest of the world in when you can pull all that off, Ronald?'

Hinks turned to Creegan, breathing heavily, his mouth open.

'Are you up there somewhere?' Creegan glanced at the ceiling. 'Where the special people live?'

'The law says you've no right to be here.' Hinks's voice shook. 'You're breaking the rules.'

'Nobody knows I'm here, Ron.' Creegan spoke calmly, watching Hinks's eyes. 'They all think I've gone home sulking because we lost you.'

Hinks pushed past Creegan. He went downstairs again, hurrying, as if that might help.

'And you couldn't prove I was here even if you did your best,' Creegan said, following more slowly this time.

At the foot of the stairs Hinks stopped, and again he faced Creegan. He panted, narrowed his eyes, trying to look outraged. But he managed only to look like a man on the verge of panic.

12

Taylor parked outside the house that had the Mickey Mouse in the upstairs window. There was a light on behind the curtains, just like last time.

She went up the path and knocked at the door. The blond woman opened it.

'Hi, I'm DI Taylor. Can I speak to Dave?'

'He's not here.'

'Well, did he say what time he'd be back?'

'He didn't, no.' The woman frowned. 'He doesn't live here, you know. Can I see your warrant card?'

Taylor got out her ID and held it up.

The woman peered at it. The frown cleared and she smiled. 'We're divorced. He lives in a flat down Stamford Road.'

Taylor blinked. 'I'm sorry, I should have checked.'

The woman peered at her. 'Are you OK?'

'Yeah.' Taylor nodded and backed away from the door. 'Sorry to have bothered you.'

As she went back down the path the woman said, 'If he calls, I'll tell him you're looking for him.'

Taylor got in the car. As she started the engine she was telling herself, for the umpteenth time, never to make assumptions about Creegan.

* * *

Hinks was standing with his back to the wall. Creegan was less than two feet away, staring at him. The dog was still whining in the vestibule.

'What do you spend your money on?' Creegan said. 'Your salary goes into your account and you take out five hundred quid a week in cash. What are you buying these days, Ron?'

'Books,' Hinks said, with a trace of defiance. He edged out from under Creegan's scrutiny and walked into the sitting room.

'Of course, he's an academic. Books! You've got a Visa card, Access card, and you've got a Diner's card. But you buy your books with cash. Yeah, you spend as much on books as I do on child maintenance.' He went into the sitting room and faced Hinks again. 'Did I tell you I had kids?'

'I'm not interested in your private—'

'*Two*,' Creegan said, nearly shouting. Then he added, softly, 'Girls.' They stared at each other for a long, silent moment. 'For five hundred quid a week,' Creegan said, 'I keep two houses going. Where's your second house?'

'I beg your pardon?'

'Well, you've no garage here.' Creegan walked forward, obliging Hinks to back up. 'And there're no kids here. They're somewhere, Ronald.'

Hinks had his back against the door jamb. Creegan stepped very close.

'Look,' Hinks breathed, 'you're in enough trouble. Please let me go. This is . . . this . . .'

'This is abduction,' Creegan hissed. 'This is what being held against your will actually feels like. And you'll be happy to know I'm not a violent man.' He put his hand on the door jamb near Hinks's head, creating a

barrier. 'You are going nowhere. I want Eddie Franklin,
Jerry Casper and Stephen Lord.' He put his mouth close
to Hinks's ear and whispered, 'Now.'

He stepped back sharply and pulled open the front
of his shirt. 'No wires. And there're no witnesses.
Talk to me.'

Hinks looked around the room suspiciously. He looked
at Creegan again. He asked if he could have a drink.
Creegan told him to go ahead.

Hinks went to a wall cupboard and took out a bottle
of single-malt whisky. He poured himself a large one,
put the bottle down and recapped it. He looked at
the drink against the light, then took a sharp gulp
from the glass. He stood breathing deeply with his
mouth open, then he took another swallow, more slowly
this time.

'You're getting ready for work,' he said. He looked
at Creegan and almost smiled. 'You're having a shave.
What are you thinking?' Again he took a good long
sip from the glass and stepped closer. 'If this person
dies or that person suffers, it's down to me? Or the
world looks awful, and you've done nothing to protect
it. When your job is, by definition, protection. Is that
on your conscience?'

'I've learned to avoid that trap.'

'Then you're kidding yourself.' Hinks's voice was
firmer now as the whisky took hold. 'The hallmarks
of your job and mine are virtually identical. We learn
by failure. We're both at the mercy of evidence.'

The tick of the big clock in the hall sounded louder
in the momentary silence.

Creegan said, 'Marc Volper and Kristian Mann died
because you failed?'

Hinks's face was impassive.

Creegan shook his head. 'You were eleven when your best mate died. When you *watched* him die. You could have helped him, couldn't you? You were less than two minutes' walk from the nearest house.'

Creegan began slowly circling Hinks as he talked.

'But you didn't walk. You didn't run. Nobody heard you screaming. I bet you can't even remember why you killed your best friend. Just that you could, so you did.'

He was facing Hinks again.

'And you got away with it. And that was your first taste of a totally unique power that nobody but people like you really want. Do they live? Do they die?'

Hinks had difficulty speaking. 'If . . . if these people died,' he said, 'surely they died because you failed? Your people?'

He drained the whisky glass, turned to the open cupboard and poured himself another.

'Oh, because nobody *stopped* you? Ah, come on, Ron, you're a big lad. If you didn't know that was wrong, how come I'm here, having to play games? Your game.'

Hinks smirked. 'In your position,' he said, 'I'd be very angry if I was involved in a game I didn't know the rules of.'

Creegan stared at him for a second, then slapped the open cupboard door against Hinks's face. As it rebounded off his skull Creegan grabbed him by the lapels and pulled him close. Blood oozed from Hinks's nose.

'Listen to me, you freak. I don't want to hear why people think you did it. They'll call you all sorts in court. Socio this, emotionally psycho that, but you're not, Ronald! You're as sane now as the day you were born.'

Creegan tightened his grip on the jacket lapels and shook Hinks once, hard, making the blood splash down on to his chin.

'You were born a sick, twisted bastard. Some people are. And that's all there is to it. Where's the pride in winning a game you wrote the rules for?' Creegan shook his head. He released his grip on the jacket and stepped back. 'Your biggest achievement in fifty years is overpowering children. How in God's name could a normal person be proud of that?'

Hinks fumbled out a handkerchief and dabbed his nose with it. 'I'm not in charge of the game,' he said, almost in a whisper.

'Oh?' Creegan peered at him. 'Voices? You gonna go for voices in court?' He scowled. 'Screw yourself, Hinks, you've not a chance. The only voices you'll be hearing are the parents wanting you dead.' Creegan brought up a stiff index finger and jabbed Hinks in the chest three times as he said, 'You sick – twisted – *bastard*.'

Hinks shuddered. 'I don't think you're in a position to judge anyone objectively,' he panted. 'A few minutes ago, you were telling me you weren't a violent man.'

The dog barked. Creegan became stock-still. The dog barked again. Creegan looked as if something momentous had occurred to him. He watched Hinks dabbing at his bloody nose. He snatched the handkerchief from him.

Hinks gaped as Creegan turned and walked smartly along the hall. As he passed the table he snatched up the tin with the dog's treats in it. He went out into the vestibule and shook the tin at the dog, then opened the front door.

'Come on, Henry! Good boy, Henry!'

He ran down the path, rattling the tin. The dog

followed. Hinks dashed to the front door. He looked terrified.

'Henry!' he roared. 'Henry! Come here!'

'Good boy,' Creegan shouted. 'There's a good boy!' He kept rattling the tin.

For a moment the dog was confused. When Hinks shouted its name at the top of his voice it began to run towards him, but then Creegan rattled the tin, louder than ever, and the dog turned again and ran to him.

'Henry! Henry! Here, boy! Here, boy!' Hinks was dancing with rage at the door of the house, hanging on to the railing, screeching at the dog. 'Come here! *Here, boy! Henry!*'

Creegan rattled the tin in the dog's face and simultaneously grabbed its collar, pulling it down the path to where his car was concealed. He opened the door, jerked open the tin and threw a treat into the back. The dog leapt in. Creegan slammed the door, ran round to the other side and jumped into the driving seat.

He stuck the porta-light on the roof and threw the engine into gear. As he tore down the path to the road, Hinks stepped in front of the car, waving his arms. Creegan accelerated. Hinks got clear with inches to spare.

Out on the road Creegan turned on the blue light and gunned the speed to eighty. Heading for the tower blocks, he threw the bloody handkerchief into the back for the dog to sniff.

Police cars and an incident van were still parked in the square at the centre of the high-rise development when Creegan arrived. Police officers came and went on the stairs and landings, prepared to work all night if they had to.

Creegan got out of the car and removed the belt from his trousers. He opened the back door, leaned in and looped the belt through the dog's collar.

'Henry. Henry. Come on, boy . . .' He picked up the handkerchief and let the dog sniff it again. 'Come on, Henry.'

They started running, Creegan and the dog, the animal moving decisively, seeming to be aware of where it was. Creegan held on to the belt and let himself be led. They ran past the incident van across open ground to the stairs at the block of flats furthest from the carpark.

Creegan reined the dog in momentarily as he scrounged a crowbar and a torch from a constable. Then he was off up the stairs, the dog bounding ahead, knowing where it was going, panting and whimpering with excitement.

They went up two flights. They passed police constables entering flats and coming out of others. On the second landing the dog stopped. It stood wagging its tail, suddenly not so sure, looking left and right along the landing. Then it was off again, heading for the stairs.

On the next landing it stopped and sniffed the air. It barked twice and ran one way, then the other. Creegan held on to the belt, trying not to tug, letting the animal follow its instinct.

They went up another flight. The dog stopped. Now it looked lost. It stood panting and whining, looking at Creegan. Then its flanks tensed, it put up its head and sniffed. It yelped and ran for the stairs with Creegan charging behind.

'You find him,' Creegan grunted. 'Good boy, show me where . . .'

They went up and up, along dingy passages between flights of stairs, into smelly dark corners and out past rusting air vents.

'Good boy! Come on! Good boy!'

They got to the top floor. The dog dragged Creegan through a maze of steaming vents and massive water tanks with sweating pipes. Then it stopped again, looking around.

'Come on, Henry, you show me.'

Creegan knelt and let the dog sniff the handkerchief. Then he took the belt off its collar and let it go free. It ran around a corner, then another, and stopped in front of an alloy door at the top of a short flight of steps.

Creegan clambered up the steps and rattled the door, gauging the strength of the lock. He put his shoulder to the edge and heaved. The lock broke and the door swung open. In front of him was a flight of alloy steps. The dog ran up them ahead of him and stood snuffling at a heavy door. Creegan turned the handle and pushed. The door opened. He was on the roof.

The dog scurried across the blacktop to a big cube-shaped object and stood beside it, whimpering. The structure looked like a ventilation system. There was a door on it with signs that said STRICTLY NO ENTRY and DANGER.

Creegan looked up and saw a TV aerial on top of the cube. He put his face to horizontal slots that looked like vents. He shouted.

'Stephen? Jerry? Eddie?'

His voice came back at him. They weren't vents.

He turned and ran at the door and began attacking it with the crowbar. The front plate was heavy sheet steel and the lever handle holding the door in place was stiff.

He battered at it, using the crowbar like a hammer. The handle moved by stages and finally swung clear.

Creegan tugged on the handle with both hands. The door seemed to be stuck. He spread his feet and tried again. The door moved a fraction. He heaved, groaning with the strain. There was a sudden hiss as air flooded into the airtight box and the door swung open.

Creegan stepped into a white-tiled sarcophagus. A television camera was set into the wall above his head. He stood by the wall transfixed, staring at the three small figures in the corner.

'Oh, please,' he said, his voice scarcely audible.

13

Ambulances came. Paramedics applied on-the-spot treatment for oxygen depletion and hypothermia. Swift diagnostic checks were made and the readings transmitted to an Intensive Care Unit. Then the boys were blue-lighted away to hospital with outriders fore and aft. Throughout the operation Creegan stood outside the tower block, looking shocked and helpless, tears on his face as he watched bustling emergency teams conduct their urgent business.

From a distance Taylor watched Creegan, seeing his pain, trying to understand the intricacy of his feelings. When finally she approached him there was nothing she could say. She simply put her hand on his shoulder and squeezed it gently.

During the course of the night it was announced from the hospital that Jerry Casper, Stephen Lord and Eddie Franklin had responded to emergency therapy and were expected to make a full and rapid recovery.

By early afternoon Eddie Franklin was fit enough to be interviewed. Creegan and Taylor went to the hospital. Creegan sat on the bed; Taylor took a chair at the side. They kept it as informal as they could. The questioning was cautiously framed to elicit the facts without causing

Eddie distress, but it turned out that he could not recall very much.

'Is that all you remember, Eddie?' Taylor asked him. 'Didn't see anything? Didn't hear anything?'

'Just a sharp pain, like an injection, in my leg.'

Creegan was nodding, feigning interest in Eddie's collection of football cards. 'You said he pulled your hair?'

'Not then,' Eddie said. 'I wasn't really awake. My hair *was* being pulled. Not really pulled. Like, you know if you put Sellotape on and rip it off?'

Taylor nodded. 'Yeah?'

'Yeah.' Eddie grinned.

'I bet that felt really weird.' Taylor moved her chair nearer the bed. 'Could you see who was doing that, Eddie? If I showed you some pictures, do you think you might recognise one of them? If you really concentrate?'

She produced three six-by-four colour prints, each showing a different man. One of them was Hinks. She fanned the prints and held them up in front of Eddie.

He stared at the faces.

'No,' he said, and shook his head.

It was the same story with Jerry Casper and Stephen Lord. They remembered nothing useful.

The sense of relief at finding the children was soon obscured by the maddening probability that Hinks could not be successfully prosecuted. For half an hour that afternoon senior officers of OSC battered at the unyielding structure of law protecting a man they all knew was guilty of abduction and murder. In the end Creegan appeared to snap.

'He *is* guilty!' he shouted, and punched the conference table with the side of his fist. 'The only way we knew about Marc Volper and Kristian Mann was because of the calling cards, the shoes.'

He paused, seeming to lose his way. When he spoke again there was the hint of a stammer.

'The only way we found victims was because of Ronald Hinks's work records, and the only reason we knew about him was because his car was in . . .' He stopped, then started shouting again. '*His very distinctive bloody car* was in Greenwich Park when Eddie Franklin was abducted!'

'Circumstantial,' said Steve Carroll, one of the two OSC lawyers present.

Creegan looked helplessly at Commander Enwright, who sat in his usual chair at the top of the table, his face impassive.

'His dog,' Creegan tried. 'His own bloody dog led us to the last three victims, sir.'

Nicola Bruce, the other lawyer, was shaking her head. 'Look,' she said, 'Hinks has more grounds for harassment than we have for a conviction.'

Creegan was on his feet now and wandering round the table. 'The dog knew exactly where it was going,' he said. 'It was following its owner's scent.'

'With the greatest respect,' said Steve Carroll, 'we can't put a dog in the witness box. And if we could, it's circumstantial.'

Creegan stared, his brows gathering. Suddenly he ran at Carroll. He grabbed him by the lapels, nearly jerking him out of the chair and yelling in his face. 'I wouldn't pay you lot with bloody washers, do you know that?'

'Creegan!' Enwright shouted.

Creegan wasn't listening. He still had a grip on Carroll. 'You couldn't make shit stick to a blanket – you *tossers*!'

'Creegan!' Enwright bellowed. 'That's not how we do things!'

Creegan let go of Carroll and walked to the other end of the table. He was seething.

'Just sit down,' Enwright said.

Creegan stood where he was.

'Sit down!' Enwright shouted.

Creegan looked at him for a second, then he turned and stormed out of the room.

Enwright looked at the others as the echo of the slammed door faded.

'Continue,' he said.

Taylor, as angry as Creegan but controlling it better, looked across the table at the two lawyers. 'You're not suggesting that Kessler will sustain defence for a freak like Hinks? He's a geneticist. I know they're not ten a penny but he can't be that gifted.'

'Kessler's worth billions,' Nicola Bruce said. 'If Hinks goes down, their name goes with him. They'll spend what they need to represent his innocence.'

'If they win,' Carroll said, 'their loyalty pays off; if they lose, they're sunk. They will not lose.' He looked at Enwright. 'You've given us nothing to fight with.'

'They've applied for the release of his passport,' Kreitman said. 'It's just going to be back to square one as far as Hinks is concerned.'

Marion, the psychologist, sitting alone at the bottom of the table, spoke up for the first time. 'He *will* do it again,' she said.

* * *

Later, in the office, while Kreitman worked on his computer to cut down the tension, Rivers watched the television news.

'The parents of three abducted children are calling their rescue a miracle,' said the newsreader, 'and they're praising the policeman who saved them. They say Detective Inspector David Creegan from the Organised and Serial Crimes Unit should receive a commendation.'

Rivers nodded. A film clip came up on the screen. It was Carol Franklin, her husband and Eddie, happily reunited.

Carol said, 'We'd all just like to say thank you for bringing our kids back safe and sound.' She grinned and cuddled her son.

The newsreader reappeared. 'The police,' he said, 'seem to be no closer to charging anyone with the offence.'

That evening Creegan went to the home of his ex-wife, Kerry, to see his children. For a long time he sat upstairs with them in their room, playing games, reading them snatches of stories from their favourite books. When Ruby, who was five, fell asleep, Creegan sat on the floor in the glow of the night-light, a richly coloured globe of the world, with three-year-old Louise on his knee. They sang 'Three Little Men in a Flying Saucer', keeping it very soft, so that they wouldn't wake Ruby. They sang it over and over, Creegan stroking Louise's hair as she rested her head on his chest.

When Louise became too sleepy to sing any more, Creegan put her gently to bed.

He went downstairs. Kerry was in her dressing gown, sitting at the kitchen table. He sat down beside her. She watched him carefully. He still looked as if he was in shock.

'I'm sorry it's so late,' he said. 'I, ah . . . I didn't know where else to go.'

Kerry smiled. 'I'm glad you came here.'

Her live-in boyfriend appeared from the lounge, wearing shorts and a T-shirt. He put an opened bottle of beer in front of Kerry and one in front of Creegan.

'Ta, Barry.'

'If it wasn't past closing, I'd be out buying you champagne, Dave. Cheers.'

Creegan smiled at him. 'Can I stay?'

'Sure,' Barry said. 'I'll make the sofa up.'

Kerry raised her beer bottle to Creegan. 'Well done,' she said. 'You're a hero.' Then, sounding faintly cynical, she added, 'Again.'

Less than an hour later, Barry and Kerry heard sounds downstairs. Barry went down, wearing only his shorts. Kerry came behind him, pulling on her dressing gown.

'Dave?' Barry said, going into the sitting room. 'You all right?'

The sofa bed was empty. Outside there was the sound of an engine being started. They went to the window and saw Creegan's car pull out and drive away.

Not far away, Taylor was alone in her car. She had been crying. Her mobile phone was pressed against her ear. She heard Creegan's recorded voice.

'Hi. Sorry I'm not in. But if you leave your name, number and the time you called, I'll get back to you as soon as I can.'

'Creegan,' she said, 'just ring me. You selfish bastard.'

She switched the phone off, then threw it on the floor.

She looked out of the window, wiping her cheeks, fighting back a fresh wave of tears. She wondered, bleakly, if he believed he was the only one blowing a valve.

Creegan drove for more than an hour, along brightly lit stretches of motorway, then on to dimmer suburban streets, and finally out along dark countryside lanes. It was close to midnight when he arrived at Ronald Hinks's house.

He switched off the engine. For a moment he sat still, staring through the windscreen. Then he took out his pistol, checked the magazine and took off the safety catch. He put the pistol back in his shoulder holster and got out of the car.

As he approached the house he could hear classical music. He moved round to the back, picking his way carefully, staying off the gravel. At the back door he stopped. He could still hear the music. He turned the door handle gently and pushed. It was unlocked.

He went in and closed the door, moving soundlessly. He waited. The dog didn't come.

He made his way carefully across the kitchen and stopped in the hallway, ten feet from the half-open sitting-room door. The music was loud now, blaring. In a nook behind Creegan, unseen by him, the dog lay asleep in its basket.

Creegan pulled out his gun. He took a steadying breath, then marched up to the sitting-room door. He pushed it wide open and levelled the gun.

He stared. Hinks was slumped over his desk. There

was a hole in the side of his head. Blood had leaked out across the desk and papers. An armchair and a polished table near the desk were spattered with blood.

Creegan looked stunned. He stared from Hinks's body to the curtain. It moved slowly in the breeze from the open window sash.

The music stopped. The only sound now was the ticking clock and the soft jangling of wind chimes hanging at the window.

Creegan lowered the gun. He looked at Hinks's lifeless face, then he looked at the chimes. He saw that they were made from wafers of dull-glinting bronze, fashioned in the shape of clouds.

PART TWO

14

On the morning of the PR event, Taylor swiped in at reception ten minutes earlier than usual. On the way to her office she saw Kreitman come out into the corridor carrying two pages of a Metropolitan Police fax. Behind him in the communications room Rivers was removing the final page from the fax machine.

'Three patients at St Barnaby's died within half an hour of each other,' Kreitman told Taylor. He fell into step beside her. 'All suspicious circumstances. Four o'clock this morning.' He handed her the fax. 'This came through from DCI Judy Brennan. You know her?'

'She hates me,' Taylor said. 'They've obviously got no suspects and they know it's a press nightmare.'

'All high-dependency patients,' Rivers said, coming up behind them with the rest of the fax. 'Cause of death's heart failure but the *cause* of cause of death is up for grabs.'

'No it's not,' they heard Creegan say.

Rivers shrugged apologetically to the other two. 'No it's not,' he said.

They entered the office shared by Creegan and Taylor. Creegan was standing with his back to them. He was looking in a mirror as he tied his tie.

'Well,' he said, 'the toxicology reports on the first two revealed five milligrams of digoxin. And since neither patient was prescribed digoxin, I think it's a bit shy to call it suspicious circumstances.'

They all knew their basic pharmacology. Digoxin, the most commonly used form of digitalis, was a heart stimulant that could be administered by mouth or intravenously, exerting a contracting force on the muscles of the heart. In a large enough dose its effects could be fatal.

'The patients were on different wards, so it wasn't opportunism.' Creegan turned to face the others and put on his jacket. 'They were specifically targeted.'

Rivers was staring at him, openly puzzled. 'How do you know all this?' He turned to Taylor and Kreitman. 'What the hell time does he get up in the morning?'

'I watched the report on breakfast news,' Creegan said. 'Then I rang around.'

Rivers sighed. 'I think you need to get laid. You might spend more time in bed and less time showing everyone else up.'

Taylor was using a strip of Sellotape to remove threads and specks from her black trousers. 'Tell Brennan we'll take the case,' she told Kreitman, 'subject to Commander Enwright's approval.'

Kreitman didn't look happy. 'Can't we palm it off on Ducassi's team? I can't stand hospitals.'

The phone rang. It was Enwright's secretary calling to say everything was ready.

On the way to the door Creegan stopped Rivers and made to straighten his tie. Rivers was glad of the assistance. He held his chin up out of the way. Instead of straightening the tie Creegan pulled it off-centre and left it that way. It was a comic moment, neatly timed to cut into the tension of the occasion, and it added another strand to Taylor's understanding of Creegan. She now knew that when the pressure was off, he could lighten up to a point where he was hardly recognisable.

They entered the conference room to enthusiastic applause. The occasion was designed to let OSC fly its flags for the press, and a number of distinguished newspaper and magazine journalists were present. Badges of commendation had already been awarded to Creegan, Taylor, Kreitman and Rivers at a more private ceremony; today was an opportunity to bathe them in a little public glory, which couldn't fail to reflect agreeably on the organisation.

The team sat at a long table with the commander at the centre. Flashes popped intermittently as Enwright addressed the press.

'Now I know you're all going to write about crack teams and the élite working practices of the OSC, and call all these people heroes,' he said, 'but I can assure you that no one here feels like that.'

'Speaking for himself, of course,' Creegan muttered, and got a laugh.

'Those children were rescued by solid police technique, driven by a very high standard of information-gathering,' Enwright continued. 'That's the point of this unit. We have to deal with this kind of stuff every day. So I'm glad you're all here to see where we hang out. But please, try not to use adjectives like élite or special. Not least because it prejudices funding if the Home Office thinks we're all smartarses. Thank you.'

There were other speeches. A Cabinet spokesman delivered a chain of platitudes about policing in an age of burgeoning technology and dwindling human values; a leading criminologist aired his enthusiasm for the philosophy of the OSC, and a member of the Scotland Yard brass pretended to do the same.

When the talking was finally over, Creegan, Taylor, Kreitman and Rivers posed in a tight group, holding the boxes with their badges while photographers fired off dozens of shots.

Creegan slipped back to the office as soon as people began circulating. Taylor saw him go and decided to do the same. On the way out she paused a moment to listen to Rivers deliver a line to a good-looking female journalist.

'If there is any friction between us and regional police forces,' he said, 'it's because it's a new relationship. Now, I don't know how you are with relationships, but in my experience you have to give and take, you know, until you find your own pattern.' He pointed to a couple of chairs in a corner. 'Do you want to sit down?'

Taylor moved away, smiling. When she walked into the office, Creegan was bent over his desk, flipping through the file on Ronald Hinks.

'Listen,' she said, 'well done.' She held up the box with her badge. 'You deserve this more than any of us.' She stepped closer. Creegan was staring at a black-and-white picture of Hinks on the top of a clipped sheaf of papers. 'I know it didn't turn out like you wanted, but you did a superb job.'

Creegan looked up. 'Do you know what the coroner's verdict was on Hinks's death?'

'I put a copy of the report on your desk last night. They've recorded suicide.'

'I don't think that's the case,' Creegan said.

'Why not?'

Enwright appeared in the doorway. 'The bodies from St Barnaby's are being examined in an hour,' he said. 'I've got a journalist telling me we're involved in the investigation.'

'Only on your approval, sir,' Taylor said.

'Fine. Don't you think one of the team should be there?'

Taylor looked at Creegan. He looked back at her, his face expressionless. Taylor went and got her coat.

The brightly lit areas in the autopsy room were on the examination tables and along the worktops and sinks. Otherwise the place was gloomy with a prevailing odour of blood and freshly dissected tissue.

The pathologist had finished the third autopsy shortly before Taylor and Kreitman arrived. Two attendants had the body in an anteroom where they would replace the organs, sew up the body and wash it. In the autopsy room the first and second fatalities lay on examination tables, half covered with sheets. They had already been stitched and cleaned.

'It's the same cause of death as the first two,' the pathologist told Taylor.

Kreitman raised his eyebrows inquiringly.

'Cardiac arrest induced by an abnormal presence of digoxin,' the pathologist said.

Taylor nodded to a camera on a tripod. 'What were you photographing?'

'Oh, I saw it on the first one. It could have been anything.' He put his hand under the shoulder of one of the bodies and turned it on its side. 'Use the lens.'

Taylor positioned a big illuminating magnifier opposite

the point on the dead man's shoulder where the pathologist was moving the tip of his finger.

'It's a small patch of skin where the hair's been removed. It's fine body hair, so you have to look.'

Taylor peered. She could see the hair like fine stippling on the skin. The regular pattern was broken abruptly by a long rectangular bald patch. She moved aside and let Kreitman look.

'It could be a burn from a resuscitation paddle, but it's unlikely,' the pathologist said. 'They could've been shaved for some medical procedure. But if they have been, it's new to me. I really don't know until I've talked to the consultants. But it's on both these bodies, in roughly the same place.'

Kreitman asked when he would have a look at the third one.

'When I've had something to eat.' He turned to the door, undoing his apron. 'You're welcome to join me.'

They looked at the tall, blood-spattered figure for a moment, then declined.

Later, walking along a corridor at St Barnaby's hospital, Taylor briefed Creegan on what she had learned so far.

'They're all patients of the same consultant. Elizabeth Walker. She manages this ward and the Mary Peters wing.'

'Has she been interviewed?'

'No. She gave a statement. And what she doesn't mention in it, and what she's famous for, is being an outspoken expert on the subject of euthanasia.'

'Was she on duty?' Creegan said. 'Bearing in mind it takes digoxin four hours to do that kind of business. So, um . . . that's . . . what's that?'

'Well, it's midnight.' Taylor checked her notes. 'She was on duty until midnight.'

They interviewed Dr Walker in her office. She was somewhere in her late thirties, fine-featured with long brown hair held back with a tortoiseshell clasp. She wore an elegant light brown suit with a darker brown sweater. She was cautiously polite.

'Elizabeth,' Creegan said, 'you're the consultant in charge of all these patients, yeah?'

'I'm probably one of five consultants in charge of any of these patients.'

'But they've all got your name above their beds.'

The doctor's careful little smile withdrew. She stared at Creegan.

'You're not the only one being questioned,' Taylor assured her.

'Good.'

'Dr Walker . . .' Taylor handed her the details of the patients who had died during the night. 'In your personal opinion, were these people murdered?'

Dr Walker looked at the list and pushed it back. 'I'm not a detective. I don't have that kind of judgement.'

Creegan said, 'What are your current opinions on euthanasia, Dr Walker?'

She sighed. 'The same as my old opinions on euthanasia, which you've obviously familiarised yourself with. So, what's the question?'

'Are some patients more valuable than others?'

Dr Walker got up and went to a washbasin in the corner. She turned on the tap and put her hands under the flow. Creegan and Taylor waited, knowing she would eventually reply. She was too civilised to ignore the question – too opinionated, too, Taylor guessed.

'All doctors,' Dr Walker said, 'are capable of looking at fifty grand's worth of equipment keeping a mixed grill warm, and thinking what a waste.'

She took a towel and dried her hands carefully, turning to face Creegan and Taylor. Her little smile had returned.

'I'm rare in having diagnosed a man PVS – persistent vegetative state – who's now cleaning windows in Colchester. So the subject's complicated, Inspector.'

She put down the towel and went to the door. 'I've got a ward round. I'll be free again in a couple of hours.'

15

Every table and chair in St Barnaby's staff canteen had been commandeered. Throughout the afternoon dozens of police officers interviewed scores of medical and nursing staff. In addition to the routine verification of identity, interviewees were asked what time they came on duty the previous day, which of their duties and assigned procedures were carried out under supervision, and which of them were unsupervised. They were asked, also, if they had unrestricted access to drugs. One interviewee could be processed every five or six minutes. Kreitman was on his twenty-third interview in two hours when a curly-haired young man sat down opposite him.

'You're not getting cramp?' he said, grinning, trying for easy familiarity but not managing it. He nodded at the interview notes on the desk. 'Looks like *War and Peace*.'

Kreitman consulted his list. 'Jim Tookey, staff nurse?'

The man shook his head. He produced a plastic ID badge and held it up beside his face. 'Carl Burgess, hygiene supervisor on High Dependency. Or ICU, depending on when you first started work here.'

'You're not on the list, Carl.'

'Oh, right.' Burgess was clearly disappointed. He

swallowed. 'I . . . I thought you were seeing all, er, all the staff?'

'*Qualified* staff,' Kreitman said.

'That's fair enough.' Burgess tried not to look stung. 'So I'll . . . send the next one in, shall I?'

'Yeah,' Kreitman said. 'That'd be a great idea.'

Burgess got up and left. Rivers, sitting at the table behind Kreitman, had watched and listened. He took a note of Burgess's name.

Early that evening, in their office at OSC headquarters, Rivers brought up an investigative point with Kreitman.

'Remember the weird guy at the interview – Carl Burgess?'

Kreitman thought for a second. 'Sort of hygienist or something.'

'Well, he's a cleaner.' Rivers waved a time-sheet print-out. 'We should see him. Look at this. Last week he should have had two days off. On both of those days he's accounted for in other people's statements. I've checked with Personnel. He wasn't paid for that time, he wasn't even asked to go in. What do you think?'

Kreitman shrugged. 'I've done two months with four and a half days off.'

'That's only because your wife's gone off sex.'

Kreitman narrowed one eye. 'I can't wait for you to have a kid on the way.'

Rivers waved the possibility aside. 'The women I see have got less maternal instinct than a house brick.' He grinned. 'Look, Jonathan, people like you make yourselves ill waiting for things to go wrong for people like me. Life's not like that, mate.'

*   *   *

Creegan and Taylor were on their way to the mortuary. Taylor was driving. They had been travelling for six silent minutes when Taylor spoke.

'Creegan, I know we haven't worked together long. But you've moved me on. You've changed the way I think about things.' She paused. 'What I don't envy about you is your communication skill. You're crap.'

He chuckled softly.

'You've got to stop locking me out,' she said.

Creegan looked at her. 'OK.' His face was serious again. He let her negotiate a bend, then he said, 'I went to Hinks's house. I went to kill him.'

'Jesus, Creegan . . .'

Taylor hit the brakes, making the tyres squeal. The car jolted to a halt.

'Creegan, I'm sorry.' Taylor took a deep breath, looking at him sidelong. 'You don't want to tell me this. I don't want to hear it.'

'I loaded the gun,' Creegan said. 'I went to his house.'

Taylor opened the door and got out. She walked ten feet from the car and stopped with her back to it. Creegan got out too. He stared at her across the top of the car.

'Shut up, Creegan,' she warned him, keeping her back turned. 'This isn't fair.'

'And when I got there,' Creegan went on, 'he was already dead.' He sighed. 'He'd murdered kids. I wanted him dead. And he was dead. Great.'

Taylor turned and looked at him.

'Not great,' he said. 'A piece of shit like him's turned me into something I thought I could never be.'

Taylor walked slowly back to the car and leaned her

arms on the top. 'So why are you the only one saying it wasn't suicide?'

'Because Hinks wasn't in possession of a conscience.' Creegan stared off into the shadows beyond their patch of streetlight. 'He would never have topped himself, because he never blamed himself.'

When Creegan had been keeping all this to himself, Taylor observed, he had been almost placid. Now that he was letting it out, he was agitated. So much for the soothing power of confession.

'Who are you saying did it?' she asked.

'I don't know. And I'm trying to work out whether they're weaker than me or stronger than me.'

Taylor studied him for a moment. She had been wrong earlier to think the pressure was off. It hadn't gone, it had changed. It was still there, compressing his mind and spirit.

She said, 'If this case is dragging you under, pull out. If the question is whether or not you can trust yourself, don't struggle with it. Trust me. I trust you. You're the only one I've ever worked with.'

They got back in the car and Taylor drove them to the mortuary, feeling better for her own small act of self-revelation.

When they arrived, the pathologist told them he had found a mark on the shoulder of the third victim from St Barnaby's, and it was the same as the marks on the first and second bodies. He gave them a set of photographs showing the areas of skin in question, greatly enlarged. A number of black dots were visible on each shot. The pathologist said he was waiting for analytical confirmation, but he believed the marks were ink.

Creegan and Taylor waited until the laboratory results arrived. Then they went back to OSC headquarters, where Creegan shut himself away for an hour with the photographs.

Late that evening the team gathered in the conference room, where Creegan used the overhead projector to show them what he had discovered about the pictures.

'There were bits of adhesive found at the edges,' he said. 'Same kind of stuff you find on Sellotape or masking tape. It doesn't correspond to any medical procedure carried out on any of the victims.' He pointed to the black dots distributed across the shaved area of skin. 'This is ink.'

He sat down at the projector and began writing in ballpoint on the photograph. The others watched the image on the screen as he joined up the dots.

'Let . . . me . . . go.' He read each word as he filled it in, then sat back and looked up at the screen. Once the significance of the ink dots was visible, it was hard for the others not to see how they made words.

'The words are more traceable on that one than the other two, but it was written on all of them. Probably transferred from the back of a piece of Sellotape.'

Kreitman looked at his notes. 'Eighty staff worked directly on all the victims. If the message had been there for any length of time, surely that's worth commenting on. But nobody has.'

Taylor said, 'It's not on any of the scene-of-crime photos.'

'Yeah.' Creegan nodded. 'The message was placed on the victims' backs. All three were coma patients. And it looks like the writing's been cleaned off.'

'But the only person who had physical access to all the bodies,' Taylor said, 'was Dr Walker when she pronounced them dead.'

Creegan looked at her. She could see he had arrived at that conclusion before she had.

At three minutes after four the following morning, an elderly male coma patient in the High Dependency Unit at St Barnaby's suffered a sudden cardiac arrest. The alarm was raised at once and an emergency team was at work within two minutes. They made vigorous and prolonged attempts at cardiac resuscitation, but these measures failed and the patient was eventually declared dead.

The police were called. Preliminary statements were taken from night-duty staff. Forensic and photographic teams moved in and isolated a whole section of the unit before setting to work. When they had finished, the body was removed to the police mortuary and yellow crime-scene tape was strung out around the dead man's bed area.

OSC were at the High Dependency Unit by 6.30. Rivers arrived looking haggard and weary. He stood by the spot where the man had died and gazed at the empty bed behind the tape. He turned aside and saw Taylor several yards away doing the same.

Then Rivers's annoyance at being dragged out of bed suddenly found itself a focus. He stared at the uniformed constable who had barely glanced at him when he came in, and who was now in deep conversation with a young female nurse.

'Am I a brain surgeon?' Rivers snapped. 'Heart surgeon? Cuddly toy?' He glared at the constable, who looked bewildered. 'Why haven't you asked to see my ID?' Rivers held up his card to make the point, then went glowering off to locate a coffee machine.

Creegan, meanwhile, was wandering around the other end of the unit, which was still operational. He stopped near the bed of a young man who wore a neck brace. His eyes seemed to be the only part of him that moved. Then Creegan noticed that the tip of his right index finger was enclosed in a pressure-sensitive cuff, which was connected to a computer mounted at the foot of the bed. A nurse sat by the bed and watched as the patient selected letters of the alphabet from the screen display by moving the tip of his finger inside the cuff. It took him a couple of minutes to create the on-screen question *What's going on*?

'It's nothing to worry about,' the nurse told him. 'They're just being nosy.'

Creegan smiled as he stepped up to the bedside. 'Can he hear you?' he asked the nurse.

'If he's in a good mood.'

'Do you think he could have heard or seen anything that happened here last night?'

'See if he likes you,' the nurse said.

Creegan went round to the other side of the bed and leaned down so the patient could see him. He glanced at the name above the bed. Gary Keane.

'Gary, in the early hours of this morning something happened here. Did you see anything out of the ordinary? Anything out of the main routine?'

'One question at a time,' the nurse warned.

Creegan nodded. 'The first.'

Gary made the computer beep twice.

'That means no,' the nurse said. 'A four-word answer could take about fifteen minutes.'

133

'What happened to him?' Creegan said, then caught himself. He looked at the patient. 'I'd ask you directly, Gary, but I'm under pressure here.'

At that moment Taylor called him.

'See what I mean?'

The nurse looked at Gary. 'Can I tell him?'

The computer beeped once.

'He fell off a roof on a stag night,' the nurse told Creegan. '*His* stag night. Didn't you, Gary?'

Creegan looked squarely at the lively eyes in the motionless face. 'Look, um, if things calm down a bit, can I come back later?'

A single beep.

'I'll see you later, then.'

Creegan walked away. The nurse watched him go. When she looked at the screen again Gary had typed three exclamation marks in a row.

'Well,' the nurse said with a smirk, looking at Creegan again, 'I wouldn't say no.'

16

Gloved hands pressed adhesive tape against Gary Keane's shoulder. When the tape was rubbed firmly in place, one gloved forefinger and thumb raised a corner and pulled it off again. A message was now printed in black ink on Gary's shoulder.

As he was rolled on to his back he stared up at the person handling him. Gary's face lacked all expression, but his eyes began to radiate concern. He turned them downward as far as he could and saw a gloved hand with a syringe. The needle on the end of the syringe punctured the plastic line through which electrolyte support flowed into his bloodstream. Gary watched as the plunger of the syringe went down and another liquid began to flow into the supply line.

Scissors now appeared in the assailant's hand. Gary saw them snip the communication cord from his finger cuff and tuck the end under his lifeless finger, creating the illusion that the device was intact.

The attacker now adjusted Gary's bedding and tucked his sheets in at the sides. Gary stared, unable to move or make a sound, and as he stared the assailant walked slowly away.

Minutes later Gary's nurse came back from Dietary Supplies carrying a plastic screw-top bottle.

'Sorry, Gary,' she said, 'we're out of orange. It's got to be vanilla. And if you don't like it, tough shit.'

She began attaching the container to a syringe which she used to feed Gary through a mouth tube. She looked down at him and smiled. She was not aware that his eyes pleaded with her.

'Your fiancée's coming tonight. And I don't want any more dirty words out of you on that computer, you hear me?'

She peered at him, detecting something different. 'You hear me?'

She glanced expectantly at the computer but it made no sound, and no message appeared on the screen. He was in one of his moods, she decided.

Three children trooped across the path in front of Dr Walker's house, screaming and shoving. As Creegan and Taylor got out of the car, Dr Walker appeared at the door and yelled, 'Will you *shut up*, please?'

The children ran indoors and disappeared upstairs, still bellowing. Dr Walker, casually dressed now with her hair down, waited for her visitors to come up the steps. She led them inside.

'The neighbours either side are all virtually deaf,' she said. 'Cause or effect, I couldn't say.'

She laughed nervously and ushered them into the sitting room. It was large and comfortable, with solid plain-wood tables and cupboards, overstuffed chairs and settees covered in autumn-coloured fabrics, and a soft fawn carpet from wall to wall. Dr Walker opened a cupboard and took out a packet of cigarettes. She lit one and went to stand by the window. She appeared reluctant to sit down.

Taylor got straight to business. On a table by the window she laid out photographs of the first three victims. 'Elizabeth, when you attended the deaths of these people, was there anything unusual about the bodies?'

'Except for the fact that they were all dead? No.'

'No writing?'

Dr Walker frowned. 'What kind of writing?'

Creegan came forward and pushed up his right sleeve. 'That kind of writing.' Lettered in ballpoint on his forearm were the words LET ME GO.

Dr Walker shook her head.

Taylor opened a polythene bag and pulled out a rectangle of sheepskin with a stiff backing. 'This is a segment of a pressure mat taken from under the first victim, James Carthy.' She pointed. 'Can you see that?'

Dr Walker looked. The fleecy surface of the mat showed clear traces of the same words as those written on Creegan's arm; this time they were back to front. Dr Walker drew deeply on her cigarette.

'This mat,' Taylor said, 'was replaced by night staff at two a.m. He died at four ten a.m. Now you're the only member of staff who had individual access to that patient between then and when he was taken to the mortuary.'

'It also shows traces of alcohol,' Creegan said. 'Did you clean that body before the police arrived, Elizabeth?'

Dr Walker sighed. 'I'd be stupid to say anything without a lawyer present, wouldn't I?'

She was taken back to OSC headquarters for questioning. The three of them waited in the interview room until Dr Walker's lawyer arrived. She was Linda Mayer, a slender, glacially serene woman with a disarmingly steady gaze. As she sat down at the table she adjusted her thin-framed spectacles and appraised Creegan and Taylor with a coolness just short of disdain.

It was agreed that the built-in tape machine would be used for purposes of evidence-gathering. For the recording Creegan identified himself, Taylor, Dr Walker and Ms Mayer. He then recapped on what had gone before, summarising the visit to the doctor's house which had culminated in this interview.

From the moment Dr Walker began answering questions, it was clear to Taylor that now she had the reassuring presence of her lawyer beside her, she was prepared to be entirely candid. She did not hesitate or avoid any question. When Creegan started to ask her about her response to the deaths at St Barnaby's, her openness came as a surprise. He asked her to detail her actions between the times of death and the removal of the bodies to the mortuary. In each case, she said, she had cleaned the body.

'You deliberately erased the writing?'

She nodded.

'Why?'

'I'd seen the writing before. It was the same writing that appeared under the arm of Constance Brewer.'

'Constance Brewer?' Taylor said. The name meant nothing to her.

'A very old lady,' Dr Walker said, 'with . . . I don't know . . . a minute chance of survival. It was in the press. This time I was fighting against the family to keep her alive. I'd seen signs of brain activity. And I won the court case. I imagined this was them showing their dismay.'

'Where's Constance Brewer now?' Taylor said.

'She died a day later from . . .' Dr Walker sighed. 'We thought it was natural causes.'

The lawyer produced an envelope and held it out towards Creegan. 'On record,' she said, 'that the following information has been voluntarily surrendered by my client.'

Taylor made a swift examination of the contents of the envelope and decided that the interview should move to a less confrontational environment. Creegan agreed. Dr Walker no longer looked like a viable suspect.

At St Barnaby's, Kreitman made his way to the cleaning supervisor's room in the basement. Rivers, meanwhile, was roaming the corridors around the High Dependency Unit, where Carl Burgess was supposed to be cleaning floors.

Beneath the door sign that said CLEANING SUPERVISOR was another, hand-stencilled, that said CARL BURGESS. It was the kind of lash-up that suggested Burgess had asked for a door-plate and hadn't got one.

The door was unlocked. Inside, Kreitman found a cosy home from home. Steam pipes crossing the low ceiling kept the place warm. There was an ancient electric kettle, three mugs and a jar of coffee on a tray by the sink. On shelves and across the battered old desktop were piles of magazines and books. Burgess appeared to like ghost stories.

Kreitman opened a drawer and began rooting through the bundle of old newspapers and magazines. Beneath them he found a medical book – *Case Studies in Emergency Medicine*. He opened it and saw a rubber-stamped rectangle behind the title page, enclosing the words 'Property of Dr Elizabeth Walker'.

Upstairs, Rivers had found Burgess. He was using an electric buffer on the floor of the busy corridor outside the High Dependency Unit.

'Carl? Carl Burgess?'

Burgess looked up and switched off his machine. 'Me, yeah.'

Rivers showed him his ID.

'You lot know how to get in the way,' Burgess said. There was hesitancy discernible through his attempt at an aggressive style. 'You got the staff here going ape-shit.'

Rivers looked mildly concerned. 'And why's that?'

Burgess swallowed and flashed a grin. 'Coppers getting under your feet when people are trying to move expensive equipment about.'

Rivers nodded and waited, compelling Burgess to say more.

'No, it's, er, it's all pretty fine-tuned round here, mate.'

Rivers nodded, still saying nothing.

'It's a fact there's a medical emergency every fifteen minutes. No, they want telling.'

'Well,' Rivers said, 'I don't actually work for the Met, but yeah, I'll certainly pass it on.'

Burgess was now suddenly co-operative, a would-be buddy. 'Look, I'm in, er, the supervisor's office. We could talk down there. I could do you a coffee if you want?'

Rivers looked regretful. 'I'd best stay where the boss can see me. I mean, you know what it's like.'

'Well I *am* the boss,' Burgess said, 'so you're fraternising with the enemy there, mate.' He laughed.

Rivers laughed too. He flipped open his notebook, playing for more time. Two nurses went past and he watched Burgess stare at their backsides.

'So,' he said, stabbing his finger at a non-existent note in his book, 'you never work the Mary Peters wing?'

'No, no.' Burgess switched his attention away from the nurses. 'Well, I say no. Sometimes if, er, we're short-staffed, I bail them out. Only if I'm in a good mood.' He chuckled self-importantly.

Rivers laughed again and was about to ask another pointless question when Burgess suddenly muttered, 'Oops.' He turned busy, pulling in the cable of his buffer, winding it around the machine. 'Old fruit in a suit,' he murmured, nodding to an administrator walking in their direction. 'Mind your backs. I'll see you around.'

Burgess moved off, wheeling the buffer ahead of him. Rivers got out his radio. Down in the basement, Kreitman's radio crackled.

'He's packing up,' Rivers's voice said. 'Looks like he's coming your way.'

Kreitman pocketed the radio. He snatched a handful of cigarette ends from an ashtray, dropped them into an envelope and twisted it shut. He put the envelope in his coat pocket, together with three medical books, then left the steamy little room.

Creegan and Taylor sat on one side of the big table in the conference room, opposite Dr Walker and her lawyer. Taylor studied one piece of Dr Walker's evidence. Creegan examined the other.

'When was this?' Taylor held up a greetings card with a stylised depiction of a heavenly ascension on the front.

Inside, in thick handwritten capitals, was the message
PRACTISE WHAT YOU PREACH!

'The day after Constance Brewer died.' Dr Walker
pointed to the letter Creegan was holding. 'That came
directly to my home address.'

Creegan read it out. '"Don't pretend to speak for
people who want to move on – if all you do is waste
time, money and resources dragging them back like
medals for you. It's not in your gift to say whether
they live or die, you stupid cow."'

Taylor looked at Dr Walker. 'You've known since
this patient died that it could have been murder?'

'No,' the doctor said. 'I suspected that someone was
glorying in my failure. That was all. Can I go home?'

'Dr Walker,' Creegan said, 'what exactly was written
on the victims?' He held up the picture on which he had
traced the words LET ME GO. 'Was it this?'

'No. It was "Let me go back".'

When Dr Walker and her lawyer had gone, Creegan
told Taylor he wanted to look at the stuff in the evidence
room set up by the police at St Barnaby's.

Taylor tagged along out of curiosity. When they got
there a uniformed constable was sealing four plastic sacks
packed with the victims' belongings. Creegan apologised
and said he had to search the bags. The constable didn't
look pleased, but he moved aside anyway.

Creegan tipped each bag out on the floor, making four
distinct piles, then sifted them. One by one he found
four cards with a design identical to the one sent to Dr
Walker. These cards all said GET WELL SOON. They
were not signed.

Creegan squatted by the piles of property and squared
the cards between his hands. He looked up at Taylor.

'"Let me go back" isn't about the victim's pain,' he said. 'It's the killer's.'

Taylor didn't understand. She watched Creegan drop the cards. His eyes had a glassy look, something more than preoccupation. He appeared to be concentrating on something painful.

He got up and walked out into the corridor. Taylor made to follow him, then decided it would be good interdepartmental politics to help the constable rebag the evidence.

Three minutes later, a nurse found Creegan sitting on a bench outside the High Dependency Unit. He was sweating and shaking.

'Are you all right?'

A young doctor, Julie Carney, came up behind the nurse. She asked Creegan if he was waiting to see a doctor.

He shook his head. 'Actually, the last thing I want is a doctor.' He held up his ID.

The nurse went away. Dr Carney stayed where she was, watching Creegan.

Taylor came hurrying along from the evidence room. 'Creegan?' She took in his pallor, his trembling hands. 'What's happened?'

He looked up at her. 'This isn't about murder.'

'Come on.' Taylor took him by the arm. He got up. Taylor thanked the doctor and walked with Creegan along the corridor.

'They've all died before,' he said.

Taylor stopped walking. 'What are you talking about?'

'They've all died before. "Let me go back."'

Taylor began walking again, staring at him.

'The killer's sending them back to where they've been

before,' he said. 'Somewhere a lot more comfortable than this.'

'Creegan . . .' Taylor had no comment that would be appropriate. Instead of responding to what he said, she got back to business. 'We've got a crisis call from Dr Walker.'

He looked at her for a second as if he didn't understand. When Taylor walked off towards Dr Walker's office, he followed her.

17

Dr Walker was obviously distressed as she showed Creegan the card that had been left on her desk. 'To my knowledge,' she said, 'I've never done anything to anyone.'

The card had the same ascension motif as the others, a design that OSC research had discovered could be bought from several retail outlets in central London. Inside the card, beneath the printed message 'With Deepest Sympathy', the words DON'T PLAY GOD, GOD PLAYS YOU were handwritten in the familiar black capitals.

Creegan studied the card for a second. 'Dr Walker, can we see the medical records of all the victims – including Constance Brewer?'

She nodded.

'Has anyone died today?' Taylor said.

'Not so far. I've asked for blood screens on all my patients, but that could take for ever.'

'We've got enough Home Office technicians to screen all your patients' blood every two to three hours,' Taylor said, picking up the phone. 'Is that enough time to act on a digoxin overdose?'

'Depends on the dose,' Dr Walker said.

Taylor made arrangements for the blood screening. Creegan got hold of a blank greetings card with the ascension motif. Inside it he wrote:

I know where you've been.
David Creegan
Died 16.06.95

Underneath the message he wrote a telephone number set aside by OSC for an automatic tracing response. He pinned the card to the noticeboard in the corridor outside the High Dependency Unit. A security camera was positioned above an adjacent doorway, looking down on the board.

It was late, but Creegan wanted to read the medical documentation on the four victims. Taylor went with him to the Medical Records department. They sat at opposite sides of a table with a reading lamp fitted centrally above it. For an hour they read every detail contained on all four files.

Finally Creegan looked up. 'All resuscitated,' he said.

Taylor looked at him briefly, then looked way again. Since his comment about the patients having died before, she had avoided any discussion of the matter. If she had learned anything about Creegan, it was that sooner or later he would communicate enough about a case to make two-way discussion possible.

She glanced up from the case papers again and he was staring at her.

'Look,' he said, 'I, ah . . . when I was shot I had chest surgery and cranial surgery, and I remember all kinds of things the surgeons said to each other. They said it

146

was impossible, but I said it happened. They laughed. So I quoted the anaesthetist as saying, "I hope he knows we're missing the match for him."'

Taylor smiled warily.

'The guy nearly passed out,' Creegan said, 'because I was unconscious, and they were digging a bullet out of my brain at the time.'

'Some kind of . . . out-of-body experience?'

'At first,' he nodded. 'Then my heart stopped. I had to be resuscitated.' He was looking past Taylor now, into the dark corner behind her. His eyes were glassy, the way they had been earlier when he had looked so ill. 'I saw a white light. And I knew that this was what my death looked like. People came by me and smiled.' He shook his head. 'They really smiled. Because it was the most right place to be. I'd never felt so welcome anywhere.'

'You look scared,' Taylor whispered.

'It was the coming back that scared me.'

'So we're looking at an ex-patient?'

'I don't know.' Creegan looked at Taylor. 'Someone who's been there before. Someone who thinks the victims would have chosen to die.'

The door opened abruptly, making Taylor jump.

'Creegan . . .' Kreitman hurried across the room. 'There's a call for you.' He picked up the receiver and said, 'Rivers? Yeah, put it through.' He handed the receiver to Creegan. 'We think it might be him. We're tracking it.'

Creegan put the phone to his ear and identified himself.

A deep voice with obvious electronic distortion said, 'David Creegan?'

'What do you want?'

'David Creegan, born twenty-third of March 1964?'

'Yes.'

'Look at his face.'

'Whose face?'

'Look at his face and tell me he's not more peaceful. Tell me you're not jealous.'

'Whose face?'

The line went dead.

Creegan looked at Kreitman, then at Taylor. He started to say something, then stopped. They could hear a distant alarm bell.

Creegan, Taylor, Kreitman and Rivers arrived at the High Dependency Unit as Dr Walker was leaning over Gary Keane's bed, holding the defibrillator paddles.

'Come on, Gary . . .' She looked at the cardiac monitor, which was showing a flat line and giving off a steady whine. She turned to the leader of the crash team, standing ready at the power control. 'Three sixty. Charging. Stand clear. Shock!'

Gary's body jerked up off the table as the current surged through his chest.

The monitor continued to whine and show a flat line.

'Charging. Stand clear. Shock!'

Dr Walker looked distraught as once more the young man's body jerked off the bed and flopped down again. As before, the monitor failed to record any sign of life.

She made to try again, positioning the paddles. Then she looked from the monitor to the lifeless face, to the red paddle burns on the pale skin of the chest.

'Asystole,' she said, putting down the paddles. 'Kill it. Patient died one seven a.m. Inform the police.'

She turned from the bed and saw Creegan and the others. 'Police informed,' she murmured, and walked out of the room.

For a while, as the emergency equipment was dismantled, Creegan stood and stared at Gary Keane's face. The once-lively eyes were closed now; the features were relaxed and placid.

Taylor was watching too, from the doorway, wondering what Creegan saw. She knew that her emotional balance was upset, that her responses were unreliable. Perhaps that was the way to be if she wanted to sense Creegan's reaction – it might be exactly like her own. What *she* saw at that moment when she looked at Gary's body, so serene in its death, was an amalgam of dignity and painless freedom.

18

Late that night Creegan joined Rivers in Burgess's little office in the basement at St Barnaby's. Rivers had been working with a forensic team to sift the contents of the office before it was all bagged for transfer to the laboratory. Among the material recovered from the bottoms of drawers and the backs of cabinets were a number of books, pamphlets and medical journals.

'So what sort of textbooks have you removed?' Creegan said.

'Neurosurgical,' Rivers replied. 'Intensive care, patient management.'

'Just medical?'

'Dr Walker doesn't remember him asking, and I believe her when she says she'd never have consented. I mean, you want to talk to this guy, he's definitely . . .' Rivers shook his head, lost for a word. 'Well, anybody who *fantasises* about being a cleaner . . . And look at this shit.' He pointed to Burgess's collection of horror stories.

Creegan was looking at a small book sticking up from a box a technician was carrying to the door.

'Hang on.'

Creegan pulled out the book. He held it under the desk

151

light and flicked through the pages. It was a home-made
diary, with all the months and days written in longhand.
The entries were mostly trivial reminders of weekly work
rotas and things to be done. Mingled with the mundane
entries were several that referred to a relationship:

Lizzy for dinner. At last!
   *Tell Lizzy can't make lunch – got to work, what
a bastard.*
   Two tickets for Saturday.
   *Lizzy thought the match was cool. Villa 3 Spurs
0!!! She wins the bet.*
   Lizzy for dinner – don't burn it!

Creegan reached for his radio and switched it on.
'Creegan.'
A scratchy voice identified itself as Control.
'Can we get hold of Burgess's medical records?'
Rivers looked at him.
'If it's him,' Creegan said, putting down the radio, 'he
knew my date of birth. I wonder what else he knows.'
Less than an hour later, two cars glided quietly into
a street of terraced houses. Taylor drove the first car.
Creegan sat beside her. Kreitman was at the wheel
of the second car with Rivers in the passenger seat.
They stopped outside a house halfway along the street.
A moment later a police van parked twenty yards
further along.
Taylor got out and walked up the path. Rivers ran
down the street and round the back of the houses while
Creegan and Kreitman followed Taylor, keeping their
distance. They stayed out of sight as she stopped and
rapped urgently on the door.

The hall light came on. The door opened a few inches. Burgess was in a T-shirt and trousers. His feet were bare.

'Yeah?'

'Hi. I'm DI Taylor. I just wanted to check a few things with you, Carl.'

He frowned at her. 'It's half two.' He looked warily behind him for a second. 'Look, I've got me bird here and it's all a bit, er, you know . . . Can't you come back tomorrow?'

'Oh.' Taylor nodded. 'OK.'

'Thanks.'

Taylor moved away and Burgess closed the door. Kreitman stepped forward and kicked the door wide open with a bang. Burgess was halfway along the hall. He ran for the back door and jerked it open.

A blinding white police spotlight hit his eyes and he stumbled down the back steps. Rivers stepped out from the group of uniformed officers and forensic technicians standing behind the light. He caught Burgess, spun him round and cuffed him. Creegan and Kreitman came to the back door.

'Been doing some unpaid overtime, Carl?' Kreitman said.

Burgess looked terrified. 'I don't know what you're talking about.'

'What have you been up to, Carl?' Creegan said.

'I've been here.'

'Yeah? Witnesses?'

'I live on my own.'

Taylor appeared on the back step. 'No girlfriend,' she said. 'No surprise.'

Creegan stepped close to Burgess, his face stark white

in the beam of the spot. 'But you have got a girlfriend, haven't you, Carl? Dr Walker. Lizzy's your girlfriend.'

Three uniformed constables marched Burgess along the hall and out through the front door.

'Get this place searched inside out,' Creegan told the others.

They worked methodically, exactly as they had done in Ronald Hinks's house, although this property was very different. This place gave away things about its occupant. To Taylor it betrayed all the marks of petty obsession and numerous unhealthy preoccupations.

There were shelves of medical books, most of them on the subject of neurology. Alongside were shelves of videotaped television programmes – *Casualty*, *ER*, *Jimmy's*, *Children's Hospital*, *Blues and Twos*. A full-size human skeleton hung from a stand in the corner beside the television set.

In a drawer Taylor found a perfume spray. She squirted some on to her gloved hand and sniffed. 'This is what Elizabeth Walker wears.'

In the kitchen were large cans and polythene bottles of detergent. There were stacked rolls of toilet paper, packets of paper hand towels, tubs of liquid soap and a drum of floor wax.

Taylor turned from the drawer where she had found the perfume and saw a wire clothes rack. Draped over the spars were a delicate white camisole, a woman's T-shirt, panties and various other pieces of female underwear.

Kreitman opened three kitchen drawers, from the bottom upwards, swiftly rummaging through the contents. When he opened the top one he didn't have to rummage.

'Bingo,' he said.

154

Creegan and Taylor came through and looked. The drawer was stuffed full with ampoules, bandages, dressing packs and syringes.

Creegan turned to the nearest forensic technician. 'Get that lot dusted and bagged,' he said. 'ASAP.'

The following morning Kreitman took Burgess to the interview room at OSC headquarters. A tape recorder was set up on the table. Kreitman told Burgess to sit down and read the sentence printed on the card in front of him. He was to speak in his normal voice, and directly into the microphone. Kreitman stood with a set of headphones in his hand, listening with one ear as the recording began.

Burgess wet his lips nervously and read: 'Look at his face and tell me he's not more peaceful. Tell me you're not jealous.'

'Again,' Kreitman said.

'Look at his face and tell me he's not more peaceful. Tell me you're not jealous.'

Without a word Kreitman switched off the recorder, removed the headphones, then the microphone, and unplugged the machine from the wall. As he took the equipment away Creegan and Taylor came in, accompanied by the psychologist, Marion.

They all sat down at the table. Creegan was directly opposite Burgess. He dumped a polythene bag on the table in front of Burgess and rolled open the neck. He then put a fresh tape in the built-in tape machine, waited for the beep, then pushed the bag closer to Burgess. Inside were the medical supplies removed from his house.

'What's all this?' Burgess demanded.

Creegan frowned. 'We say that, don't we?'

Burgess chuckled. He was still trying for a note of chummy informality, but Taylor could see the veneer was cracking. Underneath was a scared boy.

'We got it from your house,' Taylor said.

Burgess put on a heavily puzzled look. 'Whereabouts?'

'Kitchen drawers.'

'Right.' Now Burgess looked as if something was dawning on him. 'Which ones?'

Taylor held up a photograph of Burgess's kitchen and pointed. 'These ones.'

'Yeah. Yeah, well, you see, that's not mine.' He had managed to create a look of relief, except his eyes remained tense. 'That's Pete's. He's the lodger. He's straight as a die, which you, er, can take to mean boring.' He chuckled again, his eyes remaining strained. 'Only joking. And, um . . . yeah, he had, er, he had no place to stay when he came down here, so he . . . he kips round mine when he's in the area.' He stopped again to force a little laugh. 'He's . . . he's a rep. Medical rep. Which is, you know, bit of a gold mine, if you want the truth.'

Creegan took out a pen and used it to point out fingerprint-dusted items in the bag, tapping them one by one. 'That's yours. Yours. That's yours.' He stopped and looked straight at Burgess. 'So where's Pete now?'

Burgess gulped. 'Sorry?'

'Where's Pete now?'

Another gulp and a one-sided shrug. 'He took a job with Ciba Geigy. No, no, the, er, Wellcome Foundation, you know, one of the big medical suppliers. Yeah, new . . . new big car, relocation allowance, all that. He's, ah, in the West Midlands somewhere.'

Marion leaned forward, giving Burgess her reassuring

smile. 'What do you think of the people you have to clean up after, Carl?'

He stared at her. 'Meaning?'

'The patients.'

'Nothing.'

Rivers put his head round the door and nodded to Creegan, who got up and went out.

Marion was still holding Burgess with her fixed smile. 'What do you think Elizabeth Walker thinks of her patients?'

'Well, she's whatsit . . . she's . . . she's dedicated.'

In the corridor outside the interview room Rivers handed Creegan a couple of sheets of paper. 'It's a print-out of his medical data. It's thinner than mine.'

Creegan scanned it.

'No resuscitation,' Rivers said.

Further along the corridor in the incident room, Dr Walker was examining a pile of clothes and lingerie taken from Burgess's house. She handled the items with the capped end of a pen. Kreitman stood by, looking uncomfortable.

'That. Yes . . .' the doctor murmured, dropping one item on another. She looked at Kreitman. 'They're mine. Did you find them in his house?'

Kreitman nodded.

Back in the interview room, Marion had listened to Burgess's answers to her questions about Dr Walker and she had used them to launch a more probing question. 'She works hard, Carl. Which gives you and Lizzy no time at all.'

Burgess looked very nervous. 'I don't know what you're talking about.'

'You know, Carl,' Taylor said, producing his diary.

157

She flicked through the pages. 'For lunch. For dinner. For soccer. For sex.'

'No,' Burgess whined, trying to grin, 'that's a different Lizzy, that. That's a girl I know. That's a totally different Lizzy.'

'So . . .' Taylor laid several photographs of lingerie in front of Burgess. 'If we showed her these belongings, Dr Walker would say, "No, they must belong to another Lizzy".'

'Don't!' Burgess blurted, sagging with shame. 'Please don't!'

The door opened and Creegan came in. 'It's not him,' he said.

Marion frowned, openly annoyed at the interruption. Creegan went to the table and leaned down beside Burgess.

'Carl, you'll be served with a court order to stop you going within two miles of Elizabeth Walker. Do you understand?'

Burgess nodded.

Taylor and Marion gathered their things and left. Creegan, Kreitman and Rivers joined them back in the office.

'I haven't even finished my assessment,' Marion said.

'Look, the guy we're after knows what it's like to have died and come back,' Creegan said. 'To have been dragged back – that's the whole point of the messages, the letters. Burgess hasn't any relevant history.'

'We can put him in all the right places at all the right times,' said Rivers. 'What about the medical equipment?'

Taylor said, 'All that stuff had been used before he

nicked it.' She sighed. 'All he removed from the hospital was stuff that had been used by Elizabeth Walker.'

Kreitman wasn't swayed. 'At least wait until we finish the voice analysis.'

Creegan shook his head. 'Waste of time, Jonathan. It's not him. If we lock on to Burgess, we're wasting time, energy, everything.'

'Let's send him home,' Taylor said.

'For what it's worth,' Marion put in, 'he wouldn't be top of my list.'

Kreitman and Rivers went back to their office. Kreitman was seething.

'He's a liar, he's a thief, he's obsessive about the target, and he's the only member of staff that we can put into the frame. And he's on the streets.'

The fax machine beeped and a sheet of paper came rolling out.

'It's bloody ludicrous,' Kreitman went on. He took the fax off the machine and glanced at it. 'If Creegan hadn't been there, Taylor would never have let that happen.' He paused, staring at the fax. 'And he's got form – for violence, 1994. Domestic assault on his mother. She dropped the charges.'

Rivers took the fax and looked at it. 'I'll get Creegan,' he said, going to the door.

'No.' Kreitman took his jacket off the back of his chair and put it on. 'We check it out first. And if Burgess needs pushing, we push.'

'Wait.' Rivers looked wary. 'I don't think he needs pushing like Ronald Hinks needed pushing.'

'Nobody's saying he does.' Kreitman opened the door. 'Nobody's saying that at all.'

19

Burgess came back from the off-licence clutching a bottle of Bacardi. When he let himself into the house he found Rivers and Kreitman waiting in the living room. Kreitman sat in a chair with his arms folded; Rivers was standing.

'You left the back door open, Carl,' Rivers said.

Burgess looked startled.

'How's your mum these days?' Kreitman said. 'Was it a broken wrist or arm? I can't remember.'

'She fell,' Burgess said. 'She only blamed me because she didn't want me leaving home.'

Rivers smiled thinly.

'She said that,' Burgess insisted. 'She told the police that. Check.'

Kreitman got to his feet. He moved close to Burgess. 'How can you say that you're in love with Dr Walker when you're leaving her in all this shit?'

Burgess tried to look sceptical, then had to gulp before he spoke. 'What shit?'

'Do you know what happens to her now?'

'No.' Burgess looked at the floor, unable to hold Kreitman's gaze.

'Do you care?'

'No.' After a second Burgess looked up. 'What?'

'Common denominator with all the victims is her.' Kreitman spoke softly, moving closer. Burgess had his back to the door jamb. 'The single most important piece of evidence points to Dr Walker. She was there when they died.'

Burgess looked from one to the other. He had no more front to hide behind. He was scared. He turned and walked smartly along the hall, going nowhere, simply evading the weight of Kreitman's words. He went into the kitchen and stood by the worktop, still holding his bottle. Kreitman and Rivers followed him. They came in and stood on either side of him.

'She helped those people die,' Kreitman said. 'She murdered them.'

Burgess shook his head. 'She wouldn't do that. She's not like that.'

'Are you?' Rivers said.

'No.'

'So if it's not you, it has to be her.'

Burgess made a sound like a child's whimper.

Kreitman said, 'Will she cope with prison, Carl?'

'She's innocent.'

Kreitman didn't seem to hear him. 'Will you write to her in prison and tell her how you let her down?'

'She didn't do it!' Burgess whined.

'You keep saying that, Carl,' Rivers sighed, 'and we keep wondering how you're so sure about it.' He put his face very close to Burgess's. 'I can't make my mind up whether you forgot to be normal or remembered to be screwy. You know?'

Kreitman and Rivers stepped back. For a second they

looked at Burgess in silence, then they turned and left the house by the back door.

Burgess watched them go. As he shuffled back to the living room he caught a pathetic reflection of himself in the hall mirror, clutching his bottle of rum.

Back at OSC Kreitman began running the recording of the killer's message through a mini-lab on his computer, varying the frequency, trying to find the true, undistorted level of the voice. Rivers stood alongside, intrigued by the process.

One four-word phrase provided an ideal piece for analysis. 'Look at his face . . .' The skewed bass rumble became metallic as Kreitman diminished the mid-tones. He switched in another filter, watching the visual display as the voice ran again, clearer this time, higher in pitch. 'Look at his face . . .'

Kreitman used the keyboard to insert a routine that would skim away another layer of distortion. 'Look at his face . . .' Now the voice sounded almost natural, although the display showed there was still a measure of electronic distortion, enough to provide a disguise. Kreitman took the frequency level up another fraction, watching the responses at both ends of the audible range, careful not to introduce new distortions of his own.

'Look at his face . . .'

Now the voice sounded entirely human, but rather slow. More fiddling and frequency adjustment produced a much more natural effect. Kreitman ran more of the message at the new frequency.

'Look at his face and tell me he's not more peaceful. Tell me you're not jealous.'

It was a convincing reproduction of a human voice – or almost so, according to the visual evidence on the screen. The voice was not familiar, and it was in a much higher register than they had expected.

'That doesn't sound much like Burgess,' Rivers said. 'Unless he's got his bollocks trapped in a door.'

Along the corridor, in the office shared by Creegan and Taylor, Commander Enwright had just told them that Dr Walker wanted to remove herself from the hospital.

'I think that's a big mistake,' Creegan said. 'Look, either the hospital loses a very highly skilled practitioner, which in basic terms means they're going to lose a lot of patients, or we lose access to the killer. Walker's the source, she's the attraction.'

Enwright spread his hands. 'It's not my choice, it's what Walker wants.'

'Talk her out of it,' Creegan said.

Taylor nodded. 'I agree.'

The phone rang. Creegan picked it up and identified himself. The killer's distorted voice spoke to him again. 'You could've gone back any time you liked,' it said.

Creegan signalled Taylor, pointing at the other phone. She picked it up and hit the contact button for Control. 'Trace Creegan's phone,' she said, then hit another button which let her share his line.

'What are you hanging around for?' the voice asked.

Creegan said, 'Can you explain the question?'

'You died, you went where you belonged, and you came back because you were forced to. There hasn't been a single day when you didn't think that was a mistake.'

'You feel that?' Creegan murmured.

'You know I do.'

Creegan paused for a moment, then said, 'What do you want?'

'Help,' the voice rumbled. 'I just need some help.'

'How can I do that? What do you want me to do?'

'You need help like I need help.'

'Maybe you're right,' Creegan said. 'What do you want me to do?'

'You'll find out.'

The killer hung up. As Creegan and Taylor put down their phones Rivers came bustling into the office. He looked excited.

'We've got the voice,' he said. 'It's a female.'

Burgess had consumed half the bottle of Bacardi. Being drunk always made him loud and belligerent, but for once he was being so in public. He strode down one of the corridors he regularly polished at St Barnaby's, glaring at doctors and nurses as they passed.

'Do you have any idea who I am?' he yelled at a white-coated houseman. 'Hmm? No.' He watched the man go past and almost walked into the wall. 'Of course you wouldn't, stuck-up bastard! Well, you *will* know me.' He ploughed on, heading for the High Dependency Unit. 'I tell you, every doctor in this place will know who I am! I'll tell you that! I'll tell you that! Stuck-up ignorant bastards!'

He kicked open the swing door and marched into the unit. He looked around until he saw a patient on life support and went straight for it. He grabbed the sides of the respirator trolley and jerked it forward, knocking over a water jug in the process. Water spread in a pool around his feet.

A police officer manning the CCTV monitors saw what was happening and took off for the High Dependency Unit. Inside the unit three nurses were running towards Burgess. He grabbed the respirator's power cable where it was attached to the wall, then realised it was a sealed unit. He seized the other end, at the back of the respirator, and tugged. Nothing happened. Again he tugged, much harder this time. The cable jerked out of the respirator, bare wires protruding from the end. The alarm began to scream.

'You're evil!' a nurse shouted.

Burgess glared at her, brandishing the cable. 'You know me now.'

Nurses were concentrating on the patient, panicking to get another respirator in place. Now he had disabled the machine, Burgess didn't seem to know what to do.

'Tell her I did it,' he shouted to a nurse. 'Tell her to tell them that I did it. Bastards!'

'The guy's mad,' somebody shouted.

'She's innocent!' Burgess shouted back.

The surveillance officer came running into the unit. He approached Burgess, then stopped when he saw the situation. He looked from the bare wires to the puddle around Burgess's shoes.

'Move away from the patient,' he said.

Burgess's face crumpled. He gestured with the cable. 'She's innocent.'

'Put your hands where I can see them,' the officer said.

Burgess brought up his hands, letting the cable fall to the floor. One of the wires sparked as it touched the water.

'Now, move,' the officer said. 'Come on, keep moving.'

Burgess walked towards him, groaning, mumbling to himself. He started to say something else to the officer, then he stepped on the end of the cable. He screamed. The current blasted through him and flung his body across an empty bed.

Creegan got home a little after nine. As he passed the telephone on the hall table he hit the answerphone button and listened while he took off his coat, jacket and tie in the bedroom.

The mechanical voice told him he had three messages. The first was from a woman he knew well.

'Carmel from Video Shack. I rang yesterday. You should've brought two films back on Wednesday, *The Third Man* and *Delicatessen*. Can you ring, please?'

Message two was from Criminal Intelligence – could DI Creegan ring Frank on extension 4134 when he was free?

During the playback of the third message, which was from Kerry, Creegan took a screw-top bottle of Pepsi from the fridge and drank down half of it in three gulps.

'Dave, it's me. The kids have asked if they can stay with you next weekend. Let me know if you're up to it, but I warn you now, Louise is talking about you buying bunk beds. Is that your idea or hers? Give me a ring. And if you want to go for a drink, we're around all weekend. Lots of love. 'Bye.'

Creegan went to the bathroom and turned on the shower. He returned to the bedroom, took off his shoes and went back to the bathroom in his stockinged feet.

Inside the bathroom he suddenly swayed and grabbed the shower curtain. Under the strain of his weight it came away from the rail. He landed on the floor in a sitting position and tried to push himself up. His hands didn't seem to be under his control. For a time he sat motionless, looking dazed. After a minute he fell over and lay sprawled, his head on one side, only his eyes moving.

Footsteps came along the hallway from the spare room. A young woman walked into the bathroom and knelt beside Creegan, positioning herself where he could see her. She was smiling gently as she put her mouth close to his ear and spoke.

'People are wrong,' she said softly. 'Places are wrong. You disagree with about seventy per cent of what goes on here. *Here.*'

She took a sterile-packed syringe, an ampoule and other items from her pocket. She pushed up Creegan's shirtsleeve, exposing his upper arm. Next she unwrapped the syringe, uncapped the needle and drew up a quantity of liquid from the ampoule. Then, from a sterile packet, she took a coiled plastic tube with a butterfly needle on one end. A port on the other end was designed to fit over the end of the syringe when the needle was removed. She pushed the butterfly needle carefully into a vein in Creegan's arm, fitted the syringe to the other end of the tube, and drew a little of his blood up into the coil.

She paused and smiled at Creegan with something like familiarity. Then she pressed down on the plunger of the syringe, injecting a quantity of a drug into his bloodstream.

She sat back, regarding him calmly. Light from the hallway caught her blond hair, back-lighting it, making it shimmer like a halo. Her face was placidly attractive, with very wide blue eyes. She was a woman Creegan had seen fleetingly a few times, but he had only spoken to her once. She was Dr Julie Carney, an anaesthetics registrar.

'I know you can hear me,' she said. 'You can blink. Once for yes. Nothing for no. I'm right, aren't I?'

She waited, but he did not blink.

'Can you honestly say this was worth coming back for?'

Creegan blinked once.

20

Taylor was driving carefully through heavy rain when her mobile rang. She snatched it up off the passenger seat.

'Taylor? Enwright. Have you got Creegan with you?'

'I've just dropped him off at home,' she said.

'I've tried bleeping him, got nothing. Listen, Eric Santer from the Home Office must have read the papers. He's coming round on his way from work. He wants to meet you all.'

Taylor frowned. 'I'm meant to be doing some research.'

'No you're not. You're off on a date. I won't spoil your fun. Half an hour. Please. Get Creegan.'

Taylor made a little scowl. 'Fine,' she said.

She switched off the phone and threw it on the seat. At the next red light she checked her make-up in the mirror. She decided to wipe off some of the lipstick.

Moving again, she tried to call Creegan. His mobile number was Code 3 on her phone. She hit the button and listened to the number connect. She let it ring for twenty seconds then killed the connection and hit another button.

'Taylor to Control.'

'Control,' a gruff voice said. 'Go ahead.'

'Is Creegan static or moving?'

There was a pause. She heard a keyboard being worked, then a loud beep.

'No, he's at home,' Control said. 'Well, his warrant card's at home.'

Julie Carney washed her hands carefully in Creegan's bathroom and dried them on one of his fleecy towels. She put on a pair of rubber gloves and went back to where he lay helpless on the bathroom floor.

'There's an ancient Jewish sect – Sadducees,' she said, kneeling beside him. 'If you cheat death and return to earth, you're taking up space that doesn't belong to you. To them it must look pretty overcrowded round here.'

She put two gloved fingers against the side of his neck, locating the pulse. When she had found it she took a matchstick from her pocket and impaled it, at its middle, on a drawing pin. She then laid the flat head of the drawing pin precisely at the spot on Creegan's neck where she had found the pulse, directly over the carotid artery. What she had created was an impromptu pulse monitor. With each beat of blood along the artery, the ends of the matchstick jerked visibly.

'I'm not Jewish,' she went on. 'So obviously you're safe enough with me.' She watched the steady jerking of the matchstick. 'What I can't understand is how you live with yourself. Have you ever felt that welcome before? I know you haven't since. I don't know what keeps you here.'

She removed the syringe from the slender tube leading into his arm and replaced it with another, much larger syringe. She pressed the plunger firmly and before the syringe was empty Creegan's eyes had closed.

Julie watched the matchstick on his neck bobbing from

side to side. She stared at it intently. It stopped. Then it bobbed one last time.

She sat back on her heels and studied Creegan's face. Her own face had an expression of wonderment and curiosity.

The telephone rang. For five seconds she didn't appear to notice it. Then she moved, suddenly all efficiency, unbuttoning Creegan's shirt. She put the heel of her hand on his breastbone and put her other hand on top. Leaning her weight on her stiffened arms she began rocking her hands back and forward, making his breastbone move, stimulating his heart.

Her hair tumbled forward as she worked. Now she didn't look so serene. She looked worried. She pulled open Creegan's jaw and lowered her open mouth on to his. She blew air into his mouth, sealing her lips on his, forcing the air into his throat. She raised her head, took a deep breath, and repeated the procedure. She did it six times, then rocked his breastbone again, panting with the exertion.

She stopped and looked at him. He was lifeless.

She scrambled to the corner, snatched up her bag and took out another syringe with a long capped needle. She pulled off the cap with her teeth and positioned herself over Creegan's chest. She brought down the tip of the long needle carefully, positioning it over the left side of his breastbone, at the space between the fifth and sixth ribs. She took a sharp breath, held it, and pushed the needle down into Creegan's heart. As blood began to trickle across his chest and down on to the floor she thumbed the plunger and drove it to the bottom of the barrel. She withdrew the needle slowly, staring at Creegan's face, searching it for a sign of life.

173

There was a loud banging on the door. Julie jumped back, staring out into the hall. She snatched up the big syringe and the needle cover and hid behind the bathroom door.

The letterbox flapped open and Taylor called through the gap. 'Creegan. Late call to show your teeth. Someone from the Home Office wants to see us.'

The flap went down again. Julie was torn between the need to get out and the necessity to bring Creegan back. She crawled across the floor to him and began rhythmically pumping his breastbone, grunting as she strained to jolt life into his heart.

'I know you're there!' Taylor shouted through the front door. Julie scuttled back out of sight.

Outside on the step, Taylor was about to give up. She turned away from the door, then decided to take one last look through the letterbox. She pushed up the flap and put her face as close to the door as she could. All she could see was the open living-room door and light from the bathroom streaming on to the hall carpet. She panned down, thorough as ever, and saw a spent syringe lying on the floor near the bathroom door.

'Creegan! Oh, shit!'

She stood back from the door and yanked out her radio.

'Taylor to Control. I need help at Creegan's flat.'

She pocketed the radio and pulled her gun from the holster at her hip. Standing back, she aimed the gun, supporting her right hand with her left, and fired a single shot into the door lock.

The door swung open as the echo of the shot died. She ran in and found Creegan on his back in the bathroom.

His shirt was open and a trickle of blood ran from the front of his chest down on to the floor.

'Oh, Creegan,' she whispered, 'what the hell have you done?'

She put the gun on the floor and began giving Creegan mouth-to-mouth. Kneeling there, she was unaware of Julie Carney moving out from the shadows behind her. Taylor continued to force mouthfuls of air into Creegan's motionless chest as Julie reached down and picked up the gun. She put the muzzle on the back of Taylor's head. Taylor froze.

'Don't turn around,' Julie said nervously. 'If you move, I'll shoot you.'

Taylor knew better than to try anything. She stayed motionless. There was agitated breathing and the hurried sounds of things being gathered and dropped into a bag. The pressure of the gun remained on the back of her head. Then suddenly it was gone. Taylor stayed as she was, crouched over Creegan's body, until she was sure the intruder had left.

Police cars, unmarked cars, an ambulance and a team of paramedics were at Creegan's flat within minutes of Taylor raising the alarm. Commander Enwright arrived with Kreitman and Rivers as Creegan was being transferred to the ambulance.

Enwright found Taylor standing by the back doors of the ambulance. 'How's it looking?'

'Well . . .' She shrugged. 'He's alive.'

'You saw her?'

'No. Listen . . . she got my gun.'

Enwright pointed to the stretcher as it was secured inside the ambulance. 'Go with him,' he told Rivers.

'Take two officers to cover him. Armed. And get to me every fifteen minutes. You understand?'

Rivers nodded.

Enwright turned to Kreitman, who had been quizzing two uniformed officers. 'How did she get into his home?'

'She told the caretaker she was his wife. He said she seemed distressed.'

Enwright looked astonished. 'He let her in? Has he still got his job?'

Creegan was rushed to the nearest hospital, St Margaret's. On arrival he was taken to the Intensive Care Unit where, flanked by protection officers, he was put on a ventilator. A specimen of his blood was taken for high-speed toxicology screening.

Rivers, standing by the bed, spoke quietly into his radio. 'Can we get hold of Dr Walker? Dr Elizabeth Walker from St Barnaby's. Also we've got a closed circuit covering the noticeboard in the main canteen at St Barnaby's. Get the tape. Get it to Enwright.'

Thirty minutes later, in the conference room at OSC headquarters, Enwright, Kreitman, Taylor and Marion, the psychologist, listened in silence as a machine in the centre of the table played back the taped conversation between Creegan and the killer. Now the distortion had been removed from the recording and the woman's voice sounded normal.

You died, you went where you belonged, and you came back because you were forced to. There hasn't been a single day when you didn't think that was a mistake.

Taylor asked Enwright if he knew about Creegan's near-death experience.

'Yes. I knew his wife blamed that for the breakdown of their marriage.'

'The equipment we've picked up from his flat was fairly specialised,' Kreitman said. 'She'd have to be pretty senior to know how to use it.'

'She sounded scared,' Taylor said.

Enwright's secretary came in and handed him a Jiffy bag. Enwright pulled a videotape out of the bag and put it on the table. He looked at Taylor. 'So where did Carl Burgess come into this?'

'Burgess is out of the frame now, isn't he?' Kreitman said.

'Well, in and out,' said Enwright. 'He tried killing a patient at St Barnaby's.'

'Different pattern,' Marion said. 'He literally tried to unplug him in front of witnesses. Out of his tree. I think we'd be wasting our time looking for a connection between him and the person on the tape.'

Kreitman was frowning. 'What's Burgess saying?'

'Nothing.' Enwright pushed the videotape towards Kreitman. 'He electrocuted himself. Died two hours later.'

Kreitman looked troubled. He sat staring at the wall.

'Are we looking at this tape?' Enwright said. There was no response. 'Kreitman?'

Kreitman shook himself. He got up and put the hospital surveillance tape in the VCR, which was hooked up to a large-screen projection unit. The black-and-white image of corridor traffic came up on the screen. The noticeboard with Creegan's card was visible to the left.

'The card was never removed from the board,' Kreitman said, 'which is why nobody leapt out.'

They watched several people pass the board. One or

177

two looked at it and moved on. One young woman seemed to look more intently than the others, and as she moved on she was glancing back at the board.

'Can we see her again?' Taylor said.

Kreitman didn't hear. He was staring at a case folder on the desk. It had a picture of Carl Burgess on the cover.

'Jonathan,' Taylor snapped, 'spool back.'

'Sorry.' He fought down a yawn. 'I'm tired.'

Taylor sniffed. 'We're all tired.' She watched the screen image run backwards. 'There,' she said, pointing.

Kreitman froze the frame. They all stared at the young woman in a white coat.

Creegan opened his eyes slowly. He still couldn't move his body, but his eyes were perfectly mobile. He looked up at the doctor who was taking an interim tox-screen sample from his arm. His eyes widened. The doctor was Julie Carney.

She stared at him expectantly. 'Did you see anything?' she whispered. 'Blink once for yes.'

Creegan continued to stare.

A junior doctor approached the bed. 'His eyes are open,' he observed.

Julie slid smoothly into her clinical role. 'Patient regained consciousness at nine forty-two p.m.,' she said, consulting the clock above the bed. 'Check the pattern on the neuro chart.'

Rivers came forward. He was staring anxiously at Creegan, at the blank expression and the eerie stillness of his body. 'Creegan? It's Rivers. Can you hear me?'

There was no response. Creegan continued to stare

178

at Julie. Rivers spun round as the curtain was pushed aside. Dr Walker came in and announced herself.

'I've been asked to take the case,' she said.

Rivers nodded and turned to address the other medical personnel working around the bed. 'He's now a private patient of Dr Walker. No drugs or treatment without her spoken consent.'

Dr Walker smiled at Julie. 'No offence. I'll tell you about it when I'm allowed to.'

Julie said that was OK. She turned and left the unit.

During the following twenty minutes Dr Walker set up specialist monitoring on Creegan's respiration and blood pressure and ordered electrolyte and haemoglobin analyses. When the findings from the toxicology screen arrived she studied them very carefully.

'He's been given atracurium,' she told Rivers. 'We use it to paralyse patients during surgery.'

'Paralyse?' Rivers looked startled.

'It wears off. But you see this . . .' Dr Walker tapped the coloured graph that accompanied the test results. It showed the presence and percentages of metabolic residues that were not normally found in the body. She pointed to one jagged blue line labelled 'epinephrine'. 'This is adrenalin.' She shook her head. 'God, this is . . .'

'What's she done to him?' Rivers said.

Dr Walker studied the graph for a second longer. 'I think she stopped his heart with digoxin then resuscitated him. We'll need to keep a check on the heart rate.' She looked at Creegan, at his anxious eyes. 'It's all right,' she said, smiling.

Kreitman arrived. 'Dr Walker, can I talk to you?'

She was already setting up a heart-rate monitor. 'I'll need about half an hour longer,' she said.

Kreitman pushed a print-out from the surveillance video in front of her. 'Do you know this woman?'

Dr Walker nodded. 'Julie Carney. She's an anaesthetic registrar.'

Rivers gaped at the picture. 'She was here tonight,' he said. 'She was working on Creegan when I got here.'

21

Police cars closed on Julie Carney's house from both ends of the street. They came with flashing lights but no sirens. Taylor's unmarked car arrived behind them. She parked close to the house, a neat-fronted place with no attempt at character, on an estate of economy-styled first-buyers' homes. She could see Kreitman already on the step, gun at the ready, waiting as a lock specialist used glinting steel instruments to open the door.

Taylor got out of the car and entered the house behind Kreitman.

The smell in the hallway was the first thing they noticed. It was musty, with a hint of something rotten. Kreitman switched on the living-room light.

Taylor gasped. The place was filthy. Unwashed clothes, takeaway boxes, empty bottles and used tissues were scattered where they had been abandoned.

The kitchen was worse. Piles of unwashed dishes, covered in half-eaten mouldering food, were stacked in the sink and on the drainers and worktops. Bin-bags bulging with rotting waste were lined along the walls and out into the hallway.

Kreitman went to the bedroom. The smell there was different, a fetid human odour, as bad in its way as the stench in the kitchen. The bed-linen was greasy and stained and apparently hadn't been changed for months. Stacks of medical books and pamphlets lay on chairs, on the window-ledge and around two linen baskets overflowing with unwashed clothes.

Taylor stood in the living room, looking at the only clean things in the place – Julie's starched white coats, on hangers along the curtain rail, and a few laundered outfits in cellophane bags.

She turned in a slow circle, responding to the awfulness of the house, the strangeness. Every mirror had been whitened with Windolene. On tables and on a sideboard there were framed pictures of medical and pharmaceutical events and parties, the ordinary accretion of a young doctor's life. In every picture, Julie Carney's face had been scratched out.

Taylor went to the bathroom. A solitary small bar of soap sat on the ledge of the washbasin. A dirty towel hung on the rail. She opened the cabinet. It was bare except for a stack of cardboard boxes in one corner of the bottom shelf. They contained unused ampoules of digoxin.

Kreitman came from the bedroom with a handkerchief to his nose. He held up a clutch of bank books. 'She's cleared out all these accounts. She's wandering around with about two grand, and your weapon.'

Meanwhile, in Commander Enwright's office at OSC headquarters, Dr Walker sat in front of the desk, drinking coffee from a mug, watching Enwright pace back and forth and listening as he and Marion explained the situation. They had told her there was little doubt that Dr Carney was responsible for the hospital deaths, and that she had deliberately made it look as if Dr Walker was the killer.

'But I don't understand,' Dr Walker said. 'Why would Julie Carney want to do all this to me?'

'Swindon General, 1984,' Enwright said. He came and sat at the side of the desk. 'You treated an eighteen-year-old girl after a traffic accident. Her heart failed, you resuscitated her.'

Dr Walker shrugged. 'I was a Casualty junior then. I've no idea how many people I—'

'Her name was Julie Farrah. In 1987 she married a man called Steven Carney.'

'Oh my God.' Dr Walker looked shocked.

'According to her personnel records,' Marion said, 'she's refused three permanent jobs to remain a locum. A possibility is that she wanted to remain a locum to stay around you. When you've moved house, she's moved house. She's followed you.'

'Look,' Enwright said, 'she's never attempted to damage you personally, but we can't take any risks. We'd like to move you and your children into a safe house until this is over.'

Creegan was propped up in bed in a side ward at St Margaret's. In the fourteen hours since he had been brought there his colour had improved, but to Taylor, sitting by the bed, he still looked very ill. He was motionless, his eyes wide open and staring at nothing.

'She must've been in the flat when I got home,' he said.

Taylor was unsettled by his stillness, but she didn't let it show. 'Did she say anything?'

'She wants to know if there's anything waiting for her if she dies again.'

'And what are you going to tell her, Creegan?'

183

The door opened. Kerry and her boyfriend Barry came in. Kerry bent and kissed Creegan's cheek. She looked tearful.

'I came last night and they wouldn't say what had happened,' she said. 'They still won't tell me.'

'I'm sorry,' Taylor said, meaning it. 'The information we're carrying has to stay classified.'

Kerry frowned. 'I'm security-cleared, aren't I?'

'Er, *you* are,' Taylor said.

Barry caught on at once. 'I'll get some coffees,' he said.

Taylor got up and followed him out. They got coffee from the machine in the corridor and sat down on a bench. Barry sensed Taylor's curiosity, which appeared to coincide with a need on his part to talk to somebody. He explained that he was an independent builder, and he now lived with Kerry and her children.

'I thought she was a single parent. Well, she is a single parent. Then I realised Dave was coming round every second day, at least, to see the kids.'

Taylor didn't hide her surprise. 'And you stayed?'

'No. I called it off. Then he turns up at my house one night.' Barry smiled faintly, recalling it. 'Says he thinks I've let his family down. If I knew anything about kids, I'd know that they need continuity. If I really cared, I'd move in and be around for them.'

'Does that leave you anywhere to go?'

'When I start feeling like his best man on loan, he stops coming round for a bit. He makes room for me.'

In another wing of the hospital, in the personnel office, Rivers was searching through filing cabinets crammed with the records of medical staff. Kreitman sat at a desk. He was obviously preoccupied. He had been that way all morning.

'Carl Burgess?' he murmured. This was the first time he and Rivers had been on their own together since the previous afternoon.

'I heard,' Rivers said.

'He *could* have been the killer. His form, his profile, his mistakes.'

'Nobody's arguing,' Rivers said, 'are they?'

Kreitman shook his head. He looked troubled.

Something occurred to Rivers. He looked at Kreitman. 'Did you log the visit to his house?'

'It's in the computer.'

'Can you get it out of the computer without leaving a bloody great hole?'

Kreitman nodded. He still looked troubled.

Rivers found what he was looking for. It was the personnel file on Julie Carney, with a four-set of identification photographs clipped to the front.

'Here we go,' he said.

They left. The hunt for Julie Carney was now a major priority.

Elsewhere, Julie had realised that a number of people would be looking for her, and she was taking steps to thwart them. The previous night she had put through a call from a hotel bedroom to Creegan's house and left a message on his answering machine. On this occasion she had not disguised her voice, and as she delivered the message she tried to kill herself with a lethal injection. But she couldn't do it. She ended up crying pitifully into her mobile phone.

She had known before she tried that she lacked the

185

courage to end her own life. It was something she could not do on her own.

Now she planned to leave London, but first she paid a visit to a hairdresser, who at that moment was holding up a mirror to the back of Julie's head to show her the effect of her transformation.

Julie appeared unwilling to look in the mirror.

'Don't be so shy,' the hairdresser told her. 'You'll go home tonight and knock him for six. You will.'

Julie looked at the mirror in front of her.

'There.' The hairdresser angled the other mirror to present the best view. 'How's that?'

Julie stared at herself. Her long hair was short now, and it had been dyed from light blond to a dense brown.

'It's fine,' she said, looking as if she hated everything she saw.

'I hope your protection's better than my home security,' Creegan said as he let Taylor and himself into his flat. The door had been fixed and the place was tidied.

Taylor put down the overnight bag she had brought. She watched Creegan tap the replay button on the answering machine. It told him he had one message.

'So how's your cooking?' he asked Taylor.

'I don't cook,' she said.

Julie Carney's voice came on the answering machine. 'David Creegan. By the time you get this message I'll have moved on. You died on the sixteenth of June two years ago.'

Creegan and Taylor sat down, listening.

'Nothing's worked out for you since. I hope you know what it took for me to bring you back. You looked so peaceful . . . I wanted to leave you. I envied you.' Julie paused. 'You left me that message on the noticeboard thinking you were being clever. "I know where you've been." Well, I know where you've been, David. What I want to know is how you condemn me for what I've done? You believe, don't you?' The voice wavered, then she began to cry. 'You believe, don't you, David?' She went on crying for several seconds before the connection was broken.

Taylor got out her radio and called Control. 'Carney's left a message on Creegan's machine. She's using her mobile. Find out what time that was. Get a location.'

She put down the radio and joined Creegan in the kitchen, where he was removing every bottle and can of drink from the fridge. Taylor got a roll of bin-bags, and while she filled them with food from the fridge and cupboards, Creegan poured every one of the drinks down the sink.

Later, after a hasty supermarket trip for replacement supplies, they followed a lead passed on by Enwright. It took them to a primary school in Hendon. They waited in the teachers' carpark until a dark-haired man in his thirties came out and walked towards his car.

Creegan stepped forward. 'Steve Carney?' The man just looked at him. Creegan held up his identification. 'DI Dave Creegan from the Organised and Serial Crimes Unit.'

Taylor held up her card and identified herself.

Steve Carney looked glumly from one to the other. 'Is this to do with Julie?'

They took him to Julie's house and showed him the squalor that had been her recent lifestyle. Carney looked stunned. It was Creegan's first visit and he looked surprised too, even though he had been warned what it was like. Carney walked from room to room and finally came back to the living room, where Creegan and Taylor waited.

'Any idea where she might have gone?' Taylor asked him.

He nodded at the front window recess. 'I was in the middle of papering that when I left.' He looked at Taylor. 'I haven't seen her since. I don't want to.'

Creegan said, 'Did she hurt you, Steve?'

Carney looked unwilling to talk any more, but finally he said, 'She came at me, over and over again, about me being depressed. What a dump the world is, how small I was. Weeks and weeks and weeks and weeks. She drove me round the bend. Julie's completely . . .' He sighed. 'Look, I'm not . . . I can't help you. All right?'

He opened the back door and walked to the bottom of the garden. Taylor followed him, weaving her way between the fluttering yellow lengths of crime-scene tape. She stood a couple of yards away, giving him space.

'Had you known each other long before you got together?'

Carney looked at Taylor. 'What's she done?'

'She's a murder suspect.'

Carney took it in without looking surprised. 'I met her at the Point of Light Foundation. It's a self-help group for . . . zombies. She did research for them.'

'Did she ever talk about her near-death experience?'

'Julie's obsessed with death. I don't know why. I don't want to.' Carney put a cigarette in his mouth and lit it. 'What I can't figure out is why she went to so much bother if all she wanted to do was damage me.'

In the house, Creegan had been going over the OSC file on Julie Carney, which he had brought to read in the car. He had now reread a traffic accident report from 1984. He noted the name of the police officer who reported the case and called Control to see if they could get the man's telephone number. Within two minutes they were back on the line with the number. Creegan rang it and waited.

'Sergeant Linguard,' a voice said.

'Keith Linguard?'

'Am and always will be. What can I do for you?'

'DI Creegan here from the OSC in London.'

'Oh. I *am* honoured.'

'Keith, you attended a traffic accident in Swindon when you were a constable. It was back in '84. You probably won't remember. Eighteen-year-old girl. Her name was Julie.'

'Julie Farrah,' Linguard said at once. 'I remember that one.'

22

Julie Carney stood on a street of terraced houses in Mold, North Wales. She clutched a clipboard and carried a leather bag over her shoulder. She flashed a friendly smile at an old man who had opened the door of number 53 to her. He was Mr Swan, the householder, and he explained to Julie that his wife was asleep.

'Well, I'm not in a hurry,' Julie said. 'Maybe we can make a start.'

'She went back to sleep just ten minutes after you rang.'

Julie tapped the clipboard. 'You could help me fill in this questionnaire.'

Mr Swan led her through to the main downstairs room, long and narrow with a window at each end. The room served as kitchen, living room and a bedroom for Mrs Swan, who had suffered a stroke. She lay pale and motionless in a single bed at the far end of the room.

'Do we need to bother her at all if it's just a questionnaire?' Mr Swan asked.

'Oh, not particularly.' Julie looked at the old woman. 'I just need to check her over, take a sample of blood. It'll take two minutes.'

She went to the bed. Mrs Swan was awake now.

Her eyes followed Julie as she sat by the bedside. The eyes were the only part of herself that Mrs Swan could move.

'I can only manage the stairs twice a day,' Mr Swan said, filling the kettle at the sink by the front window. 'So the bed had to come down here.'

He worked with his back to the two women, putting biscuits on a plate, topping up the sugar bowl from a packet.

'This isn't living, is it?' Julie whispered to Mrs Swan. The eyes widened a fraction.

'Handier, really,' Mr Swan was saying. 'The cooking, the washing. They're putting us a shower in the old pantry.'

Julie opened the little medical case she had brought and took out a syringe. It was already full of liquid. She uncapped the needle and made a sad little smile. 'Who are you here for, Dorothy?'

'Money coming from the lottery,' said Mr Swan, drying a cup. 'I never bought a ticket in my life. Now that's what you call lucky.'

He put the toe of his slipper on the pedal of a flip-top bin. The lid stood upright as he emptied used tea leaves from the pot.

'Take a deep breath,' Julie whispered to Mrs Swan. 'Can you smell that? That's what the world smells like. You can't wait, can you?' She put the tip of the needle on the thin old arm. 'You don't have to.'

Mrs Swan made a sound as the needle slid into her arm. It was a small broken sound, like a muffled whimper. Julie pressed the plunger home.

Mr Swan turned from the sink. He looked surprised. 'Was that her?'

He came to the bedside as Julie was closing her case.

'Was that her?' he said again. He looked at his wife. Her eyes were staring at Julie. They were closing. 'She's not made a peep in six months. What did you do to her?'

'She's tired,' Julie said.

Mrs Swan's eyes were closed now.

Mr Swan beamed. 'You can come again.'

The full OSC team was present when Creegan walked into the conference room and sat down in a wheelchair waiting by the door. To loud applause and cheering, Rivers pushed him to his place at the table.

'You do realise,' Rivers said, 'you're officially on file as a murder victim. So I've eaten your biscuits.'

Creegan adjusted his position as the noise died down. The wheelchair was a good gag but not very convenient. As he propped his elbows on the table he did a double-take on a folder with a picture of Carl Burgess on the front. The word DECEASED was printed across it.

At the opposite side of the table Kreitman held up a sheaf of stapled photocopies and began to distribute them.

'This document is a membership register for the Point of Light Foundation, a self-help group for—'

'Existentialist electricians,' Rivers said. The others laughed.

'For people who have had near-death experiences,' Kreitman continued. 'Julie Carney was paid by the organisation to collate this register. It gives names, addresses and clinical details of all their membership.

We know she owns a copy of this, but we can't find it at the house. So, she must have it with her.'

'Assume she's on the offensive, not on the run,' Commander Enwright told the assembly. 'I want everyone in this register notified to contact us if she gets in touch.'

A secretary came in while Enwright was speaking. She whispered to Taylor. Taylor got up and followed her out of the room.

Enwright invited Marion to let them hear whatever psychological input she might have.

'Carney's requesting help from Creegan,' she said, 'but he, according to her own beliefs, doesn't belong here either. She's treating him as if he's special, but forgive me, he's no more special than the victims she terminated.'

Taylor came back in. She held up a fax sheet. 'Julie Carney's on the move. She used a credit card about four hours ago, in Clwyd, North Wales. Now the prints match, the signature matches. But the store assistant swears she's got dark brown hair.'

Enwright told Rivers to issue a new description. As Taylor went back to her seat, she dropped a folded note in front of Enwright. Creegan was watching. He also watched as Enwright read the note, refolded it and threw a quick, cautious look at Creegan himself.

'We've got two people listed for North Wales,' said Kreitman, consulting the Point of Light register. 'They're in Mold and Clwyd.'

'Make contact,' Creegan said. 'And put everybody on the register under surveillance.'

Kreitman and Rivers got the necessary information together in less than a minute. Control connected Kreitman with the police authority for Clwyd. He warned them that

Peter John Crowther, of Castle Row in Clwyd, might be at risk.

Simultaneously Rivers was connected with the police station controlling Mold district. 'I'm DC Mark Rivers at OSC in London. We've got an urgent request for assistance on your patch. Dorothy Swan, 53 Cranmaer Road, Mold. She's seventy-two. Now we think she might be at risk from a Julie Carney. Carney. That's C-A-R-N . . . What?'

Rivers put his hand over the mouthpiece and whistled to Creegan, who was heading for the door. 'A seventy-two-year-old woman, Dorothy Swan, died two hours ago in Mold. She took a visit from a doctor claiming she was doing a survey on stroke victims. The doctor took a blood sample.'

Creegan told Rivers to get all relevant details and log them. He left the conference room and stood outside, waiting. Eventually Taylor came out.

'Where's Enwright gone?' Creegan said.

'To his office, hasn't he?'

'What was that note you slipped him?'

Taylor immediately looked contrite. 'I'm sorry. I didn't want you thinking it was on display.' She sighed. 'Your medical records were left in a café in Euston. She's drawn attention to some sensitive elements.'

Creegan nodded curtly and walked straight down the corridor to the commander's office. When he marched in, Enwright was at his desk, leafing through the medical records. Creegan leaned down over the desk and spun the file round to face himself. He saw yellow highlighter marks over sections of psychiatric information:

. . . *increasingly difficult to communicate with his wife.*

No confidence in dealing with his children.

'Have you seen any of this before?' Enwright said.

Creegan shook his head and flicked to another page.

Constant nightmares.

. . . *admitted that he had, on occasion, contemplated suicide.*

Creegan stepped back from the desk and began pacing.

'In 1984 the van that hit Julie Carney was in the middle of rush-hour traffic,' he said. 'The cop who was first on the scene said then, and he says now, it was a suicide attempt. She wants to try again. She thinks I do too.' He looked at Enwright. 'That's why I'm special.'

Minutes later, Enwright walked into the gents' toilet and found Creegan staring at himself in the mirror. His gaze was fixed on the scar above his eye. He stepped smartly away from the mirror.

'I know I'm not the first to say it,' Enwright murmured, 'but if you're feeling too exposed by this case, I can easily put you on to something else.'

Creegan waved the suggestion aside. He rinsed his hands and towelled them. 'She won't try again unless she definitely knows there's something worth going back for.'

'Fine.' Enwright nodded. 'Tell her there is. Tell her you saw the fireworks. Point her in the direction of the tallest building we can find and tell her we'll even watch her.'

'Could you?'

Enwright smiled and shook his head.

'And what if,' Creegan said, 'she's so scared she just wants a bit of company on the journey?'

Kerry Creegan parked her car in front of the house and

196

herded the two children through the gate ahead of her. She was halfway along the path when she heard the gate close again. She turned and saw a young woman with dark brown hair, clutching a clipboard. She smiled at Kerry.

'Mrs Creegan? It's Dr Farrah.'

'Yes?' Kerry was conditioned to be suspicious of strangers, especially when they ventured past her own front gate.

The young woman flashed a plastic-covered identity card. 'One forty-five? Community health screening?'

'Yeah?'

'You'd forgotten. It's the second time today that's happened.' The young woman shrugged. 'There's a meningitis outbreak at All Saints primary.'

Kerry frowned. 'I don't know anything about it.'

'Well, it's routine checks. You were meant to have had a letter. But . . .' She shrugged again. 'I can come back tomorrow if it's easier.'

'No. Please . . .' Kerry had made her evaluation. This woman was all right. 'Come in.'

She went to the door and fished out her keys. 'This is Dr Farrah,' she told the children. 'Say hello.'

23

Creegan was in the office. He had been reading the file on Carl Burgess. Now, as he called up the master file on the computer, Kreitman came in and put a wad of papers on Taylor's desk.

Creegan looked up. 'Jonathan? What went wrong with Carl Burgess?'

'Nobody knows.' Kreitman went to the coffee jug on a table by the window. He poured himself a mug and sugared it. 'He just went ape-shit, tried killing a patient. Botched it.'

'Yeah, and when he did, he said directly to a cop, "Tell her to tell them I did it. Tell them she's innocent."'

Kreitman was facing Creegan across the room, the coffee mug halfway to his mouth.

'The "she" is Dr Walker, obviously,' Creegan said. 'Who's "them", do you think?'

Kreitman was beginning to look hostile. 'If there's a proper question in there, ask it.'

'Was Burgess leaned on after his release?'

'No.'

'You agreed with his release?'

'No.' Kreitman tasted the coffee. 'At the time I thought

he was hot for the hospital murders. You know I did. And you know I was wrong.'

Creegan nodded. 'OK.'

Kreitman turned and walked away. Then he stopped. 'No.' He turned back. 'Apologise. You wouldn't speak to your plumber like that.'

Creegan looked surprised. 'Jonathan, I apologise. Unreservedly. It was a question, not an accusation.' He waited until Kreitman was at the door then he added, 'It's just that we've got two separate Burgess files on the hard drive. One's empty, one's not.'

Kreitman nodded, working to stay calm. 'Control "R" for reveal. One's a back-up, the other's not. We don't clear it till after the post-mortem.'

Kreitman walked out. Creegan looked at the computer screen. He held down the control key and tapped R. Both Burgess files now looked identical. He looked at the doorway, wondering.

'Can you lift your hair up for me, Ruby?'

Julie Carney was on her knees on the living-room carpet at Kerry Creegan's house, doing a cursory medical examination of the two little girls as they stood before her.

'That's eczema round there,' Kerry said, coming from the kitchen. 'She's just growing out of it.'

'Tell you what . . .' Julie unhooked her stethoscope and handed it to three-year-old Louise. 'Have a listen. See what your sister had for lunch.'

Louise put the stethoscope on and pushed the end of it against Ruby's stomach.

'What symptoms should we be looking for?' Kerry asked. 'Can I get you a coffee or something?'

'Do you know, you're the first to offer.' Julie got up and wandered across to the fireplace. 'Thank you.' She paused, remembering the first question. 'Any headaches, neck stiffness, sensitivity to light, get your GP out.' She looked at the pictures of the girls on the mantelpiece. Dave Creegan was in one of them. 'Did you want girls?'

'How do you take it?' Kerry called from the kitchen.

Julie looked at her blankly.

Kerry held up the jar. 'Your coffee?'

'Oh, no, I won't, thanks. Can I just have water?'

Kerry stared for a moment. 'Sure.'

'Was he there for the birth?' Julie asked.

'Five minutes before the first. Three minutes after the second.'

'Shame.'

Kerry nodded. 'That was one more than I expected.'

She poured mineral water in a glass for Julie and hot water on to her own instant granules, using a little domestic bustle to deflect this woman's dreaminess and her odd lack of focus.

Julie was studying Creegan's picture again. 'Is he kept very busy?'

Kerry deflected the question with another. 'Do you have any children?'

The idea seemed to startle Julie. 'Er, no, it's not that kind of job. Too many nights.'

Now Kerry was confused. 'As a community doctor?'

Barry's van had drawn up at the front of the house. The children ran to him as soon as he came in.

'Look what I got,' Louise said, pointing to the stethoscope dangling from her neck.

Barry picked her up while Louise danced around his legs.

'Barry,' Kerry said, 'this is Dr Farrah.'

'Hello,' Barry said brightly.

Julie made a jerky little motion with her head. She wasn't quite able to smile back.

'Do you know what Ruby had for lunch?' Louise asked Barry.

'What?'

'Fish fingers.'

Julie sat still, unsmiling, watching the enactment of simple domestic life, observing a genuine sociological composite. A family.

At eight o'clock that evening Commander Enwright's secretary brought a classified box file to him. He was still at his desk, working by the light of a single reading lamp. The secretary waited, but Enwright said he would file the documents himself.

When she left he flipped open the box and picked up Creegan's medical file. He was about to drop it inside when he noticed a torn-off page, separated from the rest and tucked in at the back. He pulled it out and looked. At the top was a label bearing Creegan's address. The label had been loosened. When Enwright lifted the corner he saw Creegan's old address printed underneath.

Enwright snatched up the phone. He called Creegan on his mobile and told him Julie Carney had got hold of his ex-wife's address.

Creegan rang Kerry's number. It was mid-evening; she should be there clearing up after putting the girls to bed. Barry should be there too. But the phone rang and rang.

Taylor and Creegan got in Taylor's car. He drove while Taylor put out an alert. Three police patrol cars were diverted. Creegan estimated it would take him another three minutes to get to Kerry's place.

Taylor called Unit One. 'How near are you?'

'Coming down South Malton towards the dual carriageway.'

'There must be somebody closer,' Creegan snarled. 'Get somebody closer!'

'All units,' Taylor called. 'Anyone closer?'

The radio crackled. 'Affirmative. Unit Two. We're two streets away. We're on it.'

'Where are they?' Creegan demanded.

Taylor asked for their position.

'Turning into Broom Road now.'

'It's number sixty-one,' Creegan shouted, throwing the car into a bend. 'Sixty-one. Ask if the lights are on.'

Taylor put the radio to her mouth. 'Do you see any house lights?'

Static crackle, then, 'Er, just the front bedroom. Front bedroom.'

'They've answered the door!' Creegan yelled. 'Ask if the van's outside.'

'Just break in,' Taylor told Unit Two. 'Repeat – break in.'

'Are we authorised?'

'Yes!' Creegan yelled at the radio, fighting with the steering. 'You're authorised! Do it!'

At the house, two policemen kicked in the door as another police car screeched round the corner and braked at the gate. Neighbours were emerging from their houses, gravitating towards the action.

Policemen ran into the house with torches, calling for

Mrs Creegan. They went clattering through the living room and kitchen, calling out, their torch beams sweeping walls and floors.

Taylor's car skidded round the end of the street and slid to a halt by the gate. Creegan got out and ran up the path. Taylor was behind him.

In the hall he paused for a split second, then ran upstairs. He burst into the main bedroom. No one was there. As Taylor came up the stairs and strode into the bedroom he went to the window and looked out. Across the road, Kerry and Barry stood gaping at the house. The girls were with them, both dressed up as fairies, as were most of the children pouring out of the house behind them. The boy at the front wore a big badge that said I'M 5 TODAY!

'Oh, shit,' Creegan groaned.

Much later, in the middle of the night, the phone in Creegan's flat rang. Taylor was still staying with him for security cover and she was first out into the hall. Creegan emerged from the room opposite. They stood for a moment and surveyed each other's night attire: Taylor wore a set of red tartan pyjamas; Creegan had on red pyjama bottoms and a white T-shirt.

Taylor leaned on the wall while Creegan went into the living room and picked up the receiver.

'Creegan.'

'I only wanted to look,' Julie Carney said.

Taylor saw the sudden tension in Creegan's shoulders. She had the feeling he wanted to shout at the phone. Instead, he took a careful breath then said, very softly, 'You don't look.'

'Is that what you're hanging on for?' Julie said. 'Your family?'

Creegan sighed. 'Julie . . .' He signalled Taylor. She came and turned on the recording machine. 'Give yourself up.'

It was as if he hadn't spoken. 'I don't know why,' she said, 'they seem perfectly happy without you.'

'Look . . .' Creegan sat down. 'We checked your phone bills. And you know what's really weird? Two phone calls in three months. And both calls to work.'

Julie said, 'Have you seen your girls with that man – Barry?'

'You're gonna need a lot more friends than that to stay on the run.'

'That man being you but better? I'm right, aren't I? You don't fit in. You don't fit anywhere. That's normal.'

Taylor, listening in on a headset, went to the fridge and got two bottles of beer. She uncapped them and brought one to Creegan.

'Do you think you're normal, Julie?' Creegan chuckled. 'See, I don't pretend I am, but I am a bloody long way off you.'

'Not according to your medical records. Had you seen them before?'

Now Creegan began to sound angry. 'Did you want them to shock me? Did you?'

'Patients are always shocked when they see notes. I think it helps sometimes to be reminded about what you've got way down.'

'You do, Julie, do you? Well, that's great. Where do we start reminding *you*? Swindon, 1984, when you attempted suicide?'

He paused, listening. Julie said nothing.

'You're killing people because you believe that they

205

believe they're better off somewhere else. But you wanted to die before that. I've seen your records, black and white.'

Another pause. Still no response.

'You haven't got the guts to do it again, Julie. Which is just about the only positive thing that I know about you.'

Julie hung up.

Creegan put the phone down. He glanced at his watch. 'It's ten to four.' He groaned. 'I'll never get back to sleep.'

He looked at Taylor, sitting in the armchair next to his. Slowly she turned and looked at him. They stared at each other.

Creegan said, 'Do you fancy breakfast?'

In the kitchen they made a buffet of cheese, tomatoes, pickles, hot toast and scraps from the fridge. As they ate, Taylor found she was enjoying it much more than she had expected. They washed the food down with beer and for a while they said nothing.

Creegan broke the silence. 'Did you work with Rivers and Kreitman before this?'

'Rivers,' Taylor said. 'Once, during his training. Why?'

'They're good.'

'And? But?'

Creegan chewed for a minute. 'If you were on an armed raid and you had to choose someone to cover you, who would you choose?'

Taylor didn't hesitate. 'Rivers. His reactions are quicker.'

'Kreitman's more experienced,' Creegan pointed out.

'True.'

'If you needed to get somebody to tell the boss you're

206

going to the dentist, when really you're going shopping, who would you choose?'

Taylor frowned at him. 'What is this?'

'Go on.'

'Kreitman. Why?'

'I'm going shopping tomorrow,' Creegan said. 'And I'll bet you'd be useless.'

Taylor burst out laughing.

24

A team meeting was scheduled for 10 a.m. in the conference room. Creegan had asked to be excused. Rivers had made no such request, but he was absent too. As the others took their seats, Kreitman pointed to a document on the table in front of him.

'What's this?'

'It's a transcript of a conversation between the killer and Creegan,' Enwright said. 'Three fifty a.m. today.'

Kreitman pointed to where portions of the text had been blacked out. 'Why is it masked?'

'The other bits are classified.'

Kreitman frowned. 'Even from us?'

'She got fairly personal with Creegan,' Taylor explained. 'He's happy to lead her with that stuff, but I don't think he wants it broadcasting.'

'Right.' Enwright pulled his chair closer to the table. 'I'd like to get started, please. Where's Rivers?'

'He's checking a lead on Julie Carney,' Kreitman said.

Taylor threw a sidelong glance at Kreitman. She caught a whiff of a lie.

Elsewhere, Creegan was in a position to know that it *was* a lie. He was standing among the trees in a North

London cemetery, watching a funeral fifty yards away. Very few people were present – just the minister, the gravediggers and one mourner, Mark Rivers.

'We have entrusted our brother, Carl Burgess, to God's merciful keeping,' the minister said, his voice toneless, 'and we now commit his body to the ground, in sure and certain hope of the resurrection to eternal life, through our Lord Jesus Christ, who died, was buried and rose again for us. For Him be glory for ever and ever. Amen.'

Rivers stood a few feet apart from the others, staring at the coffin, occasionally looking round the deserted cemetery.

The minister closed his prayer book and stood aside to let the gravediggers lower the coffin. Rivers moved off a little further, got out his cigarettes and lit one. Creegan watched, seeing him look around again, uneasy, fidgety, as if he were anxious to have this over and done with.

Creegan left the cemetery shortly after Rivers. On the drive back into central London his mobile phone rang. He had it hooked up to the hands-free set. He touched the button and identified himself.

'I've overdosed three people,' Julie Carney said. Her voice was calm. 'If you don't believe me, all three blood samples are in a Red Star box delivered half an hour ago. Test them if you like, but that might waste time you haven't got. They're not my patients, it's not my hospital.'

'You sent them to the office?'

'Look inside.'

'I'm not in the office,' Creegan snapped. 'Look, what are you talking about? What three people?'

'They've got less than three hours before the digoxin kills them.'

Creegan slammed on the brakes, snatched up the phone and got out. He stood by the car with the phone to his ear, his hand covering the other ear. 'I don't believe you,' he said. 'You've never told us in advance.'

'I've never needed to. I want you to meet me. If you help me, I'll give you those three names and absolutely nobody gets hurt. But you come on your own and you don't speak to a single person or my mind goes blank.'

'Come where?'

'My house.'

Julie hung up. Creegan stood for a minute, frowning, drumming his fingers on the car roof. He got back in and rang the office. Taylor answered. He asked her if a parcel had been delivered for him. She said no, then corrected herself. There was a Red Star parcel in his in-tray, she said. Creegan hung up and drove to Julie Carney's house.

It took less than ten minutes. As he came in sight of the house with its yellow festoons of crime-scene tape, the phone rang. It was Julie. 'The back,' she said, and hung up.

Creegan stopped the car several yards from the house. When he reached the back garden he paused on the lawn, took out his gun, then gently opened the French window. He stepped into the filth and mess of the living room.

'Where's the gun, Julie?' he called.

'I'm in here,' she called back.

'Where's the gun you took off DI Taylor?'

'There's a bag on the chair in there.'

Creegan looked around, saw the black leather bag. He flipped it open and took out the gun. He went into the hall, pocketing Taylor's gun, holding his own at the

211

ready. Julie Carney was sitting in a wooden chair by the desk in an open area that had been set up as an office. She wore a sombre black dress. In her hand, resting on the arm of the chair, was a syringe. It was attached to a coiled tube leading up to a needle in a vein just under her left collarbone. The needle was taped in place.

She looked at Creegan. Her face was blank. 'I said if you do as you're told, everybody gets what they want.'

'Well, I did what you asked,' said Creegan. 'So you give me the names of the people you've hurt.'

'You get the names when you've done this.' Julie looked down at the syringe.

'What's in it?'

'Two seconds to reach the brain and you can go away again.'

'No . . .' Creegan shook his head. 'You do it, if that's what you want.'

'I've tried.' Now her face wasn't so blank. She looked tearful. 'I can't. I get this far, and . . .'

At approximately that moment at OSC headquarters, Rivers noticed a puddle of blood on the floor.

'What happened?' he asked Taylor, nodding at the puddle.

Taylor looked around. The parcel in Creegan's in-tray was leaking, one corner of the wrapping paper bright red. A few minutes earlier she had picked it up and looked at it, curious to know what might be inside. She had put it down again and it toppled from the top of the tray on to the desk. She had put it back, but it was clear now that the fall had disrupted something inside the parcel.

She took a pair of rubber gloves from a drawer and put them on. Carefully she opened the parcel and unwrapped the bubble plastic inside. There were three phials. One was broken. The other two were intact and full of blood.

'Ring the lab,' Taylor told Rivers. 'Get them tested.' She picked up the phone on her desk and dialled Creegan's mobile number.

It rang as he stood in front of Julie Carney, caught in an impasse. He reached for the phone.

'Don't,' Julie said.

He took the phone out slowly and switched it off. 'I think we've got a logistical problem here,' he said, half smiling, keeping his voice low. 'Where are the names, Julie?'

'You first.'

'Are they in your bag?'

'You'll get the names.' Julie began to look anxious.

'Have you written them down?' Creegan started pacing, picking up papers, scanning the scribbles on them.

'You'll get the names,' Julie said again.

'You haven't, have you? Because you've no intention of giving them to us. If I honour the deal, you're dead within two seconds.'

'You'll find them.'

Creegan stopped pacing and stared at Julie. 'I don't believe you. You don't think those people want to live. They'll go like the rest did.'

'They *won't*,' Julie said, tearful again. 'I promise.'

Creegan stepped closer. 'If you were looking for somebody to trust, and you were looking at us two, who would you go for? I haven't killed anybody. I haven't lied to you. I've never broken a promise in my life.' He came closer still. 'Trust me.'

Julie's eyes grew wider as he crouched in front of

her and reached out, almost touching the hand with the syringe.

'I know what it's like to get that far,' he said softly. He held up a finger and pointed it at his temple. 'I once had a gun this far from my head. I heard the bullet going into the chamber. And I squeezed it, and squeezed it. But I couldn't.' He paused, letting his fingers close gently over hers. 'If there had been somebody like you there, I'd have trusted them, Julie.'

There was a long look between them. Julie was reading his eyes.

'St Bede's,' she said in a small voice. 'Sylvia Goldman, ward seventeen. Frank . . . Frank Whittaker, High Dependency Two.'

'St Bede's?'

Creegan's finger hovered over the plunger. Julie looked at it, then at him. She nodded.

'Doreen Brown, in the breast unit.'

'St Bede's?'

She nodded again, trembling, her eyes wide as she watched Creegan's fingertip begin to lower on to the plunger of the syringe.

Then he moved back abruptly and stood up. He pulled out his radio and thumbed it on. 'Creegan to Control.'

Control acknowledged.

'Commander Enwright,' Creegan said. 'Urgent.'

'You bastard!' Julie screamed. 'You bastard!'

Enwright came on.

'Take these details down,' Creegan said. 'They're all patients at St Bede's. They've all been OD'd by Julie Carney. Sylvia Goldman, ward seventeen. Frank Whittaker, High Dependency.' He paused, frowning to recall the last name. 'Doreen Brown, breast unit.'

'OK,' Enwright said. 'We've traced you to Carney's house. Are you safe?'

'Send a van. I'll bring her in.'

'No!' Julie howled. She leapt out of the chair and ran to the kitchen, still clutching the syringe.

'Taylor's on her way,' Enwright said. 'She's got a team with her.'

Creegan pocketed the radio and ran through to the kitchen. Julie was lying on the floor, her head and shoulders propped on the door of the grimy cooker.

Creegan hunkered down in front of her. She cowered away from him.

'Julie, I wasn't lying about the gun. You know why I got that far and couldn't? It's the same reason you can't. You can't want to die *enough*.' He held out his hand to her. 'Come on.'

She jerked away. 'No.'

Creegan sighed. 'Julie . . .'

'Did you know your ex-wife's pregnant?' she said.

'What?' The sidetracking left Creegan looking bewildered.

'She told me.' Julie watched him as she spoke, reading his eyes again. 'I said I was a community doctor and we were screening for meningitis.'

Creegan glared at her with something like anger.

'She wanted to know if there was any risk to the baby. So if you're hanging on for your family, I wouldn't bother. I don't think you belong there either.'

A police siren sounded in the distance. It got closer.

'Did you see anything the second time?' Julie asked.

Taylor's voice came on the radio. She asked Creegan where he was.

'You can tell me now, can't you?' Julie said.

'Creegan,' Taylor's voice said, 'tell me where you are.'

He pulled out the radio. 'Kitchen,' he told Taylor. Then to Julie he said, 'Yes.'

Taylor was coming into the house followed by Kreitman, Rivers and two other OSC officers. They moved cautiously, guns at the ready. Taylor led the way stealthily through to the kitchen. She looked in and saw Creegan, standing stock-still. She followed his gaze to the floor. Julie Carney lay there with her thumb pressed firmly on the plunger of the syringe. She was dead.

The three overdosed patients at St Bede's were located and emergency treatment was started at once. They were given intravenous antibody fragments to trap the digoxin in their systems and carry it safely away through their kidneys. The first one to recover was Sylvia Goldman. Word was passed by Control to Susan Taylor, who was at that moment supervising the removal of Julie Carney's body to a waiting ambulance.

A minute later Creegan came out of the house. He stopped on the way to his car and looked at Rivers, who was in conversation with Kreitman. Rivers caught the look, a stare that seemed to penetrate him. He didn't understand, and he was clearly unnerved.

Taylor, standing by the ambulance, saw the silent exchange. She didn't understand, either. She watched Creegan go to his car, get in and drive off, but not before he had another hard look at Rivers.

PART THREE

25

The Plough was a shabby, homely pub in the Kent countryside. It always did fair business on weekends and this one was no exception. The Sunday night crowd had been in a supping mood and even the late-stoppers were doing as much drinking as talking. Local custom, reinforced by a perpetual need for profit, dictated that on Saturday and Sunday nights Ted McCaffrey and his wife Eileen allowed a few trusted, free-spending customers to stay late and have after-hours drinks. Now, at ten past midnight, as Ted pulled pints and Eileen went round emptying ashtrays and collecting glasses, their seventeen-year-old son, Jack, let himself in through the back door.

No one apart from Eileen paid any attention. Jack, a slight, snub-nosed lad with small eyes and thick dark hair, didn't naturally attract people's interest. Most of the time he appeared surly and intense. In the bar he only ever smiled and became lively when he was too drunk to be coherent. Tonight Eileen watched him shuffle in and go straight up to his room without glancing at her or his father. She looked annoyed, but as usual she said nothing.

Jack's bedroom was a space where serious money had

been spent to create just the environment he wanted. The CD machine was top quality and it was backed by a good amplifier and state-of-the-art speakers. His PC, hooked up to a maximum-speed modem, was switched on and running a screen saver that depicted a spider crawling along a web. Clothes, none of them cheap, were scattered casually about the place. It was a room on which Jack had put his stamp, and when he entered it, he changed.

He shut the door and leaned on it for a second. His face lit up as if he had suddenly heard great news. He stepped away from the door and took off his jacket. His shirt was soaked with fresh blood.

He dropped the jacket and quickly stripped off his shirt. He held it bunched between his hands and buried his face in the folds, drawing the fabric from side to side across his nose and cheeks. When he lowered the shirt his face was streaked with blood.

He reached down to the jacket and from the inside pocket he pulled a long carving knife. Blood was caked and clotted along the edge of the blade.

He went and stood by the open window, grinning and panting. He stared out at the darkness and held aloft the shirt in one hand, the knife in the other. With a huge intake of breath he threw back his head, then let out a roar that tailed off into hysterical, gleeful laughter.

Jack McCaffrey was king of the night.

Eight miles away from the Plough, in another seventeen-year-old's bedroom, with another PC running a screen saver, Vince Wilson sat on a chair, stripped to the waist, with a clean shirt spread on the floor between his feet. Vince had a more conventionally teenage appearance than Jack, and at that moment his youthfulness was intensified by a look of tight-lipped fear.

Vince held a long sharp kitchen knife in his right hand. It was spotless and it gleamed. He took a deep breath, held it in, and brought up his left arm. With a swift stroke he drew the knife across his elbow, where the scar wouldn't show. Skin parted along the edge of the blade and rich blood surged out through the cut.

Vince winced and gasped. He leaned forward, holding his bent arm out, letting the blood dribble and pool in the folds of the shirt at his feet.

A full team was present in the conference room at OSC headquarters. On the big screen high on the wall opposite the end of the table a videotape was being projected. The screen showed a close-up image of a young Japanese boy. It was a strange, sinister image, the talking head of a human being whose eyes appeared scarcely alive.

At the end of the table one of the team lawyers, Steve Carroll, stood watching the screen. In a rich Belfast brogue that contrasted sharply with the clipped Japanese delivery from the speakers, Carroll provided a running translation of the boy's words.

'I am not ashamed. Why should I be ashamed? I did my duty.' Carroll used his handset to freeze the picture. He turned momentarily to address the others. 'And this name keeps cropping up. Amathus. It's not Japanese.' He touched the handset again. The picture moved and the boy spoke. 'I did what Amathus wants. She's lost. We're all lost, lost in the world. But Amathus found us, she's calling. And I followed the rules. I found the blood.

I touched it. And she's not finished. There's blood to come. Better blood.'

The Japanese boy looked straight at the camera and said, in English, 'Game over.'

Carroll froze the face on the screen. He sat down.

'Lee Yamaguchi,' Creegan said.

He stood up, lifted a remote control of his own and walked along the side of the table.

'Fourteen years old, from Rumagaya, sixty miles north of Tokyo. He was caught carrying a knife outside some stables, ten miles from his house. He attacked a horse. A stallion. It received a vertical slash from the knife on its left flank. Now that was one of six horses attacked that night.'

Creegan pressed his remote control. Lee Yamaguchi's face disappeared and a map of Japan appeared on the screen. A red mark had been inserted above Tokyo.

'In chronological order, the Rumagaya stables came first. Then England, three separate incidents.' A map of Kent appeared with three zones marked. 'Gorse Farm, John Jericho Stables, Collinswood Stables. Then America.' A North American map came up with marks at northern and south-eastern locations. 'One, thirty miles outside Lexington, Kentucky, and finally, Jamestown, North Dakota.'

'Who the hell saw the connection?' Taylor asked. 'It's a miracle anyone noticed over that distance.'

Commander Enwright smiled. 'I wish I could say it was a brilliant piece of observation, but it was software. A pattern recognition programme, sorts through isolated crimes. If there's a link, it's sent here.'

'The six attacks didn't all happen at once,' Creegan went on, 'but technically they all happened at the same time. As midnight of the twenty-fifth moved across the time zones, so each attack was triggered. It was co-ordinated.'

Marion asked if Yamaguchi had said anything more about Amathus.

'Not a word,' Creegan said. 'Just the name, over and over again.'

'We've got a profile on Lee Yamaguchi,' Marion said. 'His parents sent him to an educational psychologist two years ago. He's a loner, an introvert, with one obsession. Computers. Spends hours every day surfing the Net.'

'Well, even if it is an Internet campaign,' Creegan said, 'the attacks in this country have got a physical connection.'

He pressed the remote control again, bringing up a world map, flagged to show the global distribution of the incidents.

'Look how spread out these things are. Japan to Dakota. But in this country, they're all within forty miles of each other. So our three attackers are *together*. Must be.'

After the meeting Creegan, Taylor and Rivers stood in the dimly lit computer room and watched as Kreitman logged on to the Internet.

'If Amathus isn't in the title,' Kreitman said, 'it could take for ever to find. There's a million voices in cyberspace, all chattering away. It's the edge of the world out there.'

A bleeper went off.

Kreitman sighed. 'Rivers, give it a rest.'

Rivers looked at him. 'It's not me.'

'It was funny the first time.'

'It's not me!'

Kreitman went on staring at Rivers, then he reached into his jacket pocket and pulled out his own bleeper. He pressed the button and read the screen.

'Shit.'

'Is it Judith?' Rivers said.

'Yeah.'

Creegan came forward, curious. 'What?'

'Um, it's the baby,' Kreitman said. 'It's not due for another week.' He reset the bleeper and put it back in his pocket. He made an effort to return his attention to the computer screen. 'Look, OK. If . . . if it isn't in the title, every website has a fifty-word description. Amathus might be there.'

'Never mind that,' said Taylor. 'Just go, you daft sod.'

'OK.'

Kreitman got up, trying to smile through the worry on his face.

Taylor slapped his arm. 'Good luck.'

Kreitman went to the door. Rivers followed him.

'All the best.'

Kreitman took a second to absorb the good wishes. 'Oh, yeah. Cheers. Listen, tell Enwright I've gone. I'll come back if it's a false alarm.'

'Jonathan, go to your wife and your kid. Take your leave, everything you're owed, and forget this place. All right?'

There was an evident weight of added meaning in Rivers's words. Kreitman looked at him for a long moment then nodded and walked away.

Rivers turned and saw Creegan standing behind him.

'Lucky man,' Creegan said.

Rivers nodded and touched his tie nervously. Ever

since that day outside Julie Carney's house, Creegan had been looking at him strangely – not all the time, but often enough to keep Rivers on edge.

'My ex-wife's pregnant.'

Rivers didn't know what to do with the information. 'Is that good news or bad news?'

'I don't know,' Creegan said. 'I'm still waiting. Kerry hasn't told me yet. I only found out by accident. But the funny thing is I like this, not knowing. I don't have to commit, act pleased, upset. Don't have to get involved.'

Creegan paused. He looked around him in his disconcerting way.

'This unit's got the best early retirement deal I have ever seen,' he said, 'because they know. Reach fifty, we're burned out.' He moved very close to Rivers and stared into his eyes. 'We get too involved. All of us.'

They held each other's gaze, but Creegan's stare was stronger; it looked as if it could last as long as it was needed.

'I went to the funeral because I felt sorry for Burgess,' Rivers said. 'That's all. Maybe we did push him. All of us.'

'Did you go to the funeral of Ronald Hinks?'

'No.'

Creegan looked around him again. 'Kerry will tell me, in the end. Then I'll get involved.' He was looking into Rivers's eyes again. 'I'll have no choice. I can wait, Mark, but it's not going to go away.'

Early on Monday morning Jack McCaffrey walked into the pub kitchen wearing jeans and a scarlet polo-neck sweater. His mother was making breakfast.

'Is there any post?' he said.

Eileen looked at him. 'And good morning to you too.' She pointed to a white envelope lying on the corner of the table.

Jack snatched it up. 'Right,' he mumbled, popped a piece of bacon in his mouth and walked out again.

He went straight back upstairs and sat down at the computer table. He opened the envelope and pulled out a bundle of five-pound notes. He counted them. A hundred pounds.

He picked up the envelope again. Carefully, with nail-bitten fingertips, he peeled off the label with his name and address and put it carefully in the inside pocket of his black leather jacket.

He looked at the clock. Time to get moving. He gathered together his things for college and smiled to himself as he tucked the bloodstained shirt in the bottom of his bag.

26

Fieldon Park Sixth Form College in Kent stood in the flat, featureless outskirts of the market town of Fieldon Cross. It was a run-down seventies concrete comprehensive school, converted to accommodate four hundred sixth-form students. Half of them had arrived by 8.40 a.m.

The morning was cold and wet. Sundry groups, lagged against the weather, were scattered across the space that used to be called the playground. Lads in knots of four and six laughed and joked and moved around to link up with others they knew; girls in small gangs huddled as they caught up on each other's weekends. Here and there couples stood in corners and under overhangs, oblivious to everyone else.

Jack McCaffrey pushed his way among the throng, head down, keeping to himself.

A girl said, 'Look at him, the weirdo.'

'Weirdo!' a boy shouted.

A big lad called Mark, a would-be college personality, blocked Jack's path. His two mates flanked him so that Jack couldn't veer aside. He had to stop and face them.

'What's the matter, Jack?' Mark's tone was heavy

and mocking. He grabbed Jack's head in the crook of one arm and squeezed him close. 'What, you want to dance with me, Jack? You want to dance with me?' He spun Jack around a couple of times then let him struggle free. 'Dance with me, Jack!' he called after him. 'Dance with me! I love you, Jack! I love you!'

Others were taking up the chant. 'We love you, Jack,' a boy whispered, close to his ears, and his mates erupted with laughter.

The onslaught fell away by stages. Jack showed no anger, not even a response to sustain their attention. He kept walking, looking up only long enough to see where he would go next. Ten yards ahead of him he saw Fiona Morrison, Mo to everyone who knew her. She was seventeen, skinny, with short hair bleached white. She had tiny gold crosses for earrings and she was dressed entirely in black. Jack took a roundabout route in her direction. When he was close enough, she saw him but gave no outward sign. Jack gave no indication that he saw or knew her. He walked straight past.

'Eleven,' he said, aiming it right at her ear.

Mo promptly walked off in the other direction. She was aiming now, homing on a target, going by the twisting route. She slowed down as she neared her objective, Craig Jones, sixteen, a gaunt-cheeked youth with unruly fair hair. He looked a good deal less hard or would-be cool than Jack or Mo. She walked past him. 'Eleven o'clock.'

Jack watched the exchange from a distance. He turned away with the trace of a satisfied smirk and headed for the college doors. Then he heard a furtive scamper of footsteps behind him. Craig Jones had sidled up alongside.

'I haven't seen Vince. There's no sign of him,' Craig muttered.

Jack turned on him. 'Shut your face.'

'He comes in on the same bus as me. He weren't . . .'

'Craig.' Jack held a finger up under his nose. 'You don't talk. Not to me, not here, do you understand? Yeah? Don't talk. That's the rules.'

Craig looked as if he wanted to say more. But he nodded and walked away. Jack carried on into the college, eyes down, his own man.

Enwright brought in a polythene forensic specimen bag and showed the contents to Creegan and Taylor. It was a letter envelope with a neatly typed name and address.

'The Rumagaya police intercepted this addressed to Lee Yamaguchi. It contained an international money order, the equivalent of a hundred quid.'

Creegan looked closely. It had been posted from London.

'The Internet checks out,' Enwright said. 'They found a website called Amathus. Rivers is downloading it now.'

When Creegan and Taylor walked into the computer room Marion was already there, sitting beside Rivers. They watched the screen turn black and the name AMATHUS come up in white letters. A voice speaking in an echoing whisper delivered the commentary, which was simultaneously printed across the screen. Still pictures, painted in vivid colours, showed a woman at several stages of a hazardous journey.

'Welcome to Amathus, chapter five. In which Amathus is lost in the Wide World, and found in the hearts of fellow men.'

'Have we found the source?' Creegan asked.

'Doing it now,' Rivers said. 'It's one of the London service providers. They'll have the name and address.'

Marion was watching the screen intently. 'It's rooted in Greek mythology. Ariadne died in childbirth, and she was buried at Amathus.'

She could have gone on to tell them that Amathus was a city that once stood among sandy hills near the site of the present-day town of Limassol, in Cyprus. The name of the city was derived from its location: *amathos* is the Greek word for sand. Marion also knew that Amathus had a famous, perhaps notorious temple of Adonis and Aphrodite – so famous, in fact, that the third-century Latin nickname for Venus was Amathusia. Marion knew that much and a good deal more about the place and the period, but she was not inclined to air the knowledge, especially in the presence of Creegan, who didn't always react well to her displays of learning.

Rivers was summarising the on-screen adventure. 'She finds herself wandering through the Vale of Misery, the Hall of Faces, all that Dungeons and Dragons bollocks. She's trying to find other lost souls, and to find them she has to pass a test, to blood herself. And that test is the scarring of an ungulate.'

Creegan looked at Rivers. 'What's an ungulate when it's at home?'

'A horse,' said Taylor and Rivers in unison.

'Thank you, Oxbridge,' Creegan grunted.

'So the players become Amathus in the real world,' Marion said, 'and they get rewarded with money. Have we got chapters one to four?'

'They must have been deleted,' Rivers said. 'I think

we can expect a chapter six,' he added, as the words
TO BE CONTINUED came up on the screen.

They turned as Kreitman walked into the room. He
looked gaunt and weary.

'What the hell are you doing here?' Taylor said. She
kissed his cheek. 'Congratulations. How's Judith?'

'She's fine. Fine.'

Creegan said, 'You look about fifty. Dad.'

'What was she?' Marion asked.

'Seven pounds.'

'Cheap for a baby,' Rivers quipped. 'Don't tell me
Enwright's called you in. We can handle this, it's
nothing, just a bunch of nutters.'

'No, no,' Kreitman said, 'I asked if I could. There's
no point sitting at home. They're going to keep her in
for a few days.'

The phone rang and Rivers answered it.

Marion frowned at Kreitman. 'Nothing wrong?'

'No, no. It's just routine. She's fine.'

'Got it,' Rivers said. He had the telephone receiver
tucked into the angle of his neck as he wrote on a pad.
'The Amathus website was created by James Stoker,
twenty-two Dunstan Terrace, White City. Thank you.'
He hung up.

'Well, that was easy,' Creegan said. He sounded
disappointed. 'Game over.'

At 11 a.m. Jack McCaffrey strode towards the centre
of a barren field three miles from Fieldon Cross. The
building he approached had been a farmhouse. It had
been empty for twenty years and now it was crumb-
ling. Parts of the roof were open to the sky. Jack
grinned and quickened his pace as he drew near to

the place. It was as if he were coming more alive with every step.

He went into the house. In a room at the back with broken windows and only part of the roof remaining he found Mo, Vince and Craig. They sat separately, silent and expressionless. Jack said nothing. He went to the corner where a battery-powered ghetto-blaster sat on the floor. He pressed the tape switch. Raucous jungle music poured from the speakers at full volume, tearing into the silence.

Jack slumped down in a corner. At his signal, all four of them dug into their school bags and pulled out bloodstained shirts. Vince was the only one who had trouble looking pleased. But he managed it, and when Jack threw back his head and let out a roar, Vince was the first to imitate him. Then they were all roaring, a wordless blaring of victory and triumph as they held their trophies aloft.

The music filled the space when the shouting died. Jack became solemn as he drew the white address label from the inside pocket of his leather jacket.

He held the label carefully between the fingertips of both hands and tore it neatly into four pieces. He put one piece on his tongue and held it there, keeping his mouth open, grinning. He stood up and approached Mo. She stood up too. They kissed. Jack's tongue slipped into her mouth and transferred the piece of label. She drew back her head and chewed gently on the paper.

Jack put another piece of label on his tongue and went with it to Vince, who stayed where he was on the floor. He tried to grin the way Jack grinned, he even pretended to be eager, but he was embarrassed and was only able to look queasy. As Jack tried to kiss him he recoiled. Jack stopped grinning. He grabbed Vince by the sides of his head and kissed him violently. Vince groaned and Jack forced the paper into his mouth with the hard probe of his tongue.

Jack stood up again and put the third piece of paper in his mouth. He turned to Craig, who stood near a window. Craig had seen the way Jack treated Vince, so when the kiss was proffered he accepted it with a grimace.

Jack turned away and began to laugh wildly. He put the fourth piece of paper in his mouth and chewed on it. He giggled as Mo began to sway and gyrate to the crazy music. Her eyes were glazed and a trickle of saliva ran from the corner of her mouth as she twirled and sidestepped.

In his corner, Vince had begun to feel strange. The LSD in the label had permeated the tissues at the back of his throat and hallucination had begun to seep into his sense of reality. Time seemed to fold in on itself. He stared at his hand then up at the hole in the roof, at the grey rhomboid of sky. He looked at his hand again and was aware he had taken off his shirt, though he didn't remember when or how.

There was laughter somewhere. He was on his feet, he wanted to go to the laughter, but there was no sign of the others. A single step seemed to propel him halfway across the room. He took six big steps and found himself looking at Craig, who was crouched motionless in an empty room.

Two or three or four more steps and Vince saw Jack and Mo. They were on an old mattress in a corner. Jack lay on top of Mo. She laughed, loud and harsh, louder than the music that still filled every corner.

Jack looked up. He pulled off his scarlet sweater and

threw it at Vince. Vince caught it. For what seemed an age he stared at the twisted garment between his hands. Then Mo cried out. Vince looked. Jack and Mo were naked and twined around each other. Vince had never seen people in the act of sex before. He stared at their heaving bodies. Soon, the brightness of the sweater drew his attention again. He leaned in the doorway and gazed at it for a long time.

Dunstan Terrace was a street of shabby old houses on the outer reaches of West London. Kreitman and Rivers approached number 22 with two uniformed police constables as back-up. One of the officers, PC Albury, had already tried to make contact with the tenant.

'There's no reply,' he told Kreitman. 'I talked to the man opposite. He said the curtains have been drawn since he moved in, eighteen months back. Never seen anyone going in or coming out, never heard of a James Stoker.'

Kreitman scarcely seemed to hear. He strode up the path ahead of Rivers and banged on the front door with the side of his fist.

'Hey, Jonathan, slow down . . .'

Kreitman banged the door again.

'Jonathan, you shouldn't even be here,' Rivers complained. 'It's not as if we can charge this man with anything.'

'The sooner we get this done,' Kreitman said angrily, 'the sooner we can get back to some proper work. Now go round the back.'

Rivers stared at him. He was puzzled by Kreitman's behaviour. To defuse the situation he simply nodded, all compliance, no more argument. He signalled to the other

constable and went with him to a gateway at the side
that led to the back garden.

Kreitman banged on the door again and waited,
tapping his foot, fidgeting. Suddenly he braced his
hands on either side of the doorway and kicked the
door open. He walked into the gloomy hall with PC
Albury behind him.

'Look upstairs.'

Kreitman checked the lights. They were dead. He
went to open the curtains but the lower edge had been
stuck down with gaffer tape. He moved around the
ground floor, staying alert, hearing Albury go up the
stairs. There was something about the house, about its
deliberate emptiness and enforced darkness, which was
disturbing.

Kreitman turned at a sound near by, then heard rats
scuttle away across the floor.

Creegan and Taylor, meanwhile, were at the office of
the agents who administered the rental of 22 Dunstan
Terrace.

'Never heard of it,' the blond secretary said.

'Well, it's definitely one of yours,' Creegan told
her. 'We need some information on the tenant, James
Stoker.'

'Mind you,' the secretary murmured, 'if I haven't
heard of it, that's a good sign. Means he pays his rent
on time. Less work for me.'

She typed in her personal code and called up the
database file on her computer screen. She was about to
instigate a name and address search, then she frowned
at Creegan.

'It's confidential this. You got permission?'

'Well . . .' Creegan sighed. 'We could go away and

get a warrant, which means we'll be back at . . . what?'
He looked at Taylor. 'Ten o'clock?'

Taylor nodded.

'So if you don't mind working late . . .'

'Oh, sod that,' the secretary said. She keyed in the
address. 'What was the name again?'

'James Stoker.'

She typed in the name and the computer began a
search. Abruptly the name vanished from the screen
and the image began to crumble. The words SYSTEM
VIOLATION came up in blood red. There was a small
commotion across the office. Taylor could see that the
same thing had happened to every screen in the place.

'What's it doing?' the secretary yelped. 'That wasn't
me!'

'It's a virus,' Taylor said. 'It's got to have been
triggered by the address.'

'It wasn't me,' the secretary howled at the others. 'I
didn't do nothing.'

At the house in Dunstan Terrace, Rivers and the
constable assisting him had used a dustbin to climb
over the locked gate at the side of the house. Inside,
Kreitman and PC Albury began a search of the main
bedroom. All Kreitman had found so far had been empty
cupboards. Albury shone his torch along the margin of
the wall and ceiling and found an electrical wire that
seemed to lead to a cupboard on the adjacent wall.
He followed the track of the wire with his torch beam,
checking to see if it branched off at any point. As far
as he could tell, it went straight into the cupboard at the
top right-hand corner.

Kreitman's mobile phone rang. He thumbed the green
button and put the phone to his ear.

'Jonathan?' It was Creegan. 'Are you in the house?' He sounded agitated

'There's nothing here. It's been empty for months.'

'Get out of the house, Jonathan,' Creegan said. 'He's waiting for us. It's part of the game.'

At that moment PC Albury opened the cupboard. As the door swung outward a cord attached to the inside pulled a pin from a device on the shelf. A red light came on and a beeper sounded.

'It's under control,' Kreitman told Creegan.

The device in the cupboard exploded. The shock wave threw Kreitman across the room. Outside Rivers jumped back as the upstairs windows blew out and flames erupted into the air. Splintered wood and glass showered down. Rivers kicked in the back door and ran up the stairs with the constable behind him.

'Kreitman!' he yelled through the billowing smoke. 'Kreitman!'

A figure appeared at the top of the stairs. Rivers blinked against the smoke and saw it was Kreitman. He was dragging the inert body of PC Albury.

Between them they got Albury outside and laid him on the ground. His face and hands were blistered and burnt black. Kreitman knelt by him while Rivers got on the radio.

'Request urgent assistance, twenty-two Dunstan Terrace! Ambulance and fire services! Officer down!'

Kreitman stared up at the burning window frame. 'Bastard!' he shouted. 'Bastard!'

Elsewhere, in a field beyond Fieldon Cross, another fire was burning, consuming four bloodstained shirts thrown into the burning logs by Jack, Mo, Vince and Craig. They lay near by in the growing dark and freezing wind, separate like strangers, unaware of the cold. They watched the fire and gazed dreamily as the sparks flew upward and died against a backdrop of bright winking stars.

27

Creegan studied the envelope sent from London to Lee Yamaguchi in Rumagaya, Japan. He held it against the light, then at an angle to the window, comparing the textures of the envelope and the stick-on address label. He examined the careful placement of the postage stamp. Finally he decided to send the whole envelope to the forensic lab for testing, although he had no idea what the lab should look for.

Taylor, in the meantime, had to argue with Enwright about the Amathus website. Enwright said that in view of the fact that the site operator's name and address were false, OSC were perfectly entitled to shut Amathus down.

'And then we'll lose him,' Taylor said. 'And he'll just disappear, and start up Amathus under a different name. A couple of months, a couple of years, it'll happen again.'

Enwright thought it over and decided to accept Taylor's point, though not whole-heartedly. Taylor excused herself and went to the computer room. Marion was using one of the machines. Rivers was on the phone.

'The domain's no good,' he told an operator. 'I need a proper address. This year would be nice.'

'How's Kreitman?' Taylor asked.

Rivers covered the mouthpiece. 'He'll be all right. It was a flash fire, burnt his hand. The constable's a lot worse. He's in Intensive Care.' He pointed to the computer screen in front of him. Inside a box at the centre of the screen were the letters PTO. 'That's the message that was sent to Amathus three minutes ago.'

'They're asking for chapter six,' Marion said.

Somebody on the other end of the phone spoke to Rivers. 'Yeah, right,' he said. 'Quick as you can.' He turned to Taylor. 'We've got the address.'

He wrote it on a pad as it was given to him: Fieldon Park Sixth Form College.

Within the hour Creegan and Taylor were at the college. They were taken to the computer room by a plump little woman who taught computer studies. Her name was Yvonne Jackson.

Taylor looked around. There were more than a dozen machines in the room, all currently showing the school's logo.

'Do you have personal log-ins?' Taylor asked Yvonne.

'We don't, no. I unlock the network every Monday morning, and it's left on till Friday night. We've had instability problems. Technically speaking, these machines are crap.'

'Great,' Taylor sighed. 'So we can't tell who's using which computer? You're going to have to introduce passwords, straight away. We need to get this lot under control.'

'Right . . .' Creegan nodded. 'Starting from scratch, then. We're looking at a gang of three, or three from a larger gang. Preferably anyone taking computer studies, or with access to this lot.'

Yvonne brought up the student list on one of the machines. 'That's all of them. Anyone can use these computers for any subject.'

Taylor said, 'How many students have you got?'

'About four hundred.'

'Any with a criminal record?' Creegan asked.

'About four hundred.'

He smiled. 'Have the staff got access?'

'Yes. If they want.'

'We could narrow it down to those people without a home computer,' Taylor said.

Creegan shook his head. 'Everything's traceable on the Net, the players will know that. They'll use the school network to hide themselves. We're going to have to talk to them all.' He turned to Yvonne. 'Can you arrange that?'

Yvonne organised the rounding-up of more than 390 students, while Creegan and Taylor prepared a questionnaire for duplication and arranged for fifty officers from OSC to be drafted in.

The interviews were conducted immediately after the lunch break. Chairs and tables were set in rows that ran the full length of the gymnasium. As an exercise in mass interrogation it went relatively smoothly, although one interviewee, Jack McCaffrey, responded with noticeable hostility.

'English, French, history, biology, IT, geography.' Creegan looked across the table at him. 'That's a lot of A-levels.'

'They're GCSEs,' Jack said. 'Resits.'

'Ah. Tough going?'

'What's it to you?'

Creegan frowned.

'I bet you passed your exams first time,' Jack said.

'I did, yeah.'

'It shows. And then you end up in the police, one box to another.'

'How do you mean?'

'Student, copper, husband, father,' Jack said. 'One box after the other.'

Creegan pushed forward a sheet of paper with the names of the locations where horses had been attacked – Gorse Farm, West Ringston; Collinswood Stables, Monkshorton; John Jericho Stables, Elmstone.

'Right, Jack. Do you know any of these three places?'

Jack's eyes flicked to the list and up again. 'No.'

At a table two rows away, Taylor was encountering her own patch of hostility from Mark, the college loudmouth. She had asked him what he got up to in the evenings.

'You asking me out?' he said, so most of the gymnasium could hear. 'Hey, Wiggsy,' he shouted to another table, 'she's asking me out.'

'What do you do?' Taylor continued, unflustered. 'Hang out with your mates?'

Mark laughed. 'Here, Wiggsy, she's asking about you. She's wants the pair of us.' Wiggsy laughed dutifully. Mark lowered his head and leaned closer to Taylor. 'Look, I'll tell you what. Tonight, outside in the carpark, eight o'clock. I'll show you what I can do.'

'Fine,' Taylor said. 'You, eight o'clock, your mate, eight-oh-one.'

Mark scowled at her. 'What's that mean?'

'Work it out.'

Later, when the interviews were over and pupils were going home, Jack confronted Vince outside the school. He said nothing. He simply stared at the boy and held up three fingers. Vince turned and saw Craig staring at him from the school steps.

For a moment Vince appeared frozen to the spot. Then he ran past Jack and caught up with the yellow bus that would drop him at the foot of the lane by the farm where he lived. He jumped on as the door was closing and found himself a seat at the back. The bus swung round, taking the country road north, and as Vince looked out of the window he saw Mo, on a landing between two school blocks. She was staring right at him.

Vince sank back in his seat, hugging his school bag. He tried not to look afraid.

Creegan, Taylor and Rivers got back to OSC head-quarters at dusk. As they came in through reception they saw that the door to the conference room was open. Kreitman sat with his elbows propped on the big table, his hands, one of them bandaged, clasped at his chin. Enwright was standing beside him.

'Look at him,' Rivers called, 'the injured hero.'

The three of them walked into the conference room. In the glow from the shaded lamps on the table, Kreitman looked deathly pale.

'You got off lightly, Jonathan,' Rivers said. 'We've been in the back of beyond.'

'Four hundred suspects.' Taylor nodded.

'And guess where they were on Friday night?' Creegan said. 'A rave, so they've all got an alibi – all off their heads, can't remember a thing.'

'He's dead,' Kreitman said. 'Albury.'

They stared at him.

'The constable at Dunstan Terrace,' Enwright said. 'Died this afternoon.'

'Shit.' Rivers looked at Kreitman. 'Sorry.'

Kreitman's expression changed. 'It wasn't my fault.'

Rivers was startled. 'I didn't mean . . . Look, I'm sorry, all right?'

'Whoa.' Creegan put up his hands, enforcing calm. 'We'll get him. James Stoker. Crack these kids, they'll lead us to him.'

Kreitman appeared to draw something from this encouragement.

Later, walking through reception with Creegan, Taylor said, 'We must have a profile of Stoker from the stuff we've got. He built that bomb. That narrows it down.'

'What, fuel oil and ammonium nitrate? That's the sort of thing anybody can pick up on the Net. It doesn't mean he's clever.'

'OK, well, he knows his technology.'

'Hang on, hang on . . .' Creegan tapped the face of his watch. 'It's six o'clock. Work is over.'

'Ah. New regime.' Taylor squeezed his arm. 'I give it a week.'

He shook his head slowly, implying she underestimated his determination. 'Have you had a good look at Jonathan Kreitman? He's just had a kid, he's still here. Me, I've got a party. I'd have invited you, but it might be a bit too wild.'

The party was in full swing when he got there. It was in Kerry's house and it was being thrown to celebrate the fourth birthday of Louise. The place was jumping. Throngs of children ran round the house, screaming, singing, shouting, blowing horns and joining in impromptu games. At one end of the living room one of the other mums was conducting a contest to see who could leap the highest. Adults, those who weren't participating in the mayhem, squeezed into corners with glasses of beer or soft drinks and watched.

Louise, radiant in a blue-and-white dress, ran up to Creegan when he waved the package he had brought.

'Present,' he shouted, 'present.'

Louise took it with both hands. She paused a second to smile, but ran off again before Creegan had time to kiss her.

'Louise,' Kerry shouted to her, 'say thank you.' But Louise had been swallowed up by the party again. 'I blame the parents,' Kerry said. 'I didn't think you'd make it. How's things?'

'They're fine. And you?'

'Yeah, fine.' Kerry saw the expectation in his look, a readiness to be informed. She did not understand, and the odd intensity of it troubled her, but she rode it out. 'I think there's a beer left, if the mums haven't drunk them all. They're worse than the kids.'

Kerry went to the kitchen. Creegan followed, pausing for a moment to watch as Louise ran to Barry and was swept up in his arms.

Kerry found him his beer. He stood in the kitchen with her, and between sips of the fizzy lager he told her about the kind of afternoon he'd had.

'There were all these students, all looking the same. They're all seventeen, eighteen years old, all miserable and paranoid. They all sounded like me.'

Kerry chuckled. 'You said it.'

'Yeah. But not any more. No more late nights. If it's not done by six, tough. I'm even switching the mobile off when I leave the office.'

'Good,' Kerry said. 'It's about time. I could almost believe you.'

'I mean it. Honest, I do.'

'Mmm.' Kerry wasn't convinced. 'Where's your phone? Go on, show me.'

He took it halfway out of his pocket and showed it to her. She snatched it from him and turned to the light.

'You liar! It's still on.'

Creegan tried to grab it before she could switch it off. Out in the living room, Barry saw the playful wrestling.

'Give us a chance, Kerry. One step at a time.'

The phone beeped as she pressed the switch.

'There,' she said. 'You're all mine. You should have done this years ago.'

'Yeah.' The look was back, but different. 'It's not too late, though, is it?'

Kerry turned her head aside. The question caught her completely unprepared.

Barry came into the kitchen. He carried a little boy in his arm and led a tiny girl with his other hand.

'This one's lost a piece of cake,' he said, nodding to the girl, 'and this one needs the loo.'

'Oh, we've run out of cake, sweetheart,' Kerry said. 'Your mum ate it all. Blame her. How about a bag of crisps?'

Kerry handed Creegan his phone back and went off to find crisps for the little girl. Barry glared at Creegan, then slowly walked out again.

28

In his bedroom at the farm that night, Vince Wilson sat in front of his computer and rapidly turned sick with fear. As soon as he switched on there was a message telling him he had mail. For ten minutes since then a continuous flow of electronic communication had come in, all of it saying the same thing in different ways: *three*; *3*; *trois*; *drei*; *iii*; *THREE?*

It came in different sizes, different colours, different fonts, filling the screen and accusing him. There was no end to the flow; it poured on to the screen in relentless, overlapping streams of type and splashes of colour. In the end Vince became frantic. He picked up a football trophy and hurled it into the screen, smashing it. As smoke spiralled out of the gaping hole in the tube, Vince grabbed a holdall and stuffed it full of clothes. When it could hold no more he zipped it shut and put on his heaviest windcheater.

He stood by the bedroom door and listened. When he was sure his parents were caught up in their television programme, he slipped downstairs and left the house.

In near-total darkness he hurried out on to the lane, the heavy holdall banging on his leg as he walked. A car came towards him, its headlights dazzling. For a while after it passed he couldn't see a thing. Then, as his vision cleared and he was able to make out shapes again, he saw the trio ahead of him on the road, coming his way. Jack in the middle, with Mo and Craig on either side.

When they were five yards away Vince stopped walking. So did Mo and Craig. Jack kept coming. He came right up to Vince and pushed one shoulder hard, spinning him, making him face the other way, towards the farm. Terrified, Vince started walking again, hearing the others behind him.

When they were past the main gate at the farm Jack marched ahead of Vince and pushed open the door of an outbuilding. He stood in the opening and waited. Vince went in, quaking. The other two came in behind him and Jack shut the door.

They stood facing Vince, shoulder to shoulder.

'Three attacks,' Jack said. 'Not four. Because you didn't do it, did you, Vince? Haven't got the nerve. So where did you get it from, hmm?' He stepped closer and the other two moved to either side of him. 'Where did you get the blood?'

'I did this.' Vince pushed up his sleeve and showed them the bandage. 'I gave you my own blood, Jack. I hurt no one but myself.'

'That's no good,' Mo snapped. 'That's not in the rules.'

'Shut up, you,' Jack told her.

'Anyone could do that,' Mo went on, her voice rising. 'That's nothing—'

'Shut up!'

She was silent. Jack looked at Vince again. 'I mean, if you'd said, if you'd come and told us, then maybe we'd have understood.'

'Yeah?' Vince glared at them with a surge of defiance. 'How? We're not supposed to meet up, that's the rules.'

'I gave you Amathus.' Jack's voice was low, a growl. 'I gave you the reward, and all the time you were lying.'

'You can't come back, Vince,' Mo said. 'You're lost.'

'I don't want to come back. I've had enough. I'm getting out. I'm going away from you, from that house.'

'What, into the crowd?' In the half-light Jack's grinning face looked hollowed out, shadowed at the eyes and mouth. 'Poor Vince, losing himself in the crowd. Parents, teachers, employees, they look at the crowd and they label them. They put them in nice little boxes. And d'you know why?' Jack put his mouth right beside Vince's ear. 'So they can know them. It's control. No one knows us, no one knows. We're beyond control, Vince. We're invisible.'

'But we're not.' Vince backed off. 'The police are here, Jack. They're *here*.'

Jack had turned and pressed oblongs of white paper into the mouths of Mo and Craig. They took the offering as if they were communion wafers. Jack turned back to Vince.

'The police know nothing. Nothing. Not until one of us tells them. You could point us out, then we're a part of the crowd, we're nothing. We go back to being nothing. I'm not going back to that. I'm never going back.'

'Amathus says the best should move on,' Vince said. 'Those that fail just get left behind.'

'Yeah, well, Amathus isn't here. There's only me.' Jack put an oblong of paper into his own mouth. He stood for a moment, his jaw moving, then his hand came out of his pocket holding an empty whisky bottle. He smashed it against a pillar and held up the jagged end, his fingers wrapped firmly round the neck.

Vince turned and ran. He went through the door blindly, pulling the holdall on to his shoulders, making it easier to carry. The others were close behind; he felt the thudding of their feet on the ground. Up ahead were the pig pens, filled with piglets. Vince leapt the rail and ran through the shrieking, scattering animals. Jack, Mo and Craig jumped into the pens too, shouting now, howling, sending the pigs in all directions as they tried to get out of their way.

Vince leapt the fence and came down among more pigs. He staggered, nearly overbalanced, and charged through the squealing beasts, hearing Jack scream now, Mo too, as they got closer, battling their way through the mud and scampering animals.

Vince jumped on to the path at the far side of the pig pens and ran as fast as he could. The others were getting high now, full of the manic energy of an acid trip, whooping and screaming, running with arms outstretched to catch Vince. In the faint light the jagged edges of Jack's weapon glinted as he waved it in the air above his head.

Vince forced himself to run faster than he had ever run before. It didn't seem to be enough. They were still close behind him, still screeching with the need to do him harm.

He crossed the path and ran into the woods, too frightened to think any more, too breathless and scared to have any sense of where he went. He ran and ran and they followed with relentless energy, howling all the way. Vince hammered forward into the dark heart of the wood, straining every resource, using fear to fuel his flight from the razor-edged glass.

Half a mile away, Mrs Wilson came to the back door of the farmhouse. Far off she could hear howling and screeching. Then, as she listened, it became rhythmic chanting. The sound chilled her.

It stopped suddenly. Mrs Wilson moved further into the yard, hugging herself, still listening. There was a sudden, piercing, horrifying screech of human voices. To Mrs Wilson it sounded triumphal, like a cry of victory.

Then silence.

Taylor came into the office at eight o'clock the next morning. She went to her desk, put down her bag, then jumped with fright at a crash from behind the open door. A man was half hidden there. He stood up and looked at her. It was Cyril Golding.

'For God's sake! What are you doing there?'

'There's a moth,' Cyril said. He fingered the visitor's ID badge hanging on a chain from his neck.

'Cyril, isn't it?'

He looked surprised. 'How d'you know that?'

'I saw it in the clouds.'

'Did you?' He came to the desk. 'It's different today, it's all red and green, did you see it? Red and green and red.'

'How did you get in here?'

'Creegan. He's gone to get me a Pepsi.'

'Has he got lots of Cyrils tucked away, or are you the only friend he's got?'

'There's you.'

Taylor shook her head. 'I don't know about that. I think I'm just a colleague.'

'There's you,' Cyril repeated.

Creegan came in. He was in shirtsleeves. He handed Cyril a silver ring-pull can. 'They only had this. Health drink.' He watched Cyril scowl at the can. 'It's pop. Morning, Inspector Taylor.'

'Good party?' she said.

'It was interesting.'

'No, no, don't tell me . . .' Taylor gave him a wry little smile. 'You copped off.'

'I might have.' Creegan took his jacket from the back of his chair and put it on. 'Cyril, you're going to have to bugger off.' He took a sheet of paper from the desk and turned to Taylor. 'Enwright wants us back in Fieldon Cross.'

'What for?'

'A kid's gone missing. Vince Wilson.'

Cyril tasted his drink. 'It's all right,' he told Creegan. 'I've said it now. Red and green. She's seen it too.' He pointed at Taylor. 'Red and green.'

Creegan and Taylor left Cyril to finish his drink.

Further along the corridor Rivers was pulling on his coat, getting ready to leave for Fieldon Cross. He looked at Kreitman, who sat at his desk, his face in shadow, staring at the computer screen. Nothing showed on the screen but the OSC logo.

'Enwright's told you once,' Rivers said. 'Go home.'

'I'll . . . I'll come with you,' Kreitman said. 'It's all waiting at home. The cot and the toys and the rubbish. It's all just waiting, till they're home. I'd rather be doing something. Just till they're home.'

He got up and walked out of the office. Rivers stared after him.

Two hours later, while OSC and a forensic unit made

a search of Vince Wilson's room at the farmhouse, teams of uniformed officers combed the surrounding fields and woods.

When the search at the house was over, Rivers transferred Vince's broken computer to the boot of his car.

'I'll take this lot back to Minto Road and see what I can resurrect,' he told Kreitman. 'You go with Creegan.'

Near by, Taylor was interviewing Mrs Wilson. She was a young woman, intelligent, level-headed and capable of expressing herself with clarity. The emotional stress of the past twelve hours was telling on her, but she had been trying hard to stay calm and rational.

'You know what they're like,' she said. 'They don't tell you a thing. He goes out some nights, comes back drunk. I don't know who he's with.'

'Did he mention anyone at all?' Taylor asked.

'You think he's dead, don't you?' Suddenly the veneer was too much to sustain. Tears welled in Mrs Wilson's eyes. 'All this. You think he's dead.'

Taylor suggested they go inside and have a cup of tea. She avoided answering Mrs Wilson's question and continued to use evasive tactics until the woman took control of herself again. They went back outside, where the brisk police activity helped to keep Mrs Wilson distracted.

Shortly before one o'clock a police team searching a wood less than a mile away found a holdall packed with clothes. It was brought to the farm.

Five minutes later Taylor ran to where Creegan and Kreitman were organising a search of the farm outbuildings. Creegan was talking on his mobile phone. He ended the call and looked expectantly at Taylor.

'The clothes belong to Vince,' she said. 'His mother's come up with a name as well. Mo, a girl he used to mention. That's all she knows, no surname.'

'They've analysed the envelope sent to Lee Yamaguchi,' Creegan said. 'The address panel's impregnated with LSD.'

At the Fieldon Park Sixth Form College, meanwhile, the introduction of user identification had caused a commotion among students, who saw the move as oppressive and aimed at curbing their privacy and their freedom. To Jack McCaffrey it was a gigantic obstacle to progress. He passed word to Mo. Later, on a deserted corridor, she passed it to Craig.

'We've lost Amathus. Two o'clock.'

'What d'you mean?' Craig turned and followed her.

'Shove off,' Mo warned him.

'How can we lose her?' he demanded. 'She's sending chapter six today. Mo, tell me.'

'They've put on passwords,' she said. 'We try and read it, they'll know it's us.'

'So what we gonna do?'

'Two o'clock, you dull little twat,' she hissed. 'Two o'clock. Now piss off.'

29

'Welcome to Amathus, chapter six,' said a computerised voice, 'in which the web of deception is no more, and the enemy stands proud in hominid form.'

Enwright came into the OSC computer room and stood behind Rivers's chair. Marion was there already, sitting beside Rivers.

'Chapter six, sir,' Rivers said. 'Stoker's in there right now.'

'What country's he in?'

'It's coming through the London service provider, but he could be anywhere in the world. We're tracing it.'

On the screen a travelling red line had originated in a blue circle with the target's address: www.amathus.com. Then it passed through a site symbol marked *Intermediate Station UK*, one marked *Intermediate Station USA*, another marked *Intermediate Station Austria*, another marked *Intermediate Station UK*, and a final symbol labelled *END NODE – LONDON SERVICE PROVIDER*.

'It's British mainland, sir,' Rivers said. 'He's using a laptop and a mobile phone. It's going to take a while to get a fix.'

Ten seconds later the progress bars on the screen dropped back to zero.

'It's gone down, sir. We couldn't trace it.'

Creegan was with Taylor and Kreitman in the records office at Fieldon Cross College when Rivers called him. Creegan listened intently as Rivers brought him up to date.

'Look,' Creegan said, 'the players are waiting for chapter six. They must know when Stoker delivers. They can't use the school computers. If they go somewhere else, we can trace it.'

Creegan asked Rivers to summarise the content of chapter six. In the background he could hear the recording being played back.

'It's describing something called the Long Walk,' Rivers said. 'At the end of which there's a final test. A hominid, a human being.'

'What's the instruction?' Creegan asked. 'Scar them?'

'No. It says kill.'

Creegan switched off the phone and turned to Kreitman. 'What have we got?'

'No student by the name of Mo or Maureen.'

Creegan's phone rang again. 'Someone's opened up Amathus,' Rivers said. 'One of the players.'

Creegan told him to call back when they had traced the caller.

Across the room from Creegan, at a bank of filing cabinets, Yvonne Jackson was trying to help Taylor.

'Anyone dealing in dope or speed, leave them,' Taylor said. 'We're looking specifically for acid, LSD.'

'There was one,' Yvonne said, flicking through the files. 'It wasn't proved.' She pulled out a buff folder and handed it to Taylor. 'That's your man.'

Creegan, Taylor and Kreitman headed back along the corridor to the main entrance. As they walked, Taylor gave them the details from the file.

'Name's Jack McCaffrey. A teacher saw him leaving at midday. Lives at the Plough public house, Charterhouse Yard, about ten miles away. At a school disco, last summer, a boy named Gareth Constantino started hallucinating, claims Jack spiked his drink with acid. No charges, nothing proven.'

'Excuse me, excuse me . . .'

They stopped. Yvonne Jackson was running after them, waving. She reached them panting. 'Frank just said there is a girl called Mo. Fiona Morrison – it's her surname.'

'Where is she now?' Creegan said.

'Don't know. Could be in lessons.'

Taylor moved off with Yvonne. 'I'll find her.'

Creegan and Kreitman were outside heading for the carpark when Creegan's phone rang. It was Rivers again.

'We've got identification,' he said. 'The name's—'

'Jack McCaffrey,' Creegan said, 'the Plough, Charterhouse Yard. Yeah, thanks, Mark, tell me something new.'

It was a ten-minute fast drive. Creegan and Kreitman got out of the car and barged into the empty saloon bar at the Plough, warrant cards in their hands.

'Police,' Creegan told Eileen behind the bar. 'We're looking for Jack McCaffrey. Where is he?'

'You can't just walk in here—'

'Here I am,' Creegan said, 'walking in. Believe it. Where is he?'

'In his room.'

Creegan and Kreitman ran up the stairs and burst into Jack's bedroom. He had gone.

He was at the hideaway out in the fields with Mo and Craig. He had brought a set of colour prints downloaded from Amathus, representing the entire sixth chapter. When they had read it all, they stood in the ruined central room of the old house, daylight streaming in through the gaps in the roof. Jack and Mo were electrified by what they had read. Craig was scared.

'Something real, Craig,' Jack said.

'What?'

'Some*one*. We can walk into this world and change it, leave it changed for ever. I mean, they all think that we're nothing.'

Craig couldn't look at Jack. 'I'd rather be nothing.'

'Oh yeah?' Jack's voice had a goading, belligerent edge. 'Do you want to go back home? Your father's dead, Craig. Your mother wants you sitting there, a copy of him.' He moved closer to Craig. 'That's all they want of us – copies. Growing old and dying in their image.' He leaned on the wall. When he spoke again his voice had softened. 'Take the walk, Craig. Do something that no one has ever done before.'

'Twenty stars for the journey,' Mo said. 'Carrying a sword.' She came forward and stood on the other side of Craig. 'Then find the hominid. And kill.'

'But who?' Craig squirmed his shoulders against the wall. 'It's not like a horse. Who am I supposed to find?'

Mo held up one of the printed sheets and pointed to a line of print. 'You'll know them when you see them.'

'You'll know them when you see them,' Jack said

in Craig's other ear. 'One of the crowd, Craig. A face in the crowd.'

'And what if I can't?'

'You'll do it,' Jack said.

He reached into his pocket and produced three pieces of white paper. He pushed one into Craig's mouth, gave one to Mo and kept the remaining one for himself.

Twenty minutes later they drove up to a little petrol station in Jack's father's car. They were all high but Mo's trip was the wildest. She stood drumming her hands on the roof as Jack filled the tank, putting in precisely twenty pounds' worth of petrol.

'Come on! Come on!' Mo squealed.

Jack hooked the nozzle on the side of the pump and jumped back in behind the wheel. Mo got in too. An angry attendant stopped what he was doing in the workshop and ran out to apprehend them. Jack swung the car round the pumps, twice, then straightened up and roared off down the road.

'Start from the centre of the labyrinth,' Jack shouted. 'London tower Trafalgar Square!'

'Buckingham Palace!' Mo squealed. 'Tower of London! Off with his head! Wooh! Yee-*ha*!'

'All units,' the radio voice said, 'suspects in blue Granada estate, heading north on A317.'

'They won't go through with it,' Kreitman said. 'They're just kids.'

He was driving, peering through the smeared screen as the wipers flailed against torrential rain. Beside him Creegan adjusted the volume of the glove-box receiver and sat back.

'Jack's seventeen,' he said.

'Seventeen's a kid, he's just a kid.'

Ten yards ahead of them the lights turned red.

'Ah, shit,' Creegan grunted. 'I had this yesterday. Three sets of lights before the turn-off. Hit this one on red, they're all red.'

'I can beat them,' Kreitman said. His tone suggested he had said something profound.

As the lights turned green he accelerated away, tearing past the car in front, climbing through the gears and slamming his foot down. Twenty yards from the next set, the lights turned red. Kreitman accelerated, going for the crossing, nothing else in sight.

'Shit!' Creegan hissed.

A car appeared in front of them, turning from their left. Kreitman braked and slid to a stop with only three feet to spare.

'OK, you don't have to prove anything,' Creegan told him, getting angry. 'Let's just get there in one piece, all right?'

Kreitman sighed. For a moment he looked like a man agonised by something only he could see. The rain pounded on the roof and he glanced up, as if the noise were too much for him.

'They're just kids, Creegan. Whatever they've become, we made them. If they're clever, we made them clever, and if their heads are full of shit, we made them full of shit. Because who have they got? Who have they got except us?'

Creegan stared, surprised at the outburst.

'That's our job,' Kreitman said, 'the only job that counts, carving out a world that they can live in.

Everything we do is for them. And we've got to be fast, we've got to stay ahead.'

The lights changed. Kreitman tore away, slamming through the gears, putting the speed up past sixty.

'Jonathan, please slow down.'

'Too fast for you, Creegan? We've got to be fast.'

He accelerated past a stream of cars, going too far over to the right, making oncoming motorists swerve.

'I'm telling you to slow down!' Creegan shouted.

'We've got to be fast, or we're letting 'em down!'

White headlights blazed in the blurred screen. Horns wailed past.

'Blood vision, have you heard of that?' The needle climbed past seventy. Kreitman had to shout above the roar of the engine. 'You go so fast, the blood comes up over your eyes, everything's red. Too fast and we'll beat them.'

'Kreitman, you have to slow down!'

They were roaring towards the next set of traffic lights. They were on green. Kreitman was like a maniac at the wheel, twisting his way past other cars, making the tyres squeal. Fifty yards away the lights were still green. Kreitman put his foot down harder. At fifteen yards the lights turned yellow.

'Kreitman, stop the bloody car!'

They sailed through a split second before the lights went red.

'Yes!' Kreitman screamed. 'Yes!'

He pulled over to the side and braked hard.

Creegan got out and slammed the door. He punched the roof and stamped to the middle of the road. He was furious, ignoring the rain. For a second he looked over his shoulder at Kreitman, sitting behind the wheel, his shoulders sagging. Creegan went back to the car and jerked open the driver's door. He grabbed Kreitman's arm and shook it.

'What are you playing at, man?'

Kreitman went on staring through the windscreen. He began to talk in a quiet, dispirited voice. 'It was oxygen, they said. I don't know. They told me and I'm listening but it's not going in. Something to do with oxygen . . . at birth. Starved of oxygen in the head, damaged in the head. Oh, she's breathing, she's living, but she's just meat. A sack of meat.'

Creegan drew back, appalled. He stared along the darkened road, rain running off his face.

'She hasn't even got the sense to die,' Kreitman said. Tears rolled down his cheeks. 'I made her. It's no one else's fault, it's mine. And she'll never know all the things I've done to keep her safe, when all she's got is a head full of shit.' He finally looked at Creegan. 'I did it for her.' He paused. 'Ronald Hinks.'

Creegan stared at him.

'I killed him to make her safe. I thought I was better than him. I couldn't understand a man who wanted children dead.' The grief surged in him. His breath caught and his shoulders started to shake. 'I do now.'

At Piccadilly Circus, under the statue of Eros in the flashing red-and-green stripes of neon light, Jack, Mo and Craig stood and watched the wandering crowds.

Jack turned to Craig. 'You'll know them when you see them,' he said, and kissed him on the mouth.

He turned to Mo. 'You'll know them when you see them.' He kissed her.

They turned slowly and walked off in three different directions, heading out, losing themselves in the crowd.

30

At one minute past nine in the evening, Jack McCaffrey ran blindly down Lexington Street in Soho, clutching a bloodstained carving knife. His legs pumped wildly; his open-mouthed panting sounded like cries of pain. As he charged round the corner on to Brewer Street he slid, nearly fell, corrected himself and carried on running to the corner of Wardour Street.

The murderous gleam had gone from Jack's eyes. He no longer had the appearance or the bearing of an avenging warrior. Now he looked pale and scared. As he ran past the end of Green Court he threw the knife into a cluster of dustbins and bulging plastic rubbish bags.

Less than a mile away Mo was running too, across Leicester Square, zigzagging through the crowds to get to the street where Jack had parked his father's car. Mo carried a bloody knife wrapped in the tattered remains of a man's shirt. As she cut through a side street she dropped the bundle into a refuse bin at the back of a Chinese restaurant.

At three minutes past nine, Craig Jones was standing stock-still in front of a young beggar who sat by a doorway on Lisle Street. The beggar had asked Craig if he had any small change.

'What?'

'Have you got any loose change, mate?'

Craig stared at him. He had despaired of ever finding one, a hominid that would be recognisable as the target, the enemy. But now . . .

'You started it,' Craig said. 'I could've walked past. You came to me.'

'Look, I don't want a Tony Blair, I just wondered if you had a few coins to—'

Craig drew a flick-knife from his pocket. He touched the button and the blade shot out.

The beggar pushed himself to his feet. 'What are you doing?'

'You came to *me*.'

Craig brought up the hand with the knife. The beggar made to dodge out of the way but Craig's arm swept sideways and the knife cut through the beggar's coat and the flesh at the top of his arm. Blood surged through the gaping slit in the coat. The beggar screamed and backed away, clutching his arm. Craig looked mesmerised by the blood. He brought up the knife again, going for the beggar's chest. From nowhere, it seemed, the beggar whipped out a length of steel chain and swung it with a crack against the side of Craig's head. Craig went down, stunned.

'Psycho!' the beggar yelled, clutching his arm again and running off into the dark.

Craig stared after him, blinking. His head swam and a throb of pain penetrated the numbness at the side of his skull.

He groaned and pressed his hands against the wall, not sure how to get back up on his feet. At the core of his pain and dizziness he knew he had lost it. The drive to assert his uniqueness was gone. One sharp act of retaliation from a down-and-out had shown Craig what he was. A nothing, after all.

He thought of Jack and the muddle in his head began to clear. He could never go back near Jack, or Mo. The penalty for failure would be swift and sure. Something would have to be done, changes would have to be made.

He looked around him, touching the lump on the side of his head. He looked at the scatter of cardboard boxes, the people crouched in doorways further along the street. They survived here, Craig thought. It was a life, of sorts. He would have to learn to do the same as them, merge with them. That way he could be anonymous, as well as a nothing.

Across the city, in the communications room at OSC headquarters, Rivers was on the radio talking to an operator at Scotland Yard's Division TO14, which controls traffic in the capital.

'We're looking for a 1984 Granada estate we've tracked coming into central London. Dark blue, Southend plates. B195 XHX.'

Rivers pushed the START button on a VCR. A second later a black-and-white traffic video came up on the TV screen. Jack McCaffrey and Mo were clearly visible in the front seat of a Granada coming up to a set of traffic lights in central London. The tape was hours old and both Jack and Mo were still in boisterous warlike mode, shouting, slapping each other and kissing with exaggerated passion a moment before the lights changed. As Rivers watched, a hand appeared from the back seat and slapped Jack on the shoulder.

Rivers switched on the radio again. 'Rivers to pick-up

units. We're looking for three kids, not two. I can see Fiona Morrison, Jack McCaffrey, and a third, no ID.'

In the narrow street where Jack had parked his father's car, Mo arrived and instantly became jumpy, looking for Jack, incapable of simply waiting. She walked to one end of the street then the other. When she turned back to do the same thing again she saw Jack and ran at him, screaming, grinning, her teeth bared. Jack made a show of doing the same. They collided by the car and wrapped themselves around each other, squealing and falling to the ground.

'I made my mark!' Mo shouted in Jack's ear.

'Does it feel good?' he shouted back.

'We did it!' they yelled in unison.

Jack struggled to his feet and ran to a wire fence. He leaned on it, hooking his fingers through the mesh. He ducked his head and vomited.

Mo came to him, panting, breathing on his face. She saw the way he looked, the sick fear on his face. She fumbled in his pocket and pulled out a length of white paper. She tore off a piece and pushed it into his mouth.

'Here,' she grunted, sliding it across his tongue. 'We can't wait here, all right? We've got to go. Right? Come on! Come on! Come on!'

She tried to shuffle him towards the car but he seemed to have lost the power to move himself. His weight against her was too much and Mo began to stagger.

A mechanically amplified voice cut through the air, startling her.

'This is the police. Stay where you are.'

Unmarked cars moved in, blocking the exits from the street. Uniformed officers came running from alleys.

'Get down on the floor!' the voice barked. 'This is the police! Stay where you are! Get down on the floor!'

Hands grasped Jack and Mo by the shoulders, forcing them down. Other hands searched them.

'No!' Jack screamed. 'No! No! No! Get off me! Get off me! Get off me!'

They were picked up like dolls and pushed, kicking and shouting, into the back of a police Transit.

Vince Wilson had telephoned his mother at the farm.

'He said he'd done something bad,' she told Taylor, 'and he daren't come home. What's he talking about?'

Taylor didn't reply. Instead, she called Control on her radio. 'Can we trace a call made to 01233 750232 this evening at about . . .'

'Nine o'clock,' Mr Wilson said.

'Nine o'clock,' Taylor said, and gave the Wilsons a confident nod.

At nine thirty Vince rang again. He was in a telephone box in Fieldon Cross.

'Mum?' He stood hunched over, facing a rear corner of the box.

'Vince?' his mother replied. 'Where are you, love?'

'I can't come home. I need money.'

Mrs Wilson began to argue.

'Mum, I need . . . just give me money.'

Outside the box Taylor rapped sharply on the glass. Vince turned, hunching even more, staring at the faces of all the policemen standing round the box with shadowy faces, looking in on him.

Vince was brought to OSC headquarters. Shortly afterwards his parents arrived. They sat with Vince between them at one side of the table in number two interview room. Taylor sat opposite. She talked as if she were addressing the parents, but she was talking to Vince.

'The only thing that stopped Vince being a part of this was the fact that he absconded, which means he's not like them, doesn't it? Which is why we think Vince is our key to finding out what actually led to all this.'

Taylor was good at convincing people they should co-operate. Her sole purpose at the interview was to make it clear to Vince that his best interests would be served by giving up his mates and holding nothing back. She talked to Vince and his parents for ten minutes, then told them to wait – a woman called Marion would be coming along shortly.

Creegan, meantime, was about to talk to the parents of Jack McCaffrey when Enwright called him into his office. As soon as the door was closed, Enwright went to his desk and picked up a document. He waved it at Creegan.

'What the hell's this report about?'

'It's what it says. I took a verbal statement from Jonathan Kreitman saying he'd murdered Ronald Hinks.'

Enwright stared at the report, then at Creegan again. 'Have you got any evidence?'

'I'm not filing an accusation,' Creegan said. 'It's a report on a conversation which landed on my lap. I think it belongs on yours, sir.'

Creegan left Enwright's office and went to number three interview room. Ted and Eileen McCaffrey were already sitting at the table. Creegan sat down opposite them. As the parents of a minor suspected of a serious crime, he told them, they were required to be party to certain legal undertakings that required their signature before the inquiry could go any further.

'And I warn you now,' Creegan said, after they had signed, 'if you want to watch these interviews, some of this stuff is going to be pretty difficult to listen to.'

'In what way?' Eileen asked.

Ted held up a flat hand. 'Don't say anything,' he told Creegan. 'I don't want to know.' He got up and left.

Eileen looked at Creegan. 'Is Jack going to prison?'

He nodded.

'For?'

Creegan pushed a brown envelope towards her, then gathered up the signed papers and left. Eileen slowly opened the envelope. The picture inside took her breath away. She gaped at it as tears brimmed and her breath caught in her throat.

Later, in number three interview room, Creegan and Taylor confronted Jack McCaffrey. He still looked pale and sick.

'Why did you do it, Jack?' Taylor said.

Creegan was shuffling the forensic photographs, occasionally tipping them in Jack's direction, letting flashes of horror cross the table. Jack was trying not to look.

'You set off from home knowing only that you'd kill someone tonight,' Taylor went on. She pushed a picture in front of Jack. 'Who told you you could kill this man and get away with it?'

'Um, well . . .' Jack stared at the table, then at the darkness beyond the pool of light on the surface. 'People living in boxes end up with a lot of sharp corners, yeah.' He gave a little shudder. 'You can't live in boxes.'

Taylor hammed surprise. 'You'll have to now, Jack. Prison's a box.'

Jack smiled, then frowned. He pressed a finger to his temple. 'I tell you, you sound like . . . you sound like God.' He laughed, his head down, staring at the edge of the table.

Creegan reached forward with one finger extended. He tapped the side of Jack's nose and said, 'Do you think the guy who sent you on the rampage is grown up, Jack? Do you think James Stoker's grown up enough to look at this lot?'

He pushed the pictures forward. Jack recoiled and shut his eyes.

'Why did you do this to the body?'

Jack wouldn't reply.

Half an hour later, when Creegan and Taylor interrogated Mo and asked her the same question, she said, 'I deserved it.'

'Yeah,' Creegan said, 'but the woman was dead. Why did you do this to the body?'

'Make your mark,' Mo said, grinning.

Late that night Creegan and Rivers went to the mortuary. Creegan looked at one of the bodies under its sheet. Rivers looked at the other one. Then they swapped.

'You're saying kids did this?' Rivers was shocked.

Creegan appeared to be simply puzzled. The pathologist was watching him, gauging his reaction. Creegan looked at both bodies again, frowning now and concentrating.

The pathologist said, 'You're only old enough to have read about it.'

Rivers looked at Creegan. 'What's he talking about?'

'This signature's been used before,' Creegan said. He turned to the pathologist. 'What was it? Ten—'

'Fifteen,' the pathologist said.

'Fifteen years ago.' Creegan shook his head, still not remembering.

'I'll give you a clue,' the pathologist said. 'It was coastal.'

'Yeah, I knew it was South.' Creegan scratched his nose. 'Atlantic or English Channel?'

'Both.'

'Devon?'

The pathologist shook his head. 'Falmouth. Cornwall.'

'They caught the killer.'

'Big case at the time,' the pathologist said. 'Male or female?'

Creegan thought hard. 'Female.'

'That was a guess,' the pathologist snapped.

31

Mr and Mrs Wilson sat in the viewing room while Marion questioned Vince. He was nervous, but Marion was coming across as a good-natured aunt, a ploy that was helping to ease the tension. She asked Vince about his first encounter with Amathus.

'It was a laugh,' he said. 'Jack found it on the Internet, multiple-choice thing. Except every time you got a section right, you were given a special password and a pay-off.'

'Drugs?'

Vince nodded. 'Money, sometimes.'

'What came up on the screen?'

'You had to say what you were most scared of, what you hated most. Cats, spiders, snakes.'

'People?' Marion said.

Vince nodded again.

At that moment in number one interview room, Taylor sat opposite Mo, confronting her with two police photographs of the people she and Jack had killed. Mo was no longer high. The acid trip was over and she was staring at bleak reality. After a moment she began to cry. She looked up at Taylor.

'I swear to God, I didn't . . . I didn't do that.' She

looked at the pictures again. 'I didn't do that,' she sobbed. 'I didn't do that.'

At 2.30 in the morning Enwright convened a meeting in the conference room. Creegan, Taylor, Marion and Rivers were present.

Enwright said, 'James Stoker, whoever that is, posted a questionnaire on the Internet that specifically targeted kids in arse-end communities.' He looked at Marion. 'How clever are we looking at?'

'More instinctive than clever,' she said. 'He used something like this.' She handed round copies of a three-page document. 'It's a bog-standard trip-you-up personality test. Questions like "Are you happy about the number of real friends you've got?" He knows you'd have to be fairly sad to want to fill one of these in. Then he offers them real friends, he offers to prove they're inseparable by giving them a secret that binds them for life.'

'Yeah . . .' Creegan got out of his chair and picked up the remote control for the slide projector. '. . . but the adventure's a second-hand quest because this, and this, and this' – he brought up three forensic photographs in rapid succession – 'are hallmarks of somebody else's crime.'

Rivers supplied the details. 'Fifteen years ago, a woman by the name of Justine Barber was convicted of murder. She had early form as a prostitute which resulted in the murder and mutilation of seven pimps. Her trial split public opinion, and she took a feminist lobby with her through the courts.'

'The murders were always selective,' Creegan said, 'but the mutilation was identical to these. She is currently serving life in Stanmore.'

It was Taylor's turn. 'The images that drew these kids to the website in the first place,' she said, 'were nude or portions of nude bodies on the screen. Never pornographic, but always depicting nipples. Male, female, but always nipples, which were jokingly referred to as stars.'

'And this,' said Enwright, picking up a sheet of paper, 'is a memorised quote from Vincent Wilson.' Enwright cleared his throat and read: 'Every time you succeed, take a star for yourself.'

At 9.30 that same morning Creegan and Taylor were ushered in through the main gate at Stanmore prison. They were met inside by a senior prison officer, a woman of serious bulk and few words who took them to Block A and led them up the metal stairs to the second level. As they went up, female prisoners cheered, shouted and catcalled at them.

The officer left them at the wide-open door to Justine Barber's cell. Justine, wearing a black sweater and black ski pants, sat at a table in the middle of the cell with her back to the door. She was listening to a shipping forecast on Radio 4.

Creegan and Taylor went in. They stood behind Justine's chair. She went on listening to the radio, engrossed.

'Justine?' Creegan said.

She reached across the table and switched off the radio.

Taylor said, 'Justine, we're investigating a series of murders, and we think you might be able to help us.'

Justine turned. Her face was strong-featured and

striking. She had deep blue eyes and neatly cut blond hair. 'Who am I now?' she asked with a faint smile. 'Vanessa Feltz?'

'Kids are involved,' Creegan said.

He paused and looked around the cell. Taylor had done the same. Justine lived in an impressive setting. In spite of the brick walls, barred window and steel door, the cell had a domestic atmosphere. Justine had managed to combine tidiness with precisely judged touches of warmth.

'Schoolkids,' Creegan went on. 'They're copying the crimes you committed in '82, and we think they've been instructed by somebody who knows your case inside out.'

To enhance the chances of Justine co-operating, the governor had granted permission for her to go outside with her visitors. After a brief discussion of the recent murders, she went downstairs with Creegan and Taylor. Two prison officers came close behind. As they descended, Taylor asked Justine if she had any contact with computers.

'Computers? It's taken me thirteen years to get a manual typewriter. I think Oscar Wilde had it before me. Do you know how many letters I have to write?'

'Look,' Creegan said, 'we know you had your supporters at the time of the murders. We need to know if you've had recent contact with any fanatics, or anybody who wanted to know about specific details of your crimes.'

They came out into sunlight. Justine took a deep breath and began to walk, strolling as if it were a morning in the park.

'Do you know why I'm still here?' she said. 'Because

I won't apologise. All those people I chose to remove were filth. So I'd be lying if I said I was sorry.' She looked at Creegan, narrowing her eyes against the sun. 'What kind of kids?'

'Normal.'

'Previously unremarkable,' Taylor said. 'The bloke behind it all's been using the Internet. He's sending out coded instructions, worldwide. The kids we're attached to all come from Fieldon Cross.'

Justine pointed at Creegan's forehead. 'What's that?'

'A bullet hole.'

'Lying bastard.' Justine turned to Taylor. 'Is he lying?'

'No.'

'Bloody hell.' Justine was impressed.

'See,' Creegan said, 'the difference between you and the kids we're talking about is they didn't have a choice. They're taking instructions from a guy who can't even do his own dirty work.'

Justine stopped walking. She looked at Taylor, then at Creegan. 'The only time I've had to deal with people like you was just before my trial. But people like you have to deal with people like me all the time, is that right? Well, if that's not dirty work . . .'

She walked away, leaving them staring after her.

Creegan and Taylor stayed another ten minutes, but Justine didn't want to talk about her case. All that appeared to matter was the amount of time she could spend in the open air.

Finally the guards led her back to her cell. Creegan and Taylor headed for the main gate.

'Well, you wouldn't ask her to baby-sit, would you?' Taylor said.

Creegan laughed, then jumped as a voice shouted harshly from a window two storeys above them.

'Oi!' It was Justine, the top of her head just visible behind the bars. 'Nineteen ninety-two to 1997,' she yelled. Through the gap in the window she began to shower letters down on to the yard.

'And I want 'em all back!'

The letters, at least two hundred of them, continued to flutter down. Creegan and Taylor crossed the yard. They began gathering up the envelopes and stuffing them in their pockets.

32

By eleven o'clock the letters were being sifted and
categorised by Taylor, Marion and Rivers, assisted by
six other OSC officers. Felt-tipped markers indicated
the categories – HETEROSEXUAL, HOMOSEXUAL,
OFFENDERS, CRIMINAL LIBERAL, MARRIAGE.
The MARRIAGE pile was far bigger than the others.

As they worked, Taylor kept looking round the room
for Creegan. There had been no sign of him since ten
minutes after they got back from Stanmore prison.

Creegan had driven out to visit Jonathan Kreitman
at home. He parked his car in the road at the front
of the neat detached house. Kreitman's car was parked
on a paved area in front of a bay window. Creegan
rattled the knocker and waited. He knocked again. After
thirty seconds there was still no reply. Creegan looked
through the letterbox, then walked round the house to
the back.

He put his face to the French windows. Kreitman was
inside, in an armchair, staring at a switched-off TV set,
holding a can of beer. There were empty beer cans and
a half-eaten pizza in its box on the couch.

Creegan opened the door and went in. Kreitman
turned, looked at him, looked away again.

'Why aren't you at the hospital?' Creegan demanded.
'For what?'

'Your wife, your baby.'

Kreitman sighed and looked at his beer can. He raised it, then decided not to drink any more. Instead he stood up and moved the cans and stale food off the couch and into a waste basket.

'I told Enwright,' Creegan said. 'I filed a report. You knew I would, Jonathan. That's why you confessed to me, isn't it?' Kreitman seemed to be ignoring him. 'See, what I know and you don't is that I went to Hinks's house the same night – with a loaded weapon.'

Now Kreitman was staring at him.

'And I am convinced,' Creegan went on, 'that I would have done exactly the same as you did. But the next thing I would have done after that would have been to go to Enwright and write my own confession.'

'Creegan,' Kreitman said wearily, 'don't tell me what you would have done, because you don't have a clue what you would have done. You didn't kill him. You didn't finish the job. *I* did.'

'You did. And you can't trust yourself any more, which is exactly why you told me. Take some responsibility.'

'For whose sake?' Kreitman made a pained smile. 'Yours?'

'No! For yours, you stupid prick. Jonathan, the report's gone in. Enwright's going to send Ballistics in here searching for evidence to connect you. Your career's just turned to shit. If they find anything you're looking at ten years.'

Kreitman turned away and walked into the kitchen. Creegan stayed where he was.

'Look, your baby was born three days ago and your life has turned shit. I haven't come to punish you, man.'

A cupboard door closed and Kreitman came back to the sitting room. He took Creegan's hand and dropped four bullets on to his open palm. Creegan stared at them.

'What's this?'

'Evidence. Same bullets that killed Ronald Hinks. They're yours. Do what you want with them, Creegan.'

Creegan gaped at him. 'It's not *my* responsibility.'

There was a sharp knock at the door. Kreitman answered it. Enwright was on the step. Behind him, parked in front of Creegan's car, were two more cars full of investigative officers. Now that the door had been answered, they began piling out and coming up the path. Creegan pocketed the bullets and turned to face the door.

'Jonathan.' Enwright glanced at Creegan. For a moment he seemed to be trying to gauge the significance in these two men being here at this time. Then he let it go. He looked at Kreitman. 'Can I come in?'

Kreitman turned and went back to the sitting room. Enwright followed and stood in the doorway.

'I want you to think very carefully before you answer me,' he said. 'Did you make a confession to DI Creegan that you murdered Ronald Hinks?'

Kreitman cleared his throat. 'I reserve the right to wait for a lawyer, sir.'

'Did you murder Ronald Hinks?'

'I reserve the right to wait for a lawyer, sir.'

'Don't move,' Enwright said. Investigative officers began to pour in through the front door. 'Just tell me where you keep your weapon.'

'In the safe, sir.'

'Are we going to find any ballistics not legally issued to you as an officer?'

Kreitman had already glanced at Creegan's hands. He would have seen they were empty. Creegan kept his head down.

'No, sir,' Kreitman said.

'Thank you.' Enwright turned to the chief investigative officer. 'OK.'

The men started moving through the house.

'You're suspended from duties pending the investigation,' Enwright said. 'If you've let me down, Kreitman, I'll kick your arse from here to kingdom come.'

'Sir.'

'Get your coat.'

Creegan threw a quick look at Kreitman, then turned and walked out of the house.

Back at OSC headquarters, the Justine Barber letters were still being read and classified. There was now clear evidence that Justine was a focus and inspiration for a number of disturbed individuals still on the outside. Creegan joined the team working in the conference room when they were about halfway through the collection. Nothing with any apparent relevance to the case in hand had turned up, but a couple of outside possibilities had been set on one side.

Rivers read aloud a snatch from one letter. '"Your continued incarceration is a travesty, and I'm doing all in my power to put things right."'

As he looked up he saw Kreitman through the window, being led into reception by Enwright, followed by three investigative officers. He also noticed that Creegan had seen them, but had shown no reaction, not even curiosity.

'Here,' Marion said, engrossed in the job on hand. 'Four letters dated July last year.'

Taylor took one of them, scanned it and started to read aloud. '"Every time you write to me, you give me hope. Every time I think of you, I grieve because the world without you gets dirtier, and I just can't look any more. And every time I think of you, I plant another star in the sky . . ."'

Everybody stopped what they were doing. They looked at Taylor.

'". . . hoping someday we can meet and be together."'

The letter was from a PO box number, and it was signed *J*. So were the other three.

Creegan was back at Stanmore prison within the hour. Justine wasn't in her cell so he sat on a chair by the bed and waited. After five minutes he heard her shouting at another prisoner out on the landing.

'You knew it was mine!' she roared. 'You should have asked! So you can just piss off from now on, all right?'

She appeared in the doorway, scowling.

'Not really a good time to ask for a favour, then, is it?' Creegan said.

Justine nodded sharply at where he was sitting. 'My chair.'

Creegan got up and sat on a stool. Justine took the chair. He produced the four letters Marion had isolated.

285

'Do you know who this guy is?'

Justine looked them over and handed them back without comment.

'Well,' Creegan said, 'he's using your reputation, Justine, and he's a lot cleverer than you.'

She smiled tightly. 'You'll get a smack round the mouth in a minute.'

'He's got his freedom, hasn't he?'

'Good luck to him.'

'Justine, the people you—'

'The people I cleaned up all deserved what they got.'

Creegan produced forensic photographs of the man and woman killed by Jack and Mo. He put them on the bed and pointed. 'Donald Freeborn – he was a fifty-four-year-old tramp. Claire MacLaghlan, thirty-year-old beggar. A lot's changed since 1982. Whatever they wanted from anybody, they didn't deserve what they got.'

Justine did no more than glance at the pictures. She looked at Creegan. 'Is this a two-way thing? Can you get me out?'

Creegan laughed. 'Well, I could get your parole reviewed when you're about seventy. At best.'

'For a day,' Justine said.

Creegan thought for a moment, then he reached for his phone. He spoke to Enwright, who said he would have to speak to a much higher authority. Creegan waited in the governor's office. After half an hour Enwright got back to him.

'The Home Office consents to Justine Barber helping on the case,' he said, 'providing her assistance remains confidential.'

In due course Justine was brought to OSC head-quarters in a police van. She was led into the building by the back entrance and taken directly to Enwright's office. She brought with her a box file containing more letters. Enwright, Creegan, Taylor and Rivers sat around the desk watching as she carefully untied one bundle.

'What are the others in there?' Taylor asked, pointing at stacked letters still in the box.

'Not his,' Justine said. 'And not yours. Do you know how many letters I get? I don't reply to them all. I know it's secure where I live but there's some freaky old nonces out there and you don't want them crowding your space, do you? I don't.'

Creegan and the others had begun sifting through the letters Justine laid on the table.

'First time he wrote,' she said, picking up a letter, 'was during the trial, when I was on remand.'

Taylor took the letter and looked at it. 'Fifteen years ago?' she said. 'How do you know?'

'Look at the writing.'

From another envelope Justine tipped a broad, plain gold ring. She held it out on her palm. 'He offered me a secret wedding. Promise for life so that I wouldn't feel lonely in prison.' She turned to Creegan. 'I told him to piss off, of course.'

Later, in the conference room, Creegan, Taylor and Rivers brought the whole team up to date on what they had learned from Justine. Among the letters spread out on the table were photographs of Justine, one taken when she was in her twenties, another on the day she was sentenced to life imprisonment. Others were news photographs photocopied and fixed in mounts to make them look like celebrity pictures. On the lower edges of each mount was written the phrase *The Biggest Star I know*.

Creegan picked up a bunch of the letters. 'Stoker sent these via a PO box, which we think is central London.'

'And the postmark,' Rivers said, 'ties in with the date that he first made contact with the schoolkids.'

Taylor said, 'According to Justine Barber, the first time he wrote to her was during her trial. He doted on her, said he'd do anything for her.'

Justine had been treated to afternoon tea, closely supervised by two affable but athletic female OSC officers. When Creegan had finished the briefing in the conference room, he came and took Justine to a room next door to Enwright's office. They were there now, Creegan and Rivers standing, Justine seated. She was ten feet from a sullen Jack McCaffrey, who sat facing her between his conspirators, Vince and Mo.

Justine had introduced herself to the trio. She had made it perfectly clear who she was. Then she waited, and after a minute of silence she let out a sigh.

'Well, that's what I call ignorant,' she said. 'I've said who I am. You're meant to give me something back.'

She stared at them in turn. Vince and Mo looked stiff with fear. Jack had his head down, trying to appear unrepentant.

'All right, hands up anyone who's scared of being sent down?'

Vince was brave enough to raise his hand first, though not very high. A moment later Mo raised hers. Jack looked up, but he didn't raise his hand.

'Why not?' Justine asked him.

'I don't see the difference.'

'No.' Justine's stare didn't waver. 'That's what's really scary.'

'Look . . .' Creegan stepped forward. 'We've got a proposition. Your crimes can be bargained down on account of the acid you were pre-supplied with.' He walked behind the row of chairs and leaned down by Jack's shoulder. 'You go to prison, that's compulsory, but the sentence can be minimised if you can get us to James Stoker.'

'Oh yeah?' Jack tried to sound defiant, but his voice was uneven. 'How's that?'

'You write the script for us to plant on the Amathus website.'

'What's your Amathus?' Justine said.

Jack wet his lips. 'It's a . . . it's a Greek myth. Theseus and . . . and the Minotaur.'

Justine glared at him. 'Is it bollocks. It was a nightclub in Plymouth where I worked as a prostitute. Eight quid a night with chicken in a basket, without the basket.' She sighed. 'You daft sod.'

Jack looked utterly deflated.

33

Kreitman was in the staff interview room with his lawyer beside him. Two internal investigators had already packed up their papers and left. The lawyer got up and was approaching the door when Enwright came in.

'Hang on a sec,' Kreitman told the lawyer. He looked at Enwright. 'Is this on the record?'

'No.'

The lawyer left, closing the door softly behind him. Enwright came and sat opposite Kreitman at the table. A single downlight reflected stark white off the papers on the table, making both their faces gaunt and shadowed.

Enwright said, 'I was a signatory to the campaign that made senior officers declare whether or not they were in the freemasons. It was a very proud signature.'

He watched Kreitman's eyes, catching his displeasure at having to hear this.

'You police by integrity,' he continued. 'And there's no such thing as two-tiered integrity, is there?'

Kreitman swigged a mouthful of his coffee and put the cup down carefully. He looked squarely at Enwright.

'I'd been to Safeway's, 1985,' he said, 'and I'd taken my dad a couple of bags of shopping. He was losing it a bit and I think I was secretly glad he needed me that much because we'd been a bit dry up until then. I got to his house and found him hiding under the kitchen table, crying. He'd been a bit off-centre for a while, but to see him actually cry really slapped me. If you knew him, you'd have been shocked. He was talking gibberish about Reagan and the Russians and the fact that Britain was bang in the middle and we were all due to perish with every new six o'clock news. He was totally petrified.'

Enwright was having trouble tracing the root of this monologue. Kreitman breezed on.

'We sent him into hospital and they found him a little psychiatric bar code for his file: Manic Depressive Psychotic. They gave him something that took the edges off. He was out within three weeks. Big relief, crisis over. I sat watching a Tommy Cooper special with him and he was pissing himself laughing. We sat watching *News at Ten* and he was pissing himself laughing. They were still at it – Russians and Reagan. I'm sitting there for the first time, thinking, Shit, it's true, these cowboys could kill us all. But my dad?' Kreitman waved his hand, miming data whizzing over his head. 'It made me swear never to look away from the truth.'

When Enwright was sure Kreitman had stopped talking, he said, 'If you look at the kind of shit we have to deal with, and all you smell is your own breath, there's something wrong, Kreitman.' He sighed quietly. 'There won't be any charges filed because I can find no evidence. But there won't be a job here either.'

Enwright got up and left.

At that moment Creegan was entering the office he

shared with Taylor. She was standing behind her desk, glaring at him.

'Shut the door,' she said coldly.

'Why?' Creegan came further into the room and saw Rivers.

'You bloody well know why,' Taylor said. 'Shut the door.'

He did as she said. Taylor squared up to him.

'Is it true Kreitman's being investigated?'

Before Creegan could open his mouth Rivers said, 'You know their baby's on the critical list?'

'There's three things I've done in my life that I'm totally ashamed of,' Creegan said. 'My mam catching me having a wank when I was fourteen, moving out of a house that I bought for a family, and, today, Kreitman.'

Rivers snorted. 'But not ashamed enough to keep your mouth shut.'

'What I'm ashamed of, Mark,' Creegan said, rounding on him, 'is that it's taken me this long to make something happen.'

Taylor frowned. 'Jonathan's actually confessed?'

'And what you should be ashamed of,' Creegan said, jabbing a finger at Rivers, 'is that you knew more than any of us, and you've done nothing!'

'I knew nothing!'

'Didn't you?' Creegan was shouting now.

'I knew nothing!' Rivers insisted.

'No?' Creegan went to his desk and pulled out a sheet of paper. He came back to Rivers and brandished it in his face. 'Then why have you made a confidential request for a transfer down the corridor?'

Rivers couldn't reply.

'Because you're as scared of your partner as I am!'

Taylor took the transfer request and read it. She looked at Rivers. 'Did he do it?'

Rivers remained silent, not looking at her. Her face twisted with disgust. She backed away from Rivers and turned on Creegan. 'How dare you proceed against Kreitman without consulting me?'

'I didn't want to involve you.'

'Yeah?' Taylor looked mad enough to hit him. 'Well, that's a really bad habit you've got.'

The door opened and Enwright came in. He stood for a moment, catching the atmosphere. 'They've tracked the box number that Stoker's using,' he said. 'Surveillance are on their way, but it needs co-ordinating.'

Taylor stormed past Enwright and left the room. He looked at the other two, then went out. Creegan and Rivers were left alone, staring at each other.

Negotiations to extend Justine's absence from prison were completed and a bulletin was planted with the news agencies. The next day billboards, newspapers and the broadcasting media were proclaiming the authorities' embarrassment over the escape of an inmate from Stanmore prison. Network radio helped spread the news to the British public at breakfast-time.

'Prison security is under the hammer again,' the newsreader said, 'after Justine Barber, sentenced to life for multiple murder over fifteen years ago, escaped last night from Stanmore in a taxi that was meant to be ferrying staff into town. An inquiry has been set up to investigate just how Barber was able to gain access to the car.'

Seated at Creegan's desk at OSC headquarters, Justine

Barber copied out a letter from a typed sheet Creegan had given her.

> *Dear J*
> *I don't want to say an awful lot because of risks.*
> *By the time you get this, you'll know what I'm*
> *talking about. I've never spoken to you but you*
> *wrote to me a number of times . . .*

The process of copying the letter into longhand was laborious. Creegan looked over her shoulder from time to time and made encouraging sounds.

'Concentrate,' he said at one point, annoying her as he pointed out a place where she had missed a word. 'If Stoker's checking his mail, this'll provoke contact. You'll make his day.'

When the letter was written, Justine put it in an envelope and wrote a large *J* on the front with the box number address underneath.

The letter was taken away, and from that point on it was handled only by people wearing gloves. A machine put an authentic North London frank mark over the stamp, after which the envelope was sprayed with fast-drying matt medium to improve the clarity of any fingerprints it might pick up.

Twenty minutes later Rivers, dressed as a postman and wearing a wool cap, took the letter to the seedy little mail address agency together with half a dozen others, collected from the sorting office that served the region.

As Rivers left the agency he looked up at a half-open window across the road. A tripod-mounted camera was just visible; one of two men standing beside it gave

Rivers a swift thumbs-up. Rivers went round the corner, crossed the road and climbed into the back of a small blue van where Creegan was waiting.

'Seventh from the left, third row down,' Rivers said.

Creegan got out his radio. 'Seventh from the left, third row down,' he told the surveillance team.

Up in the house across the way from the agency, the officer in charge of the camera focused on the pigeonholes behind the agency counter and moved the camera carefully on its swivel mount.

'Six, seven. Third row. Got it.'

His colleague did the same with a set of high-magnification binoculars mounted on a tripod beside the camera.

They waited and watched. It was a busy little agency and the officer on the camera was kept occupied photographing clients as they went in, then watching the target pigeonhole, ready for more shots if somebody claimed the letter.

The fatal slip occurred when a man put his pass card on the counter and an assistant reached into the first pigeonhole on the second shelf. Seeing it was the wrong pigeonhole, the officer took the opportunity to change the film in his camera, while there were no other clients in the agency. A few moments of relaxation followed as the man with binoculars stepped back, rubbed his eyes and watched his colleague thread a fresh film into the Nikon.

It was in that space of time that the client in the agency dropped a second pass card on the counter. The assistant read the number, took the letter out of the seventh pigeonhole from the left in the third row down and handed it to the client. He left the agency before the camera had been swung round and trained on the window again.

Three minutes later, as business in the agency became brisk again, the surveillance officers suddenly noticed that the letter had gone.

Justine was installed in a spacious cell in the basement at OSC headquarters. She sat at a table in the middle of the room, finishing her lunch and watching as a young engineer, nervous at the way she looked at him, attached the lead from a pair of telephones on the table to a junction box in the corner.

'Can I ring my mum on this?'

He nodded. 'Yeah.'

Creegan came in with a piece of information he had omitted to give Justine before.

'If he shows, he's going to want to tell you what he's done for you. So we'll have to mike you up so we can record it.'

Justine had been idly twirling her fork. Now she pointed it at Creegan. 'You said you had proof that he made those kids do what they did.'

'Well . . .' Creegan put his hands on his hips and started to pace. 'We can prove they did it for him, but we can't prove he made them do it.'

She waggled the fork menacingly. 'If you've got me hanging some poor sod because you can't do your job, I'll bloody hammer you, Creegan.'

'Oh, come on, Justine.' Creegan was showing right-eous indignation, some of it probably genuine. 'You've seen those kids. You've spoken to them. He's a pimp.'

Justine lowered the fork. She looked at her plate

and stirred the remains of her lunch without eating any.

'And if he gets away,' Creegan added, piling on the common sense, 'what's going to stop him doing it again?'

Enwright called to Creegan from the door. Creegan went out to the corridor, closing the door behind him.

'Surveillance missed him,' Enwright said. 'He's been and gone, taken the letter with him.'

'Shit!'

Beyond the cell door they heard the phone start to ring. They stared at each other. This was too soon. They weren't ready.

34

When they rushed into the cell, Justine was agitated, frowning at the ringing phone, dragging her fingers through her hair. Taylor and Rivers came barging in. Creegan signalled to them to stand still and be quiet. He pointed to the receiver beside Justine and poised his hand over the one nearer him.

'One, two, three.'

They snatched up the phones simultaneously.

'Hello?' Justine said, very quietly.

A man's voice said, 'Hello? Who am I speaking to, please?'

'Do you think I'm stupid or what?' Justine muttered. 'You could be setting me up. How do I know you're clean?'

'*You* wrote to *me*, didn't you?'

'So?' Justine scowled. 'OK, the first letter you ever wrote to me, you gave me a nickname.'

'Aridela,' the man said.

'I know what that means. Do you?'

'The Chosen, the Manifest One. It's Greek.'

'So's ouzo, love. You could've read that anywhere.'
It wasn't a logical response, but Justine made it sound as if it was.

'You worked in a club in Plymouth,' the man said. 'The Amathus.'

Justine hesitated for effect, then she said, 'OK. Look, I've no money and nowhere to stay after tonight, and . . .'

'Are we married?'

'What?'

When the man spoke again his voice was lower, throaty. 'Did my vows mean anything, Justine?'

She looked at Creegan. 'Well, I'm wearing your ring, if that's what you mean.'

'That belonged to my wife.' He sighed. 'You've kept me alive. Do you know you've kept me alive?'

'The ring said a lot.'

'You put your money where your mouth is, you set the world a standard, Justine. We all complain about the way things are going. And all that time ago, you set the standard. Justine, I *know* you know that you gave me something to believe in . . .'

Abruptly a mobile phone in the cell started to ring. Creegan stared at Rivers. Rivers looked in his pocket, shrugged. Not him. Suddenly Creegan was fishing out his own phone. It rang again before he could switch it off. Justine was glaring daggers at him. So was Enwright.

Justine put the phone to her ear again. 'What was that?' the man said, suspicious.

Justine's face showed the struggle to improvise. 'My daughter's looking after me. Just hang on.' Justine held the receiver a foot away from her face. Glaring at Creegan, she yelled, 'Will you piss off upstairs with that phone? This is a private conversation, all right? It's private.' She put the phone to her ear again. 'It's not healthy for me here. She's got three kids running around and . . . What's your name, by the way? I've only got J.'

'You haven't got a daughter,' the man said accusingly.

'Yes I have,' Justine said without hesitating. 'She was christened Lisa Theresa Barber, seventh July 1973. I had her adopted in 1974 and she was officially renamed Emma Singleton in 1975. Check.'

The man let out a shuddering sigh. 'How much money do you need, Justine?'

She frowned, thinking.

'Justine?'

'Look,' she said, 'I don't *like* this. What's your proper name?'

'Leonard.'

'Well, where shall we meet, Leonard?'

It was a moment before he spoke. 'I don't want any disappointments.'

'What do you mean?'

'I don't . . . I don't think I'm as handsome as I might have made out in . . . in the letters.'

'Look, Leonard. Do I give a shit about handsome? Handsome's what put me in Stanmore.'

Creegan had pushed his open notebook in front of Justine. Across one page he had scribbled MAKE FRIENDS!

She mouthed something obscene at him, then into the phone she said, 'What I need right now, more than anything, is a friend.'

'I am that,' the man said. 'I swear I am that.'

Justine looked sick. 'So,' she breathed. 'When?'

At ten past three that afternoon Justine was on the concourse at Waterloo Station. She wore shiny black high-heeled shoes, black stockings, a black miniskirt, a black jacket and a red round-necked sweater. Under the sweater, at the back, she wore a transceiver attached to a microphone inside the front of her jacket. Her hair was freshly shampooed and blow-dried. She wore make-up and gold earrings, one of which concealed the presence of a radio earphone. This was the best Justine had looked in fifteen years. Her striking tall figure attracted plenty of passing attention as she stood in the mainstream of travellers coming and going.

She was not there alone. Surveillance officers were all around her. Rivers was one of them, stationed ten yards away, wearing a denim jacket, puffing on a cigarette as he kept up a sullen inspection of every male who looked as if he might be approaching Justine. Others, singly and in pairs, looking like weary travellers, young mothers – with empty prams – gushing couples and grumpy commuters, maintained a sweeping surveillance of the concourse. Several were equipped with cameras and one carried a wide-angle video unit inside a carrier bag. Justine stood in the midst of it all, looking about her, half unnerved, half exhilarated by the novelty of so much space and variety.

'Nobody looks at each other,' she said. 'Look at them. I've seen rats happier.'

Behind her, one floor up in an isolated section of the Burger King, Creegan and Taylor watched Justine and picked up every word through their radios.

A man was approaching her. He wore a Russian-style fur hat and a long raincoat. He looked about sixty, soft-featured, half smiling. His eyes were fixed on Justine.

'Here we go,' she muttered. 'On your marks, get set . . .'

302

As the man came up to her she put her hand on her hip and showed him her friendliest face. 'Hello,' she said.

He didn't say anything. Instead, he made a back-and-forth jerking action with his hand in his coat pocket.

'Oh, go on,' Justine said, her face twisting with disgust. 'Piss off!'

'Get his picture,' Creegan said to his radio as the man moved away. 'Cover him to the exit.'

Justine had expended a lot of nervous energy on the encounter. She had also demonstrated to herself that she had lost some of her style, otherwise the cruiser wouldn't even have tried. As he disappeared in the crowd, Justine looked irritable.

'Here, Creegan,' she said. 'D'you know any jokes?'

He thought for a second. 'What do you do if a Rottweiler's shagging your leg?'

'Go on,' she said.

'Fake an orgasm.'

Justine laughed out loud, startling a few people walking past.

Through the radio Taylor said, 'Justine, can you try not speaking?'

'Yeah, you an' all.'

Twenty yards away a man had stepped off an escalator and was watching Justine. He faced away from her towards a leather goods shop, but twice he turned his head and looked hard at her, making sure. As he looked away the second time, Justine's gaze fell on him and she caught the furtive demeanour. She stared.

The man seemed to freeze where he stood. He was slightly built, grey-haired, with prominent eyes and a weak, hesitant mouth. He was aware that Justine had locked on to him. He glanced at her as briefly as he could. She was glaring at him.

All at once the man's courage seemed to leave him. He turned, crouching in on himself as if he wanted to be smaller. Then, without visible warning, he began to run.

'Shit!' Justine hissed. She ran after him.

'Justine!' Taylor shouted into the radio. 'Stay where you are!'

'You piss off!'

Justine began to move seriously fast. A surveillance officer tried to block her path but she shouldered him aside and kept running. As her quarry cleared the exit, Justine was thirty feet behind him, running energetically in her high heels, yelling at him to stop.

'Units six and seven, cover the exits,' Taylor said. 'Repeat, cover the exits. She's running for air.'

'Bastard!' Justine shouted, clattering across the Shell bridge, closing the gap between herself and the terrified man. 'You bastard!'

Yards behind her eight surveillance officers were already in pursuit. Creegan was at the front, moving fastest, able to see now that somebody was running away from Justine.

'Block the bridge at the South Bank!' he panted into his radio. 'Cover the South Bank! She's chasing Stoker! It's him!' He cut the radio and put on a spurt. 'Justine!' he yelled. 'Justine!'

'Bastard!' Justine howled.

The man ran out on to a paved stretch that led to a low wall overlooking the Thames. Justine saw he had no way out and slowed down, gasping for breath. She watched him reach the wall, look over it into the water.

Then he turned to face her. He was panting desperately, his mouth wide open.

'Justine,' he wheezed as she stepped close to him.

She looked into his eyes, seeing the desperate ardour, the devotion. She clenched her fist, drew back her arm and punched him in the mouth. Her arm came back again and flashed forward, punching him in the belly. He went down, and as he came up again on a reflex she punched him on the nose. Then she had him by the tie and she was battering gobbets of blood out of his nose and mouth.

'Justine!' Creegan yelled.

He grabbed her and hung on until three constables ran up and took hold of her. Another officer screened the bleeding man, but not before Justine punched him one more time on the chin.

'Come on, Justine . . .' Creegan motioned the officers to move her off to one side. He stood over the victim, eyeing him coldly. For a moment he seemed content to watch the blood pour out of the battered face. 'Get him up.'

The man was taken away in a police van. Four uniformed officers led Justine away to another van.

35

When the case notes and transcribed interviews had been collated and the charges set down, Jack McCaffrey and Fiona Morrison were photographed for the record and for the OSC file covers. Shortly afterwards the man Justine had battered, now known to be Leonard Hoyle, was also charged and photographed, bruises and all.

A police car took Vince Wilson home to his parents at the farm. No charges were to be brought against him.

Justine, in the meantime, was sent back to prison. The story of her recapture would be distributed to the news agencies in the morning.

That evening there was an impromptu corridor session between Creegan, Taylor and OSC's principal lawyer, Steve Carroll. In the interests of confidentiality, the conversation moved into the office shared by Kreitman and Rivers. As Carroll clarified the legal position in the case of Leonard Hoyle, the burden of his message became depressingly familiar.

'You can only cement a conviction if all these kids, and the international respondents, can say unequivocally that they understood the same signals from the same source, with the same result. Murder.'

'Yeah,' Taylor said, 'but we can't guarantee we get

identical statements from these people. They've all got their own agendas as to why they got involved in the first place.'

Creegan was about to pitch in when Kreitman walked into the room, wearing his coat. He looked at the three of them.

'Lap of honour,' he said. 'I'm allowed to say goodbye and collect a few bits.'

Carroll and Creegan looked embarrassed. Creegan sat on the edge of the desk, half turned away. Kreitman took a pen and a couple of notebooks from a drawer. Taylor was staring at him, willing him to look at her. Finally he did.

'You're being dismissed because of a confession we have no evidence to support,' she said. 'So why aren't you fighting?'

Kreitman said nothing.

'If you'd come to me first, I'd have made sure there was evidence. I'm sorry your family's gone the shape it has, Jonathan, but you have to know, I never want to work with you again. You've made a mockery of everything I believe in.'

Kreitman looked at her with a wounded smile. 'And all that without evidence?'

Taylor nodded. 'Yeah. We've been there before, haven't we? It means absolutely sod all.' She turned her back and walked away.

Steve Carroll asked how the baby was.

'Oh, hanging on,' Kreitman replied, 'for the foreseeable future. Thanks for asking.'

Rivers came in with a stack of papers under his arm. He put them on his desk. He glanced warily at Kreitman.

'Jonathan,' he said, 'your wife called earlier. If you want a lift to the hospital, I'll keep you company.'

'No . . .' Kreitman shook his head. 'No, I think we'll have plenty of time to call in the favours. About twenty-five years to call in the favours. That's the baby's life expectancy, by the way.'

He took Rivers's hand suddenly, squeezing it. Then he drew him forward against his chest and hugged him. The gesture was not entirely appropriate between them. When Rivers stepped back he looked deeply uncomfortable.

Enwright appeared in the doorway. 'Jonathan.'

'Yeah.' Kreitman picked up his briefcase. 'I'm just going.'

'I know. Goodbye. I'm very sorry to have lost you.'

When Kreitman had gone Enwright spoke to the others. 'We'll have to apply for another forty-eight hours. I can't get any guarantee from CPS on a conviction, so just keep at it.'

The gloom in the office thickened. They had already done as much as they could. Leonard Hoyle had a lawyer with him now and the lawyer's advice was that Leonard say nothing. As long as he made no confession, as long as he refused to affirm or deny anything, he was immune from prosecution. He already appeared to know that.

Taylor looked at Creegan. He shrugged. Rivers put a hand in his pocket to fish out his cigarettes and discovered that a familiar weight was missing from his armpit. He slapped his empty holster.

'He's got my bloody weapon!'

Creegan, Taylor and Rivers charged out of the office and down the stairs, heading for the basement.

Kreitman was already there. He was in the cell with Leonard Hoyle, who was on his knees now, as if at prayer, clad in the regulation frill-necked shirt. His head was bowed forward, staring at the spot on the floor where Kreitman had dropped pictures of the two people killed by Jack and Mo. Hoyle's lawyer cringed in the corner.

Kreitman adjusted his grip on Rivers's gun and put the muzzle to the back of Hoyle's skull. Hoyle whimpered. Kreitman glanced at the lawyer.

'You,' he said, his voice shaking. 'Just tell me, in really simple terms, why people like you find any kind of nobility in wanting to defend people like this.'

Kreitman flinched as the muzzle of another gun, Creegan's, touched the back of his head.

'Drop the weapon, Jonathan. For God's sake, don't do this. You're in the clear, man.'

Enwright, Taylor and Rivers had also come into the cell. They stood watching, scarcely breathing.

'You *see*?' Kreitman said, speaking to Hoyle, shoving the gun harder against the back of his head. 'All you get from now is favours. Where are mine? Where's the justice?'

Creegan kept his pistol in contact with Kreitman's head. 'You can't change a bloody thing, Jonathan.'

'Can you?' Kreitman rasped. 'Can *you*?'

Creegan stepped slowly round to the left, keeping his arm straight, sliding the gun around Kreitman's head until the muzzle rested on his temple. 'Not like this.'

He reached up with his left hand and pressed his forefinger and thumb tightly on the gun's retraction grips. He pulled back sharply on the slide, delivering a round to the chamber, letting Kreitman know he meant business.

Hoyle trembled violently. Sweat ran down his nose and dripped on the floor. For three seconds more Kreitman kept his weapon pressed to the back of Hoyle's head. Then he sighed and slowly lowered his arm.

Creegan lowered his weapon too. He reached out to take the gun away from Kreitman, but before he could Kreitman brought it up again and fired a bullet into Hoyle's head.

Enwright, Taylor and Rivers gasped in unison as the body slumped on the floor.

Kreitman let his tension out in a sigh.

Creegan shoved the gun against his head. Kreitman turned slowly, letting the barrel rest on his forehead. He shut his eyes tight and leaned into the pressure of the steel muzzle.

Creegan's finger folded around the trigger and tensed. Then he stepped back. He lowered the gun. He looked devastated by what had happened.

Kreitman opened his eyes. 'Twenty-five years. It's life either way, isn't it?'

He dropped his gun on the floor and held out his hands for cuffing.

Later, as Kreitman was being escorted out of the building, Creegan stood alone in his office. He opened a desk drawer and took out the four bullets Kreitman had given him. He dropped them from one hand to the other and stared at them nestling in his palm. After a minute he put them back in the drawer.

A week after Kreitman had been formally charged with

the murder of Leonard Hoyle, an internal computer message was sent by Enwright to Creegan, Taylor and Rivers, summoning them to the conference room. When they got there they sat in silence, not looking at each other. Creegan was alone at one side of the table, his back to the weak daylight from the windows. Taylor and Rivers sat opposite, two chairs apart. In front of each of them was a document headed UNIT 43160 INCIDENT REPORT. They had all read it before, more than once.

Enwright came in. He went to the head of the table and sat down, squaring his papers in front of him. His placid expression belied the troubles ahead of him. He looked at the other three, saying nothing.

Creegan said, 'I take full responsibility.'

Enwright looked at him. 'There's a hell of a lot of it. Are you sure about that, Creegan?'

'No, he's not,' Rivers said. 'What happened was my fault.'

Taylor leaned forward. 'Look—'

'I am looking!' Enwright exploded. 'This is a bloody disgrace! All of you!' He took a moment to calm himself. 'What happened in that cell was one man's responsibility. What preceded that event was – and this is totally unforgivable – knowledge of, or suspicion of, vigilantism. You'd better tell me now if any of you thinks that what Jonathan Kreitman did has any place in your job description.'

He waited for their responses.

'No,' Taylor said.

Rivers appeared to hesitate, then he said, 'No.'

Creegan stood up. 'I don't know how to answer that, sir.'

'How close any of you came to it is not news,' Enwright said, 'and it's not the issue, Creegan.'

For a few more seconds Creegan remained standing. Then he sat down again.

'Thank you.' Enwright gathered up his papers. He looked at them each in turn. 'From here on, the word "team" has a capital T, and I'm running it. All right?'

They nodded.

Enwright stood up and went to the door. Pausing for a moment, he turned and looked at the three of them, his face once again a mask for his feelings. He left the room.